Jane Tara is the author of *The Happy Endings Book Club*, as well as three novels in the Shakespeare Sisters series: *Forecast*, *Trouble Brewing* and *Hamlet's Ghost*. She has over twenty children's books published in Korea, and runs a children's travel publishing company called Itchee Feet. She lives with her partner Dom and their four sons in Sydney. Jane can be contacted via her website: www.janetara.com.

I0669270

Also by Jane Tara

Forecast: Shakespeare Sisters
Hamlet's Ghost: Shakespeare Sisters
The Happy Endings Book Club

Trouble Brewing

Jane Tara

First published by Momentum in 2013
This edition published in 2015 by Momentum
Pan Macmillan Australia Pty Ltd
1 Market Street, Sydney 2000

A CIP record for this book is available at the National Library of Australia

Trouble Brewing

EPUB format: 9781743342350
Mobi format: 9781743342367
Print on Demand: 9781760300579

Cover design by Carrie Kabak
Edited by Kylie Mason
Proofread by Melissa Kemble

Macmillan Digital Australia: www.macmillandigital.com.au

To report a typographical error, please visit momentumbooks.com.au/contact/

Visit www.momentumbooks.com.au to read more about all our books and to buy
books online. You will also find features, author interviews and news of any author
events.

For my mother, Yvonne Pfeiffer.
And my wifey, Olivia Pigeot.
The most wonderful ole witches in the world.

The gin and tonic has saved more Englishmen's lives, and minds, than all the doctors in the empire.

Winston Churchill

It sloweth age, it strengtheneth youth, it helpeth digestion, it abandoneth melancholie, it relisheth the heart, it lighteneth the mind, it quickenth the spirits, it keepeth and preserveth the head from whirling, the eyes from dazzling, the tongue from lisping, the mouth from snaffling, the teeth from chattering and the throat from rattling; it keepeth the stomach from wambling, the heart from swelling, the hands from shivering, the sinews from shrinking, the veins from crumbling, the bones from aching, and the marrow from soaking.

Sixteenth century manuscript detailing the benefits of wine

Chapter 1

Rub vodka into your chest to break a fever

Calypso Shakespeare's green eyes gazed deep into his brown ones. "What is it you want from me?"

"I just need you to give me what you gave the others."

"I can't do that. Everyone is different."

He looked at her with such despair. "My heart … it's …"

Calypso reached out and touched his arm lightly. "It's okay. You'll get through this. I'll make sure you do."

She was still for a moment, her skin translucent in the dim light; those incredible cat eyes intense as she searched the ethers for the answer.

She turned to him. "Her name was Mary." A statement more than a question.

His eyes nearly fell out of his head. "Yes … Mary."

"Bloody Mary! How dare she treat you like that!" She sprang to life and began to mix: vodka, tomato juice, a splash of Worcestershire sauce and Tabasco. She grabbed a lemon, deftly sliced it in half and gave it a quick squeeze. Her hand slipped into a jar and returned with a pinch of something that smelt of August rain. Her lips moved slightly, an incantation, as she sprinkled it into the glass.

He watched her, mesmerized. She was tall, with endless creamy limbs, her hair a tumble of deep red waves. Dressed in jeans and a simple white T-shirt, she was without a doubt the most stunning woman he'd ever laid eyes on. He'd heard of her for years – who hadn't in London? – but seeing her in the flesh was something else. She turned and smiled, the type of smile that launched ships.

"This should do the trick." A quick stir, and a wink as she slid it toward him. "Drink it in five mouthfuls – no more, no less."

He did as he was told and placed the glass back down, gently, warily. It tasted like summer, and it wasn't until that moment that he realized everything had tasted like winter for way too long. He licked his lips; it was delicious. Comforting even. And then he looked frightened. His hand flew to his chest.

"What's happening?"

"You're okay," Calypso assured him.

He doubled over and groaned. His back heaved as he hyperventilated, and his breathing became more labored. A slow minute passed, and then a sudden howl, primal, excruciating, left his body. Others turned to watch now. A few first-timers looked concerned. The room was still with anticipation.

An absolute calm settled over him. His head moved slightly to one side, as though trying to recognize something new. Finally he stood, victorious – smiling for the first time in months.

"I feel it! It's gone," he declared.

The bar erupted into loud cheers. This behavior, odd though it was, was common in Calypso's enchanted watering hole. Complete strangers made their way over to congratulate him. Their normal reserve didn't exist in the cavernous room. They'd all seen the sign on the door that said, *Anyone who says alcohol never solves anything has never been here before.*

The man reached across the bar, grabbed Calypso's hand and gave it a kiss. "You're incredible! Thank you."

"You needed to release the hurt. You can move on now. Mary didn't deserve a good guy like you. And by the way, you'll meet a lovely woman in about three months, through work. Keep an eye out for Samantha."

*

Calypso watched until the man disappeared out the door, satisfied that she'd once again helped someone with one of her magical drinks. She glanced around her bar. It was a tiny cavern of a room in the basement of her parents' pub, the King and Mistress. Calypso and her younger sister, Nell, had been raised in the King and Mistress, with its hodgepodge of rooms and corridors, its rota of regulars, four hundred years of history, and a handful of ghosts. Calypso had always mixed her magical potions behind the bar – even when she was too young to legally do so – but two years ago she had renovated an old cellar and Calypso's Cauldron was born. The room had low ceilings and was dominated by a large, ornate bar. The oak-lined walls and stone floor kept the Cauldron cool in summer, while the open fireplace warmed it in winter. There were two long, rustic tables surrounded by stools and lit with candles and by the fireplace were a couple of comfortable empire armchairs paired with genuine Victorian footstools. It was welcoming, magical and completely unique – rather like the woman who ran it.

"Ah, Calypso girl, you helped that lad. You always know what the poor sods need."

Calypso turned to Harry, one of her regulars. "I know what you need, Harry. Sleep. Go home, go on."

"I'd rather sit here and watch you mix those magical brews of yours."

Calypso unscrewed the lid of a tin and measured out some leaves. She tossed them into a teapot and steeped them in hot water. Then she placed the pot and a mug in front of Harry. "This'll help you sleep."

"Not one of those weird recipes, is it?"

"Plain old chamomile. On the house," Calypso said.

"Good. Don't want to wake up in Highgate Cemetery."

"Most people in Highgate don't wake up, Harry."

"Busy night tonight."

"Always is after I've been away."

"Ah yes, the wandering Calypso. Where were you this time?"

Calypso poured herself a glass of water collected under a full moon and leant on the bar. Her face lit up as it always did when she spoke of her travels. A wanderer by nature, she was rarely in one spot for long. It's why running her own bar suited her: she came and went as she pleased, and her patrons understood that. "Tallinn for a few days ... then I stopped and saw an old boyfriend in Amsterdam."

"How old?" Harry asked with a wink.

Calypso laughed. "Not as old as you – or as handsome."

An attractive brunette approached the bar and nervously cleared her throat before speaking. "Excuse me, I heard you ... help people."

Calypso smiled; it was the same smile that had comforted countless patrons. "I do. Take a seat."

The woman sat and stared anxiously at the gorgeous redhead whose remedies and psychic predictions were so famous. Calypso grabbed a cocktail glass. She scanned the woman for a moment and then snapped her fingers.

"When was the last time you treated yourself? You can only look after others if you first look after yourself. You need a chocolate cocktail!"

The woman realized that's exactly what she needed.

4

Calypso continued speaking while she mixed. Her eyes glazed slightly as the veil lifted. "You know, you're much smarter than you give yourself credit for." A teaspoon of grated dark chocolate from Michel Chaudun's in Paris. Some Chartreuse and port. "You lack confidence – stems from your childhood. Your mother never believed women could amount to much. Poor thing."

Calypso cracked an egg, separated and discarded the yolk, and then strained all the ingredients. Next, from a vial the color of the sky, she added two drops, ever so gently. She placed the glass in front of the woman and looked her straight in the eye. "You are going to pass this exam," she said. "And you will be an excellent doctor. Sip it slowly."

The woman placed the drink to her lips. "It's delicious. It's like I know it from somewhere."

"You do know it," Calypso insisted. "Remember that during the exam. *You do know it.*"

"Thank you," said the woman. "You have an amazing gift."

Calypso nodded. She appreciated and acknowledged her gift. It was rude not to. "Yours is similar. We're both here to heal."

"Bloody hell, this box is heavy. Outta my way!" Megan Walker pushed through the crowd and plunked a crate of vodka on the bar.

"I said I'd help you with those," Calypso chided.

"Yeah, well, you're needed here so it's my job to lug this shit around," Megan jumped up onto the bar and swung her legs over.

"What are you? A child?" Calypso shook her head. "There's a gate there!"

"But then no one gets to see my knickers," Megan teased.

"Thank goddess you're wearing jeans." Calypso laughed.

Calypso and Megan had been best friends since school; the

two class misfits who at first were drawn to each other out of necessity, but soon realized they had all the ingredients for a strong and life-long bond.

Megan was as tough as nails – on the outside. She had short, spiky hair that changed color regularly; today it was bright blue. Her nose was pierced, as were her nipples and belly button. She was quite striking, with her big blue eyes and full lips, but most guys didn't see past her boyish demeanor and numerous tattoos. Inside, she had a heart of gold and was a loyal and loving friend. Her mother had died when she was seven, so her father raised her and her four older brothers alone. He wasn't quite sure what to do with a daughter, and often turned to Calypso's mother Batty for help. The rest of the time, he treated Megan like another son. As a result, Megan was a loud, tough tomboy, who preferred jeans and boots to dresses, and watched football rather than chick flicks.

Calypso glanced at her watch. "Don't you have a gig tonight?"

"Yep, but it's at the White Horse in Archway, so won't take long to get there."

"You go. I can clean up."

"No, it's—"

"Megan, leave! Go and prepare to be pelted with tomatoes or heckled or whatever."

Calypso caught Megan's eye and they cracked up. Megan was a struggling stand-up comedian, which she joked was the same as embracing failure and poverty for life. Calypso assured her friend that she would make it one day, but in the meantime, Megan had to face a lot of heckling and taunts. Sometimes it bothered her, but mostly she took it on the chin and gave as good as she got.

"Hey, did you hear about the two nuns who were driving through Transylvania?" Megan asked in a perfect Irish accent.

"Okay, give it to me," said Calypso.

"Suddenly Dracula jumped onto the bonnet of the car and bared his fangs. The first nun turned to other nun and said, 'Quick, show him your cross.' So the other nun rolled down the window and yelled, 'Get off the fucking bonnet, you blood-sucking bastard!'"

Calypso burst into peals of laughter. "That's a nine. Best one in a while."

"Good. I'll tell it tonight and hopefully they'll be placated and won't aim for my head when they throw things. See you tomorrow." Megan gave Calypso a quick hug and bolted for the door.

Calypso lifted the vodka off the bar and started packing the bottles away. She only ever mixed with Babička vodka, a wormwood liquor based on a Czech witches' brew. Other vodka didn't compare medicinally.

A voice boomed across the room. "Where's my girl?"

Calypso grinned as her father strode into the bar and enveloped her in a hug. She was twenty-nine years old, but it was still the safest place in the world to be. Alf Patterson was the size of a bear with a heart to match. What was left of his hair had a ginger tinge, and his laugh, which constantly bounced off the pub walls, could be heard three streets away. He ruffled his daughter's hair. "How long are you in town for this time?"

Calypso shrugged. She never knew the answer to that.

Alf scanned the room. "They're all glad you're back. Anyone left to help?"

Calypso did a quick head count. The couple who'd come in a last ditch effort to save their marriage were kissing passionately in the corner thanks to marigold flowers muddled with lemon juice and sugar, topped with Boudier Saffron gin, Tanqueray gin, Liquore Strega and Licor 43, shaken then double strained. A woman who'd spent her whole life feeling like a clumsy wallflower was now dancing by the fire. A mix of champagne and clementine soaked in Cointreau and cinnamon did the trick. The two brothers who'd fought over a woman had called a truce and were laughing together. Yarrow tea to the rescue. Other people mingled, and chatted, and swapped stories about their personal potion.

"Yep, they're all done."

Alf reached up to a bell above the bar and gave it a loud clang. "My daughter is closing shop now. If you want more to drink, go into the King and Mistress. If not, bugger off."

The crowd migrated contentedly toward the front of the pub. No one argued with Alf, because no matter what he said, he always said it with genuine warmth.

He turned to his daughter. "You too. Come and have a drink. Nell's here." They noticed Harry, who'd dozed off with his head on the bar. "Poor old sod. Had insomnia ever since his wife died … although obviously not tonight. What did you give him?"

"Chamomile and a friendly ear."

Alf nodded. That was often all anyone needed. "I'll deal with him while you lock up."

Calypso wiped down the bar. She enjoyed closing time. She basked in the silence, and the satisfaction that she'd helped people. The space was hers and she was immensely proud of it. If she was honest with herself, and she usually was, she also liked closing time because she dragged it out as long as she wanted, anything to put off climbing the stairs to her rooms – alone. She gave a sigh. It was her choice to be alone now. Three years ago was a very different story. She'd been madly in love and never thought she'd be alone again. Foolish ignorance of youth! Since then, being alone was preferable to being in a bad relationship. Or worse, a brilliant relationship that ended badly.

She collected the empty glasses and stacked them in the dishwasher. Next, she gathered together the brews and herbs that she always locked in the safe – some things were simply too potent to be left out. She wandered around the room snuffing out the candles and lanterns. It was important to purify the space each day so she lit some sage and left it smoking in a saucer. Grabbing the keys, she wandered up the eleven stone steps that led to the main bar and locked the heavy wooden door behind her. The rest could wait until to-morrow. She didn't want to be alone tonight. She wanted to see her family.

Chapter 2

Dandelion wine is good for indigestion

Bettina "Batty" Shakespeare poured a soda water for her daughter Nell. "You sure you don't want a real drink, love? You look a bit pale. Perhaps you're low on iron. How about a Guinness?"

"No thanks, Mum."

While Batty was certainly no alcoholic, she believed in the power of a pint and couldn't understand how she'd ever given birth to a virtual teetotaler. Sure, Nell would occasionally partake in a small glass of red, but only if she was celebrating something. Come to think of it, she hadn't had a glass of wine for some time.

"Fine, soda water it is," Batty said.

She plunked the drink on the bar and watched as Nell reached for a coaster and placed it neatly underneath. Then she plucked a straw from the holder, straightened it, and put it in the glass. Finally, she leant over the bar slightly and took a small, dainty sip. Good Goddess, the child was borderline OCD at times.

Batty loved both her daughters. Not equally, as most mothers swore they did, because as far as Batty was concerned, loving

people equally was codswallop. She loved them differently, for they themselves were so very different, and passionately, as only mothers do. But while she certainly didn't have a favorite child, she did understand one better than the other.

Calypso was easy to figure out. She was a wild, free-spirited gypsy whose passion for life was contagious. Sure she had some issues, especially over the past couple of years, but that was understandable given what she'd been through. Even then, all her emotions, her pain and joy, could be easily read on her face. Her incredible green eyes told a million tales. Calypso was an open book and a bloody good read at that. Plus, she embraced who she was. She never struggled with her clairvoyance the way Nell always had. Like sixteen generations of Shakespeare women before her, Calypso was psychic and used it to benefit others.

Nell was different. She had the Shakespeare trademark green eyes and red hair, but they were downplayed by reading glasses and a short pixie haircut. In fact, Nell looked a lot like a pixie. There was something incredibly contained and mysterious about Batty's youngest child. While Calypso was tall and willowy and raged through life, Nell was tiny with soft curves and a more introverted disposition. She was also obsessively neat and organized, responsible and polite.

Batty had no idea where she got it from.

She looked intently at her daughter, who was wearing a quirky little dress. Nell favored vintage clothes from the fifties and sixties. One only had to walk down Portobello Road to know how fashionable they were, yet the clothes didn't give Nell a modern edge; she looked like she actually belonged in the same era as the dress. The clothes suited her because everything about Nell seemed a few decades behind. There was no brashness about her. Nell didn't wear vintage because she was progressive, but rather because she was more at home in the past. She liked the past. It didn't interfere with her life the way the future did, with the constant visions and predictions. She stayed up-to-date with technology, but the way she approached life was decidedly dated. There was something incredibly contained and mysterious about Batty's youngest child.

"How's the job hunt going?"

Nell's pale face filled with concern. "Not great, but I'm sure I'll find something soon."

Batty knew her daughter would find work eventually, she wished she'd take some time off and have some fun, but that wasn't Nell's style. She pushed herself, and always had. She'd just completed a Masters in museum studies and her dream was to be a curator at a museum, which obviously had nothing to do with being a psychic. As far as Batty was aware, Nell was the first woman in the Shakespeare line to choose work that had nothing to do with the occult.

Batty, Calypso and Nell were part of a matrilineal line descending from William Shakespeare's great aunt, Sylvie, who, with her bright red hair and extensive herbal knowledge, was always in demand to deliver babies and heal the sick. For four hundred years, the gifted Shakespeare women had worked their craft to the benefit of others. Now there were only a handful of them left: Batty and her girls, and their three cousins in New York: Gwendolyn, Lilia and Rowie. Gwendolyn and Lilia worked as psychics from their shop in Manhattan, while Rowie, who was Calypso's age, had her own television show. The New York Shakespeares, like the sixteen generations of women before them, made a living from their gifts.

Batty herself juggled being mistress of the pub with psychic readings, which she scheduled three mornings a week in the back room. And Calypso's travels were funded by her predictions and psychic healings. But Nell, who'd been born with the extra special gift of finding things that were lost, only ever used it to find stuff like Alf's car keys and Calypso's passport. Sometimes Batty wasn't sure whether it was Nell's gift that helped her to locate these items or her role as pillar of practical calm in an otherwise chaotic family.

Batty was immensely proud of her younger daughter, but nonetheless baffled by her. She lived alone in an immaculately kept studio apartment in Muswell Hill. Over the past few years she'd managed to study at university and volunteer at Highgate Cemetery. For money, she worked part time at a small museum and in the kitchen with Alf on weekends. She also had lunch once a week with Alf's mother, the formidable Eleanor. Nell's life was strictly regimented. She couldn't be more different to Calypso if she tried.

Ah, Calypso! There she was. Batty watched her other daughter make her way across the room. Every head turned to watch her pass. She stopped, joked with a few regulars, flirted with one of the more handsome customers, and then danced up behind her sister and gave her a hug.

Nell turned and the two beamed at each other. They were as different as night and day but there was a deep bond between them.

"Find another job yet?"

"Not yet, Callie."

"I don't know why you don't ask Percy for a full time job at the BMR."

Nell sighed. She'd love to work full time at the British Museum of Romance, but she knew the small museum was under financial strain and didn't want to pressure her boss – Percy had enough to worry about. She was just grateful for the hours she did get there. But Nell couldn't explain all that to Calypso, who was used to grabbing opportunities with both hands, whether they were there for the taking or not. Nell pulled up a stool for her sister. "How was Amsterdam?"

Calypso sat and took the drink Batty handed her. Batty never had to ask if Calypso wanted one – Calypso had a healthy appreciation for alcohol. She'd been known to drink grown men under the table when challenged, but she rarely got drunk. As far as Calypso was concerned, alcohol could be medicinal, or it could be used to enhance a situation, but the minute you needed it to hide or anesthetize, you had a problem.

"Amsterdam was great," she said. "Always is."

"And Jaap?" Nell knew not to ask too much at once.

Calypso rolled her eyes. "That's so over. Pity, because he's great, but he started mooning all over me like a lovesick puppy."

Batty and Nell nodded; they'd heard this all before.

"And then he started talking about how I could move to Amsterdam and open a bar there."

"Oh dear," said Batty.

Calypso raised an eyebrow for dramatic effect. "He even mentioned kids. Apparently twins run in his family."

There was a sharp intake of breath from the other two women. No more needed to be said, really. No wonder the boy got the boot.

"What about you, Nell?" asked Calypso. "Ended the sex drought yet?"

Nell giggled and a red flush crept up her cheeks. "Oh no, Callie. I'm way too busy …"

"One should never be too busy for sex," said Calypso and Batty simultaneously, which made all three women laugh.

Alf joined them and pinched his wife's bottom. Thirty years of marriage and he still couldn't get enough of her. "What are my three favorite redheads cackling about?"

"Sex." Batty said with a wink.

"Sex is no laughing matter," Alf said. "So Father McNeil used to tell us at school."

"Nell was just telling us she doesn't have time for it," Calypso said.

Alf nodded in mock earnestness. "That's the way it should be. She's my little girl and can wait until she's married." He turned to Calypso with a wink. "As for you, missy ... there's no hope. How's that lad in Amsterdam?"

"Done and dusted."

Alf refilled Calypso's glass and slid it across the bar. "Don't worry, the right chap will come along eventually." A horrified flush rushed up Alf's cheeks. He looked at Batty and Nell but they were equally mortified. "I'm sorry, love. That was thoughtless."

Calypso gave her father's arm a quick squeeze. "It's okay, Dad. I know what you mean."

Batty couldn't help herself. She had to seize this opportunity. "You know, there will be another—"

"I doubt it." Calypso refused to go there.

"Yes, but if you just gave these boys a chance, perhaps ..." Batty trailed off when she saw the look in Calypso's eyes. Would her daughter ever lose that haunted look?

Nell was the only person who could really confronted the taboo subject – her rather reticent nature made it easier for Calypso to handle. Nell would simply slip questions and statements into the conversation as if she was talking about the weather. Calypso still didn't like it, but she rarely ripped Nell's head off as she would anyone else who broached the topic.

"You'll love again, Callie. It's inevitable."

"Thank you, Oprah." Calypso rolled her eyes. "And tell me, when exactly was your last date?"

Nell wiped an invisible mark off the bar. "I told you, I'm too busy."

"The only boyfriend of yours we've ever met was that dullard from university."

"Edmund wasn't dull."

"He collected bugs."

"I found it fascinating," Nell lied. But Calypso was right; Edmund had been as dull as dishwater. He crapped on about insect habitats and preservation equipment, and devoured his monthly entomology magazines like a teen would porn. Nell tried to tell herself that his passion was admirable, and not unlike the love she had for history, but there was something disturbing about sleeping at Edmund's place, surrounded by dead bugs. And really, he had bored her senseless. Nell seemed to be a magnet for dull men. She knew she wasn't Sienna Miller or Kate Moss or one of those other gorgeous, wild women, but surely that didn't mean she should be subjected to a life of eternal boredom?

Batty reached out and patted Nell's hand. "He was as riveting as watching paint dry. You need a man who brings you out of your shell a bit, but with whom you still feel secure." She turned to Calypso. "And whether you realize it now or not, Nell is right. You will love again. And he'll be special because he won't try to compete with your past. He'll never tie you down, cage you in, or try to change you. And he'd better have sturdy shoes because he'll be chasing you all over the world."

"If there's one thing I know," Calypso paused for a moment, and looked much older than her twenty-nine years, "... no guy like that exists."

And that's when all three Shakespeare women felt the Winds of Change whip through the door. A chime pealed softly through the room, even though they didn't own one. Alf jumped about trying to catch the coasters, which were flying everywhere. The fire roared to life without being prodded. All the patrons grabbed their coats or their sweaters. The only people who remained still were Batty, Nell and Calypso, who were staring at the door. When she realised who had just entered, Calypso felt all the blood drain from her legs.

A lazy grin spread across his impossibly handsome face. "Don't suppose you've got a drink for an old friend?"

Chapter 3

Stout is high in iron

Taran Dee had been making plans all the way from New York to London. By the time the plane landed, he knew he wouldn't settle for anything less than a full apology and another chance.

Calypso would give him both. Not that she knew it yet.

Fate had thrown Taran and Calypso back together. And who was he to ignore Fate? She could be a right bitch if you ignored her. But go with her and life flowed. This trip was a perfect example. It was seamless synchronicity. He'd been thinking of Calypso for weeks – okay, he'd never stopped thinking about her – when the offer came to exhibit his work at the Gate. Not only was it a fantastic opportunity professionally, but it also meant relocating to London for a couple of months.

Calypso lived in London.

Fate.

"Is this room, okay? You can have one of the others. There are five, you know."

Taran realized Simon Apsley was speaking to him. He glanced around the room. "It's fine, Sime. I don't care where I sleep." He grinned at his old friend. "What the hell do you do with five bedrooms?"

"Admittedly, they're not in use right now. But I hope to have a family one day." Simon smiled, ever the optimist.

"Yeah, well, you've got to get laid to have kids."

Simon chuckled and blushed simultaneously. Taran knew his history with women.

Simon and Taran had met at college in the States and remained friends since. Unlike his charismatic friend, Simon was introverted and self-conscious, especially around women. Women would completely ignore him until they discovered he was an Apsley, the youngest son of Charles Apsley to be exact. Simon's great-grandfather founded Apsley Beer, one of the UK's largest breweries. Simon, his father and his three older brothers were all on the board of directors, and his father retained a majority hold over the company.

Simon was loaded, but that wasn't what defined him, not to his handful of good friends like Taran. They saw his kindness, his loyalty, his clumsy humor and his generosity of spirit. Like tonight, for instance, when he insisted on picking Taran up at the airport. He could have sent a car and driver, but he didn't. Then again, Taran could've caught a cab, but Simon wouldn't hear of it. Simon picked Taran up, because that's what friends do. At least, that's what Simon did. He was old fashioned in his approach to friendship. As a result, he had Taran's complete respect.

Although Taran and Simon appeared to be very different, they were in fact alike in many ways. They shared similar values and the same sardonic sense of humor. They both came from wealthy families with domineering mothers. They were both outcasts all through school, although for different reasons – Simon because he had no success with women, Taran because had too much. But mostly, they were both loyal to their true friends, and always to each other.

Simon also loved the way Taran took the piss out of him.

"So these five bedrooms? Ever been laid in any of them?"

"No," Simon admitted with a grin. "Knowing my luck and your track record, you'll be the one to christen them all before I even get a chance."

"Before you get a chance?" Taran howled in mock disbelief. "You've lived here for a year already. These rooms are lucky I came to visit. The walls will finally have something to talk about."

"I knew letting you stay was a bad idea."

"Oh bullshit, you've been begging me to stay because you know being my wingman is the only chance you've got to meet women."

They laughed.

"Ain't that the truth? Shall we start tonight?"

Taran shuffled uncomfortably. "I can't. I have an … ah … appointment."

"Good god, you're on English soil for an hour and you already have a date."

"What can I say? I'm irresistible."

Simon wasn't fooled. "You're going to see her, aren't you? The one you told me about?"

"Guilty as charged," Taran admitted. "I figure it's best to get it over and done with. Get her out of my system."

"Excellent idea." Simon's eyes twinkled with amusement. "You haven't seen her for a year. If she's not out of your system yet, then you're in big trouble, mate."

*

"The King and Mistress pub in Highgate please." Taran remembered where she'd said her parents' pub was. He remembered everything about her, which was unusual for him. Most women came and went from his thoughts quite easily.

"Right you are." The driver pulled out into the traffic and Taran stared out the window. He loved this part of London, and was looking forward to exploring it more. He turned his head to watch a stunning blond pass. Primrose Hill was filled with actors and models. Taran felt a surge of excitement at the thought of a new stomping ground, but then he remembered that he was on a mission to win Calypso back and his old ways of partying and womanizing weren't part of the plan.

He felt a twinge of regret, but it didn't last for long.

They drove through Camden Town toward Highgate and Taran soaked in the sights. English history never ceased to amaze him. Being a born and bred New Yorker, Taran had a healthy attachment to the future and what he intended to make of it. But being an artist, he was also a sucker for the past, and nowhere did it more beautifully than Europe. And as far as Taran was concerned, London was gateway to it all.

"In London for business or pleasure?" the driver asked.

Taran grinned. "Both."

"Which one tonight?"

"Hopefully the latter."

"Been to the King and Mistress before?"

"No, but I've heard plenty about it." It was true. Calypso had charmed him with tales about her unique childhood home.

"There's a famous little bar in the cellar. Calypso's Cauldron. The young lass who runs it is supposedly a witch."

"Is that a fact?" Taran failed to add that he was from a long line of witches himself. "I'll check it out." *And ask her why she left without saying goodbye.*

Taran thought about the time he'd spent with Calypso in New York. He was man enough to admit that he'd fallen hook, line and sinker for the stunning redhead. His mistake was he told her so. Isn't that what women wanted? He'd been accused of being emotionally unavailable more times than he could remember (by many woman he couldn't remember), but he refused to fake it or lie. All that changed with Calypso. Taran was elated to meet a woman he could be honest with without receiving a sharp slap in return. He actually liked Calypso – a lot. So he told her. He wasn't proposing marriage. Hell no! Marriage was like Seniors Week at Club Med: the last resort. He was simply suggesting they get to know each other better.

She obviously didn't feel the same way, because the following morning she was gone. She'd kissed him and sent him into the shower, promising to join him in a few minutes. Fifteen minutes later Taran hopped out of the shower, expecting to find that she'd fallen back asleep. She wasn't asleep. She wasn't there.

Every atom of his being had wanted to go after her, but he didn't. He couldn't. He was shocked that he'd been so wrong about someone. He'd felt utterly bound to her and was certain she'd felt the same way. They'd spent night after night devouring each other mentally and physically. In his mind, it was a match made in heaven. He was stunned that he'd been so wrong. But more than that, his pride had taken a fall. Its first ever. He'd never been dumped. He'd wished for it countless times, but had always been left to do the dirty work. However, this time, the one time he really wanted a woman to hang around, she'd tossed him aside like yesterday's news. So instead of charging ahead like he normally did, Taran retreated to lick his wounds. He and his ego had crawled into a little ball and stayed there for months. There had been other women, of course, but none who got under his skin like Calypso. None who came close. So now he was doing what he should have done twelve months earlier: he was tracking Calypso down to demand an explanation.

Which made him sound rather macho really. But if the truth were told, he'd been spurred into action by two separate events.

First came the offer from the Gate Gallery. His initial reaction had been sheer joy. He'd worked hard for years and this was the ultimate affirmation that he'd come into his own as an artist. But then he remembered Calypso and felt a plummeting fear. He'd be in the same city as her so there'd be no excuse not to initiate contact. If he wanted, which he did.

He kept telling himself that she wasn't the only ex he had in London. Oh no, there were quite a few English women who completely despised him, one who still stalked him, even a couple who still genuinely wanted him. Laura Williamsworth immediately came to mind, mainly because he'd dated her three months previously. He'd escaped her clutches by the skin of his teeth when her extremely wealthy grandfather fell ill and she returned to London to be with him. Or more to the point, returned to London to make sure she was remembered in his will. Taran pretended to be disappointed, bade her a mournful farewell, and promptly went out to celebrate her departure. Finding female company was never a problem, but if it was, he could always look Laura up. If hell froze over and pigs flew backward and women started ignoring him.

This trip wasn't about women. He wanted to concentrate on his work in London. Yet the idea of seeing Calypso began to nag him day and night. He couldn't believe he was being such an idiot over it all. How hard was it to call her up and ask her out for a drink? He'd never had a problem initiating contact with a woman before. But she did dump him, rather brutally as well, so she might not even want to see him. Taran decided his trip to London would not include Calypso.

But then his twin brother provided the second event, the deal-breaker. Now his relationship with his twin was at stake, Taran had no choice but to swallow hs pride and track Calypso down. Taran couldn't think about Finn's ultimatum right now. It hurt, and Finn had never hurt Taran before. It had always been the other way round. He'd hurt Finn many times over the years, and that shamed him deeply.

The cab driver broke his reverie. "Here we are. You have a good night, son."

Taran paid the driver. "Thanks. I intend to."

He closed the taxi door and then hesitated as he noticed the Winds of Change. Damn it! They were whipping around the edge of the street. It wasn't the first time he'd seen the Winds of Change, and they usually weren't for him, but even so, they always unnerved him slightly. He sidestepped them and made for the safety of the pub's entrance. The King and Mistress was exactly as he'd imagined it, with wood paneled walls and floors, stained-glass windows, and cozy booths. A number of doors lead off the main bar. Calypso had mentioned the smaller bars, the rooms, and the steep stairs that led to her parents' quarters on the third floor, and her own rooms in the attic. The fireplace in the corner had burnt down to its last embers, but the pub was warm and a welcome respite from the unusually chilly May evening.

Taran scanned the room. It was busy, but not overly so. The crowd was an eclectic mix of suits, students, arty types and, he presumed, locals. Oliver Swain was playing on the sound system, and there was a fabulous aroma of spice and freshly baked bread. No doubt that was from the kitchen, where Calypso's father reigned.

His gaze rested on the bar where three gorgeous redheads gathered. What a sight they were. The tiny one was obviously Nell. She was as pretty as a picture, and seemed quite happy to sit back and let the other two take center stage. Batty was exactly as Calypso described her. While Nell's hair was neatly cropped, and Calypso's fell in undulating waves, Batty's was more a tangle of curls. She was laughing loudly as she regaled the others with a story. Some of the patrons turned and stared, but Bettina Shakespeare had obviously been born and bred on strange stares so didn't seem to notice.

And finally Calypso. She was even more stunning than he remembered. Taran actually felt nervous, which was a first for him. He realized it was a mistake turning up like this, without warning. What the hell was he going to say to her? He should come back later – when his brain was working again.

He opened the door to leave, but the Winds of Change were waiting and whipped past him, pushing him back inside. They swooshed through the bar, sweeping the past clear from the corners where it clung. A chime pealed softly through the room, even though he couldn't see one. A man he presumed was Alf jumped about trying to catch coasters as they flew off the bar. The fire roared to life without being prodded. And three pairs of emerald eyes turned toward him.

His own blue ones locked with Calypso's and somehow he found the courage to speak.

"Don't suppose you've got a drink for an old friend?"

Chapter 4

Sip dill seed tea to soothe stomach upsets

Calypso thought she was in danger of fainting from shock – or perhaps desire. Instead she made her way over to Taran and gave him a warm hug.

"Taran! What a surprise. What are you doing here?"

"I'm in town, so thought I'd drop by." *Can I get any more inane?* he thought. "So here I am …" *Obviously, yes.*

"Come and meet my family." Calypso dragged him over to the bar and introductions were made, although they all knew exactly who he was.

"Would you like a drink, lad?"

"A beer would be great, sir."

"Now, now … I've never been formally knighted," Alf joked. "No need for formalities here."

"That's good to know, Alf," Taran said.

"What brings you to London?" Batty asked

"I've been offered an exhibition at the Gate."

Everyone was suitably impressed, except Calypso, who wanted to be sick. An exhibition meant this was no fleeting visit.

"What an honor," Nell said.

"It's not for another month, but I thought I'd come over early and finish painting. See if inspiration hits."

"Oh, I'm sure it will." Batty glanced at Calypso.

"That's a long time to be away from home." Alf thought there was something familiar about the boy. Then he realized who Taran reminded him of when he gave a non-committal shrug – it was the same one Calypso gave him regularly.

"I'm at home wherever I lay my hat. Or my paintbrush."

Calypso could see her mother was assessing the man she'd dated the last time she was in New York. Her eyebrows were raised so high they almost hit the ceiling. Calypso was furious. Taran was the last person she wanted to introduce to her family. They'd all wondered why she'd cut her trip to New York so abruptly short. Batty had questioned her in a way that made the MI5 look like lightweights, but Calypso refused to divulge any details.

"It's a man. I can see it … it's written all over your face," Batty had said.

Now it was written all over her mother's face. She was looking at Taran with unmasked delight. But then, Taran did pack a punch. He was an Adonis … or at the very least, a human incarnation of his namesake, Taranis the thunder god. The name suited him: his beauty was dark, almost menacing. His face was perfect: chiseled, masculine, and yet beautiful. He had jet-black hair, a haughty nose and intense blue eyes that teased, yet warned you to not get too close. He was tall and lean with a broad chest and endless shoulders. He carried himself like a man who was used to being watched and liked it that way. And he *was* used to it. He'd virtually grown up on his parents television show. Calypso could tell her mother had already recognised him.

Taran's parents owned an occult-based empire in the US that included everything from a successful reality show to merchandise such as T-shirts, toys and lunchboxes. The Dee family were famous before the Kardashians were born. His mother and father were the Oprah and Dr Phil of witchcraft, and just as rich.

But Taran Dee was more than just another spoilt brat living off his parents' wealth: he was a successful artist in his own right. This was no shallow man. Calypso loved his work. His paintings were deep and soulful and mythical. He had a romantic spirit that he exposed every time he lifted his brush. He was unique, and knew it.

Damn him for showing up unannounced. And double damn her mother's goofy grin.

Batty smiled broadly, her green eyes crinkling at the edges. "We're so glad to have you here, Taran. Where are you staying? We've got rooms upstairs."

Calypso interrupted before her mother got too carried away. Next she'd be offering him her oldest daughter for the bargain price of three camels. "I'm sure Taran is quite happy wherever he is."

"I'm staying with a friend in Primrose Hill."

"How lovely," Batty said, as though he'd just told her he does charity work for Sulawesi orphans. Then she turned to Calypso. "Why don't you take Taran downstairs and show him your bar?"

Calypso wanted to wring her mother's neck. She may as well have said, "How about taking Taran downstairs and bearing his children?" As much as her family loved and supported her, deep down they were still like everyone else: sure that falling in love was the answer to everything. Calypso shuddered. Not even a gorgeous hunk of manhood like Taran Dee would tempt her down that road. But she'd still take him downstairs. Anything to get him away from her family.

*

Calypso led Taran through a maze of rooms and corridors. There were two smaller bars off the main bar, both filled with comfy chairs and low tables. They made their way into a neat little waiting room and then a stylish dining room.

"My father's domain," she explained.

"Nice portrait," said Taran, referring to a gilt-framed painting of a woman over a mantelpiece.

"Nell Gwynn, mistress to King Charles II," Calypso explained. "Painted in 1670."

Taran was impressed. "Where did you get it?"

"She sat for it upstairs."

Calypso opened a heavy wood door and led him down some stone stairs. "My Cauldron," she announced.

Taran looked around while Calypso lit a couple of lamps.

"It's fantastic."

Calypso watched as he wandered over to the bar and ran his hand across it. He crouched down and admired the base of the bar, which had stained-glass inlays and was a work of art itself. He took his time, and when he was done he stood and turned to her.

"So what do I get now I'm here?"

"Exactly what you need." There was a pause, and then Calypso launched herself at him. Her arms were around him, her lips were pressed against him. He was stunned for a moment. He obviously hadn't been expecting this – not right away at least – but then she felt a ferocious heat surge through him. One hand wrapped around her waist and pulled her even closer while the other grabbed a handful of her hair.

The connection was immediate and fierce. Neither wanted to take it slowly; there was no time for games. They wanted each other straight away.

Taran tossed his jacket off and yanked his sweater over his head. He ripped at her T-shirt, and ran his hands across her skin.

"I've been dreaming of your body for twelve months."

Calypso was breathless. "Does this live up to your dreams?"

"No comparison. This is real." He unclipped her bra and lowered his head to her nipple. She groaned and went weak, so he lifted her onto a table. His hand undid the buttons on her jeans and slid them off before his fingers disappeared inside her. She went to scream but he silenced her with his mouth.

Good move, thought Calypso. She didn't need her parents rushing in here right now.

She clawed at his belt buckle until she was able to find what she was looking for. It was straining to be set free, and when it was, it was just as magnificent as she remembered. And rock hard.

"Condom," she gasped. "In that tin on the bar."

That threw him. He looked stunned, but opened the tin and removed a condom, taking his time to unwrap it.

Calypso almost enjoyed his reaction, but knew that enjoyment was nothing compared to what was coming. She pulled him close again. "You okay?"

"I don't have anything against condoms, but usually mine are tucked away in my wallet, not in a tin on a public bar."

"They're for my customers, you silly idiot. Occasionally one of my brews makes them a bit amorous, so I always have them on hand. Just trying to be responsible." She ran her tongue across his lips. "This is a first, okay? Dipping into my own supply."

He locked eyes with her and they laughed. The tension eased slightly, their breath mingled. She savored the moment, realizing she'd never wanted a man more than she wanted him right now.

He grabbed the back of her head with one hand while the other slid her hips closer to the edge of the table.

"You are so fucking sexy," he growled.

And then he entered her and her whole body filled with electric shocks and small rapturous explosions of light.

The bliss! Sex had never been this good with anyone before. It's why he was so bloody dangerous. So annoying. So frustrating ... so ... *so incredible.*

The rhythm got more heated, more urgent. Their kisses, their tongues, their moans echoed off the stone tiles.

He yanked her hair back and forced her to look him in the eye. "You just took off without saying goodbye."

He continued to plunge, deeper and deeper. "I don't do goodbyes," she gasped.

"No, but you do fantastic hellos!"

They stared at each other, and then a year of feverish, unfulfilled yearning tore out of them in one wild moment. Her head fell back and her toes curled. She began to leave her body. His eyes glazed over and she could feel he was close to losing it, too. It was enough to send her soaring over the edge. He came with her in one long, loud, unbelievable explosion. And then they slumped together on top of the table.

"Christ," he gasped. "That was amazing."

Calypso couldn't speak for a moment. She was completely overcome. She just lay there, naked on the table, trying to catch her breath. Trying not to sob. An unfamiliar calm descended, mixed with a bitter acceptance that this man was trouble. She opened her eyes and noticed their shadows were still dancing across the ceiling, thrilled to be reunited. Calypso didn't share their elation. She felt confused – guilty, although she knew she shouldn't.

"Ah, Cal, we've got a visitor," Taran whispered.

Calypso followed his gaze and noticed Enid, one of the resident ghosts, hovering in the corner. Enid stared at them in fury, as her long white nightgown floated around her.

"Who is she?"

"Enid. Jumped off the pub roof in 1944."

"I'm keeping an eye on you two," Enid hissed, before disappearing.

Taran and Calypso looked at each other in amazement, and then began to laugh.

Chapter 5

Dandelion wine is excellent for treating gout

Morning light peeked through the curtains. Taran opened his eyes and was able to take in his surroundings for the first time. Last night, when Calypso dragged him upstairs to her room, he was more interested in taking in every inch of her, again and again and again.

The room had whitewashed walls, beams, and a wood floor covered with a Moroccan rug. It was large and divided into two distinct areas. Scattered on one side were a few couches covered in pillows and throws and surrounded by packed bookshelves. The other side was the ornate bed he was now sprawled across, a dresser, a chair and a small Balinese desk where her laptop sat. There was a series of black and white photos tastefully framed on the wall: people dancing at Rio's carnival; Calypso in a Japanese alleyway; African children; a busker somewhere in Europe. He felt ridiculously smug when he noticed a sketch he'd given her framed on the far wall. They'd spent a weekend at Martha's Vineyard and he'd drawn her while she slept. It was a simple sketch but it captured her beauty and strength. Then he saw her suitcase propped near her closet. She hadn't even bothered to unpack it – clothes spilled out the top. In fact, clothes were everywhere except inside the closet: T-shirts were tossed over the chair; a few pairs of jeans lay on the floor. There was even a bra hanging off the top of Calypso's laptop. She could never be accused of obsessive neatness. Piled next to the computer were papers and photos and, on top of them all, as if ready to go, her passport. He tried to ignore how much that bothered him, but it was a glaring reminder of how difficult Calypso was to pin down.

Taran rolled onto his side and stared at the woman beside him. Her red hair fanned across the pillow. Her lips were full and pink and her eyelashes endless. She was a knockout. He'd never been this fascinated by anyone before. Back home he had a reputation for loving and leaving women. In his defense, he certainly didn't encourage women to throw themselves at him. It just happened. And it's not like he slept with all of them. Hell no! If he did, he'd never have time for anything else. And he was never cruel, just honest. He was yet to learn the lesson that they are often the same thing. His art came first and he'd never been interested in commitment. Not that such honesty ever stopped the women. It got so bad that his twin brother Finn stopped introducing his girlfriends to him. And then Taran met Tye.

Taran had been spending time with his sister in Hamlet, Massachusetts, where Tye also lived. They'd become friends, and he was attracted to her, mainly because she seemed wary of him – a challenge. Eventually she told him that she'd dreamt of the man she'd end up with her whole life ... and it was him, only with blond hair. Tye didn't know that Taran had a blond twin, and Taran took advantage of that fact. Until Finn arrived in town and Tye realized what Taran had done.

Of course, Tye and Finn ended up together, as they were meant to. But Finn was hurt.

Taran tried to argue his case. "Come on, Finn, it doesn't count. I met her first."

"And she told you she'd dreamt of me all her life. Doesn't that mean anything to you?"

Deep down, Taran knew Finn was right. Tye wasn't just any woman. "I'm sorry, Finn. I didn't think things through."

"You never do," Finn admonished. "Didn't you realize how much trouble this would cause between us?"

"How was I to know? I'm not psychic like the rest of you."

It was true. While Taran saw ghosts, he wasn't as gifted as the rest of his family. But it wasn't just about Tye. Finn was completely sick of Taran's attitude to all women, especially the ones he himself dated. Finn wasn't angry – sweet-natured Finn never really got angry – but it was the final straw.

"I'll never be able to truly trust you around Tye until you know what love is."

"Finn, you can trust me."

"You've slept with three of my girlfriends and flirted with countless more."

"Well, you have really good taste," Taran joked weakly.

"I don't want you in my life until you know what love is. Simple."

"Oh come on, Finn. I love you and Rhi." It was true. He'd take a bullet for his siblings.

"Love with a woman. Romantic love. And then you'll understand just how fragile the heart can be. And hopefully, you'll never break mine again." Finn was adamant. "Don't call, don't visit and don't email until you're in love."

Taran was devastated. Sure, he'd never truly loved a woman, but he loved his brother. Finn was his other half, and the only person who truly understood him. Finn knew Taran's thoughts before he'd finished forming them. Taran felt lost without Finn, but there was only one way to fix it – to fall in love. So he went on a series of dates set up by friends. And was bored out of his brain. He liked a challenge and women had a habit of being way too easy for him. He wished it weren't so. He craved a deeper connection, but he just couldn't find it with someone who didn't keep him on his toes.

Calypso kept him so high on his toes he felt like Baryshnikov.

When he was offered the gig at the Gate, the timing was perfect. A couple of months in London. They could get to know each other properly. Taran was certain that Calypso, the only woman he had ever truly connected with, would be the one to help heal the rift with his brother. Perhaps even the rift inside himself.

She began to stir and he pulled her closer and nuzzled her neck. He felt himself go hard and decided it was time to wake her up properly.

*

Calypso was aware of Taran's arms around her. He kissed her neck and she moaned softly. A gentle touch, soft persistent probing from behind her, and then –

She gasped as he gave her the most pleasant wake-up call she'd had in a long time. Afterwards she lay there with the sheets tangled around her and decided on the best way to approach the inevitable.

"Let's go out for breakfast," he suggested.

She stretched languorously "I can't. I've got stuff to do today."

"I thought we could hang out."

"Sorry ... no can do."

"Lunch."

"No."

"Dinner?"

Good goddess he was persistent. "I'm busy." Calypso stared at him for a moment. Oh, what the hell. "I'm going to a stand-up gig tonight. My best friend Megan is a comedian. You can come if you want."

Taran looked like he'd just won the lottery. "Excellent." And then: "Do you mind if I bring my friend Simon? I should spend some time with him."

"Not at all. The more the merrier." *And safer*, thought Calypso.

She extracted herself from Taran's arms and climbed out of bed. "So I'll see you tonight then."

"Are you throwing me out?"

"I know it's not something you'd be used to, but yes."

"C'mon babe, why don't you crawl back in the nest with me."

Calypso burst out laughing. "Does that shit work with other women?"

Okay." He grinned. "How about another shag?"

Tempting! "I have an appointment." She tossed him his pants. "So you have to go."

"You should go back to romance school, Callie. Retake Subtle Ways to Say Goodbye 101."

"In my experience, goodbyes are never subtle." Calypso tilted her head to one side. "So ... see ya!"

"I've met sledgehammers that are more subtle than you. You're like a Rubik's cube. I think I'd have to pull you apart to really work you out."

"Well, let me give you a tiny insight into how I *work*."

Taran sat up. She leant toward him slightly, but stayed just out of his reach.

"I'm not a morning person, Taran. I don't like chatter until after I've had an extremely strong coffee. So the more you talk now, the less chance you've ever got of waking up with me again."

Taran kept his mouth shut. There really was no way to respond to that.

Calypso slipped into her robe. "I'm going for a shower. You know the way out." She gave him a wicked smile. "And if not ... you'll find it."

Calypso spent twenty minutes under the hot water, trying to clear her head. It was impossible. Her brain wasn't foggy due to a lack of sleep, but an excess of Taran Dee. She regretted asking him to Megan's gig, but she wasn't in full control of herself when he was around. It's why he was dangerous. The last thing she needed was a complicated affair with Taran. She didn't want to feel more for him than she already did. She certainly didn't want to risk falling in love with him. She needed to stop seeing him ... but one more night shouldn't be a problem.

Chapter 6

Cowslip wine will cure jaundice

Taran dropped by the Gate on the way home and checked out the space properly. He also introduced himself to Helen Galloway, the gallery's head of press officer. It was her job to make sure everyone knew his show was on.

"We'll set up a series of interviews, plus invite a few critics to come and view your work just prior to the opening. We're thinking of calling it the Web of Life. What do you think?"

"Appropriate." Taran was getting a weird vibe off her and didn't like it.

Helen gave Taran an appreciative once-over. "We'll start with the female critics and it would be great if you were here when they came."

Taran's eyes narrowed slightly. He was used to people judging his looks before anything else, but this exhibition was going to change that. "I think my art speaks for itself."

"Yes, but we want them to like it, Taran."

"Whether they like it or not is irrelevant."

Helen shrugged. "You're probably jetlagged. We'll talk more about this later."

Taran arranged to meet with Helen and the gallery director and the curator later in the week and caught a cab back to the safety of Simon's.

He felt strange, off-kilter, slightly … used, which was ridiculous. Being treated like a prize Hereford by Helen didn't help, but it was Calypso's behavior that really bugged him. She'd thrown him out. She made no secret of the fact that she enjoyed the sex, but had more important things to do. Calypso was doing what he'd done countless times himself, to loads of women he'd never called again. The realization unnerved him. Had any of those women harbored strong feelings for him, only to be rejected so flippantly? He'd always prided himself on being honest, but perhaps honesty wasn't always the best policy. A tiny bit of faked affection, a touch of regret, a lingering farewell kiss would have made him feel a hell of a lot better today.

Or perhaps he needed a hot cup of Harden the Fuck Up.

Taran unpacked his canvasses in the bedroom he was using as a studio. He began to feel a familiar tingle in his fingers. Laying his tools out was therapeutic and the hurt and frustration he'd been feeling all morning began to lift.

He needed to paint.

Images filled his brain. The room around him faded as he prepared his oils. Inspiration hit! An image appeared, glorious, vivid and alive. He free fell through the layers of his imagination as his hand translated what he saw onto the blank canvas before him.

Hours passed in the blink of an eye.

A gorgeous, wild, redheaded woman came to life on canvas.

*

A few suburbs away the real-life version of that gorgeous, wild, redheaded woman was about to experience a problem.

Calypso stood behind the bar and stared at the girl sitting before her. Emily was fifteen, which was why Calypso had booked her in for a daytime appointment. As a rule, Calypso worked behind the bar during hours that suited her. But rules are made to be broken, so quite often she'd see underage clients during the day. She never prescribed alcohol (or if she did, she'd certainly never admit it), but still used infusions and tinctures and spells to fix their problems.

Emily, the daughter of two well-known television stars, was having problems dealing with her parents' very messy divorce. It didn't help that every detail of the split had been plastered all over the press for months. Emily's mother, Maxine, had fallen in love with an Australian actor and ex-*Neighbours* star she'd met while doing a pantomime. Emily's father, Bryce, was devastated. Normally it was he who chased C-list actors.

Emily's way of coping was to rebel. She stopped eating, and the whole country watched in horror as her weight plummeted. She suddenly had her parents' attention, which was nice, but instead of helping her, Maxine and Bryce turned on each other over their daughter's obvious distress. Emily upped the ante on her "issues" and began stealing, first from Harrods and Selfridges, both of which were caught on camera, and then from her roommates at her rather expensive boarding school, which got her expelled. Finally, she decided to have sex with her piano teacher's son and film the whole thing to upload online. Fortunately young Markham had offloaded to his mother before Emily uploaded online. That's when her mother brought her to see Calypso, something Emily didn't fight because if the truth were told, she was a bit tired from all the rebellion. At heart, she wasn't a bad kid at all.

Calypso watched Emily now, sitting slumped against the bar, her large brown eyes cloaked in exhaustion and misery. *This one will be a piece of cake.*

"My brews only work when the recipient desires change and healing," she said gently.

Emily glanced at her parents and Calypso sensed she couldn't back down while they were sitting right beside her. Maxine was glued to her phone, while Bryce looked as though he was about to snatch it out of her hand and smash it against the wall. It was hardly an environment that promoted healing.

Calypso turned to Emily's parents. "I think this will work best if Emily and I are alone."

Maxine looked mortified. "She needs our support and she won't have that if we're not in the room."

Calypso had to stop herself from rolling her eyes. Instead, she said, "Your support is obvious, but this will work better if she's alone."

"Fine. I can't get reception in here anyway." Maxine made her way out of the bar, with Bryce right behind her.

Calypso turned to Emily with a grin. "They're enough to drive anyone mad."

Emily gave a husky little chuckle and shrugged. "They weren't that bad before they split up."

"Okay, let's get started." Calypso scanned the pretty girl, but couldn't immediately come up with anything. Perhaps Emily was blocking her. "You definitely want to do this?"

Emily looked exhausted. "Yes, I really do."

Calypso tried again. And once more, but the veils refused to lift. She shook her head slightly. This time, it was Emily who was concerned.

"Perhaps I can't be fixed."

"Everyone can be fixed, if they want to be."

The one exception to that rule was with destined diseases and conditions. But even then, Calypso could still access that person's energy and prescribe remedies to help them cope, or to ease their pain.

Calypso felt uneasy. What was going on? Why couldn't she break through the veils to help this girl? She noticed Emily was starting to look upset as well, so she needed to come up with something quickly. She could admit she couldn't pick up on anything, but Emily would take that as a personal failure and this girl really needed help. Calypso decided to fake something now and advise that Emily came back for a second session some other time.

"Got it," Calypso announced, sounding way more confident than she felt. "You're an interesting and complex person, Emily. But I know what you need."

Emily looked relieved and Calypso knew she'd done the right thing. She set about making an infusion of chamomile and lemon balm, and also prescribed an *Avena sativa* tincture. She knew it was a cop out, but the properties of the tea and tincture would still have an effect. Sure, it wasn't the same as a magical brew, but for some reason she was incapable of producing one.

Calypso placed the tea in front of Emily and watched while she drank it. Even one of her more generic magical brews would work, the ones that were already made up and stored in the fridge. But she couldn't put her finger on the core of Emily's problems, so couldn't prescribe one of them either.

The core of Emily's problems. Her parents!

Calypso almost laughed out loud. Of course! Didn't have to be psychic to see that, which was lucky, seeing as for some reason today, Calypso wasn't psychic at all. "Emily, could you go and ask your parents to come back in?"

Emily slid off the stool and disappeared out the door. Calypso opened the fridge devoted to love spells. It was the main reason people came to her and she found herself using the same potions over and over again, so now brewed some of them in advance. Unless it was an unusual case, a generic cocktail often sufficed.

Admittedly, she hadn't been able to tune into Emily's parents either, but she'd be blind not to notice the classic signs they displayed. Maxine's affair followed hot on the tail of whispers in the press about Bryce having an affair. She was obviously trying to make Bryce jealous. It worked, because he had seethed and fumed while she tapped away at her phone. If they had no feelings for each other, there'd be no need to behave like this. Not that this was healthy behavior between two adults, but Calypso had seen all sorts of games and dysfunctions in her line of work.

Calypso grabbed two highball glasses, filled them with ice and poured in a pre-prepared spell: Aphrodite's Love Potion, a mix of Angostura bitters, brandy and pineapple juice. Finally, she dropped three caraway seeds into each glass. She was just garnishing the cocktails with cherries when the family arrived back.

"Emily has certainly made some progress today," she assured them, "but full healing can't occur without you two also finding a sense of peace with each other."

"There's more chance of peace in the Middle East," Bryce snapped.

Calypso slid the cocktails across the bar. "I always live in hope for resolution, wherever it may be. Drink these, for your daughter."

Both did as they were told. The effects were visible immediately.

"Delicious," Maxine sighed.

"Reminds me of the cocktails we had that time in Mexico," Bryce said.

The two smiled at each other for a moment, then turned away, embarrassed.

"I'm hungry," said Emily, surprising everyone in the room.

"You'd eat?" Maxine was shocked.

Emily just shrugged.

"Let's go and have some lunch, shall we?" her father suggested.

Emily and her mother smiled and spoke in unison. "That would be lovely."

Calypso advised them to bring Emily back soon for another session, on the house, and her parents agreed. It was the first time they'd agreed on anything for months. After some heartfelt gratitude, and an excessively large tip from a smiling Bryce, Calypso was alone again in the bar. She quietly locked the door and sank down onto the cool stone steps. Worry clawed at her gut. Where the hell had her powers disappeared to?

Chapter 7

Holly can be used for dream magic

Taran passed Simon his beer and they made their way from the bar to one of the tables crammed into the tiny Quinn's Comedy Club. Taran scanned the room for Calypso, but couldn't see her. He was excited, and nervous, at the thought of seeing her. Ridiculous really. He'd only left her – okay, she'd kicked him out – a few hours ago.

They took a seat and Simon looked down at the program. "Which one is her friend?"

"Megan something or other."

"I'm impressed. Stand-up's not for the fainthearted. I wouldn't get up in front of my family to yell fire."

"I don't blame you … what if they made it out of the house?"

Simon laughed. "Too true." He suddenly looked appalled. "There's only one girl on here. This isn't a double date is it?"

"I wouldn't think a stand-up comedian was your type," Taran said.

"I'm not sure I have a type," Simon admitted. "Sometimes I'd be grateful for anything."

"Then why don't you go for one of those money-hungry little social climbers who are always hanging around?"

"I may not have a clear type yet, but I know what I don't want."

Taran grinned at his friend. "I don't blame you, Sime."

"Are you sure this isn't a blind date? I would've bought flowers."

"And looked like a total dickhead. You don't give a stand-up comedian flowers."

"What do you give then?"

"I don't know? A six pack." Taran chuckled. "Being an Apsley, you could manage a whole keg."

Simon glanced at his watch. "Should I duck out now and pick something up?"

"No need. It's not a date." Taran stopped scanning the room for Calypso and focused on his friend. He realized Simon was nervous. "I don't even think I'm on a date. Calypso is playing hard to get ... or *impossible* to get. Even my invite to this thing was given grudgingly."

Simon visibly relaxed. "Nice little club, this."

Taran rolled his eyes. "Sime, it's a shithole, but as long as the comedians are halfway funny, we'll have a good night." *And as long as Calypso turns up.* He tossed back the rest of his drink and stood. "Want another round?"

"Absolutely. I could use some Dutch courage."

"That makes two of us," said Taran as he headed to the bar.

*

Calypso paid the cab driver and ran toward the club. She was late, thanks to Taran and his incredibly annoying sex appeal. She rarely suffered a wardrobe crisis, but tonight she'd torn through her clothes, despairing at them all. It was ridiculous. She didn't need to impress Taran; she should really be deterring him. But she couldn't bring herself to look anything less than fabulous. Goddess damn him! In the end she settled on Top Shop jeans and jacket, a funky little vintage shirt, and Stella McCartney boots, which cost a fortune, but came guilt free. Calypso liked to look good, but not at the expense of anything that ever had a mother. Tonight, in her high-end pleather, she looked better than good – she looked great. But she was nervous, indecisive and excited all at once, and she hated that Taran had this affect on her. She was tempted to cancel, but to cancel on Taran would be to cancel on Megan, and she'd never do that.

It took a moment for her eyes to adjust to the dim club, but once they did, they rested on Taran. It was as though he had a homing beacon attached – somewhere around the groin area – and could spot exactly where he was sitting. He seemed to sense her arrival too, because at that exact moment he looked over at her and their eyes connected, despite the dim light and the distance between them.

Calypso approached Taran's table with a determined, long, sexy stride and gave him a light kiss on the cheek. "Hi there."

"Hi."

"Am I late or are you early?"

"Both," he muttered.

Calypso waited for Taran to introduce his friend, but he remained strangely silent, so she sat next to Simon and introduced herself.

"I'm Calypso."

"Simon. And you have no idea how wonderful it is to meet you."

Calypso was slightly thrown by his enthusiasm. "Oh, why's that?"

"It's such a pleasure to see Taran at a loss for words around a woman. Usually it's me." Simon grinned at Taran.

"Your shout, mate. And perhaps you can find a speech therapist while you're at the bar."

Taran ignored Simon. "What do you want, Cal?"

"What do I want?"

"To drink ..." He was finding his feet again. Perhaps not verbally, but his heated stare made her blush.

"I'll start with a beer." Calypso gave Taran a sexy smile and turned her attention back to Simon.

Before long the show began. The MC introduced the first comedian for the night, and then the second. They were genuinely funny and the audience laughed loudly through both routines. Calypso felt nervous. She knew Megan always had to work extra hard, simply because she was female. Megan often joked that she was white, straight and female, so was automatically at a humor disadvantage. She also had both her legs ... but figured that having tiny breasts was a shortcoming she could get some mileage from. And she did.

Megan's turn, and the energy in the room shifted. It was as though they expected her to fail. A number of people got up and went to the bar. Calypso felt like yelling out, "Where are your manners?" But fortunately Megan was made of sturdy stuff and did it for her.

"That's okay ... go and get a drink, duck off to the loo ..." she said as she strolled onto the stage. She smiled sweetly at the audience. "I've actually been placed third in the lineup for the alcoholics and bladder impaired to do just that. My act isn't important. What's important is that you don't piss your pants when you laugh at me."

Simon burst out laughing.

Megan grinned and searched the audience for the phantom laugher, but the spotlight made it difficult for her to see. She settled for saying, "Thanks, Dad, but I told you to stop coming to my gigs."

She took a moment. "Evening, everyone. I'm Megan Walker ... I'm a girl. I know ... I don't really look like one. And I know what you're thinking, but no, I'm not a lesbian. I like men, although because I look like a lesbian, men never like me. It's a vicious circle. I actually had a guy hit on me a couple of years ago ..." Megan paused and stared around the room for a moment, and then: "No, there's no punch line there. I just wanted to share, because it rarely happens."

The crowd burst out laughing. They were warming to her. Simon was in hysterics and laughed long after everyone else stopped.

Megan gave an amused snort. "Excellent, my new stalker has finally arrived. I ordered one from stalker dot com a few months back, but he was faulty. Things started out okay, but after a while he ignored me, was always too tired to stalk me ... I was like, 'You never stalk me any more', and he was like, 'For God's sake, woman, can't a stalker have some peace?'"

Megan took a sip of water while the laughter died down. "I found having a stalker was like being married," she joked. "Speaking of marriage, I was reading this article the other day about these chastity clubs in America where teenagers wear a ring that commits them to no sex before marriage. What I'd like to know is if they don't have sex before marriage, when are they going to have sex? Because everyone knows you don't have sex *after* marriage! Not that I'd know, either way. I'm like the carpet in the foyer here ... Got laid once years ago and walked on by drunks ever since."

The audience grew louder and louder in its appreciation of her jokes and self-deprecating humor. Megan had a way of being tough and sassy, yet subtly sexy at the same time. Taran and Simon were in stitches. Calypso was thrilled that everyone could see what she'd always known: Megan Walker was funny. The jokes started coming out thick and fast.

"I mean, I'm not a complete loser. I date, but it's tough. Dating is hard work ... that's why it's called a blow *job* and not a blow holiday! I don't want you thinking I'm unpopular or anything. I've got loads of friends ... Hundreds. Although, I've got to say, they all let me down recently. It was my birthday, and I sent out an invite to my party. No one came. Not one single present. Nothing. Fuck them all. I'm seriously thinking of closing my Facebook account."

Megan grinned at the audience and patiently waited for the cheers to settle.

"Anyway, that's me for tonight. Anyone who's interested in dating a girl who looks like a boy, look me up on Facebook – while I'm still on it. See ya, and thanks ... it's been real!"

And with that she was gone.

Chapter 8

Raspberry wine soothes sore throats

After the show, Megan joined the others for dinner at a cozy Italian restaurant nearby.

"So you're my new stalker?" she said by way of introduction to Simon.

"Well, yes ... no ... I'd never ..."

"I appreciate the laughs." Megan leant forward and whispered flirtatiously, "I'll pay you later."

Simon chuckled and blushed simultaneously. He buried himself in the wine list until the heat left his cheeks. "Oh fabulous, they have the 2009 Ren Valley Pinot Gris here."

Megan turned to Taran and Calypso, completely unaware of the affect she was having on one of England's richest bachelors.

"They've got loads here for vegetarians, Calypso."

Calypso was scanning the menu. "The mushroom risotto looks great."

"You go for it, but I need to eat animals." Megan gave Simon a wink. "Stand-up is a bit like sex. I'm always ravenous afterwards."

Simon let out a strangled giggle, but was then mortified that he did.

Megan waved the waiter over and ordered steamed mussels, spaghetti and meatballs, a serving of bruschetta for everyone, but two for herself, and an arugula salad. The others ordered their – much smaller – meals and then Megan decided to add an order of tiramisu to hers. Simon thought she was the most delectable creature he'd ever met. He was so sick of taking women to dinner only to watch while they picked at a salad and bitched about their weight.

"Have you always been funny?" he asked.

"A sense of humor was essential growing up in my house."

"Megan has four older brothers who used her as a punching bag," Calypso explained. "The more she made them laugh, the less they tortured her."

"It's also the reason I started hanging out with Calypso. They were all on their best behavior when she was around."

Calypso and Megan shared the look of lifelong friends and laughed.

"That's utter bullshit. I started hanging around you because it took the focus off me. People never quite knew who to bully, so they left us alone."

"It's true. Alone we were victims, but together we were a weird force to be reckoned with," Megan said in mock seriousness. "She could cast spells and I knew how to fight."

Simon was fascinated. "How old were you when you met?"

"Five," said Calypso and Meg in unison.

"So you've been friends forever."

"Forever? Watch your mouth," Megan warned. "We're not that old." She took a slug of her drink and glanced at Taran. "I'm the bulldog at the gate. I'll always be around while others come and go. And *everyone* has to get past me."

Taran nonchalantly refilled everyone's glasses. "Judging from the amount of food you've ordered tonight, Megan, getting past the bulldog won't be too tough ... if I throw you a bone."

Megan's eyes sparkled. "Why thank you, Taran. It's been so long since I had a good bone."

Simon's wine went down the wrong way and he began to cough, and Megan gave him a slap on the back.

"Easy, cowboy."

"So what about you two?" Calypso asked. "How did you meet?"

Simon glanced at Taran, afraid he'd reveal the embarrassing truth about how he'd found Simon naked, chained to a bike rack, after a college initiation got out of hand.

"We met through friends," Taran said simply, and then couldn't help himself: "At a bike club."

"Do you cycle, Simon?" Megan looked impressed and tried to check out his ass.

"Ah, no … used to. I didn't like being chained to one thing."

"So he took up drinking and partying with me."

"It's true, but I was never a gold medalist like Taran." Simon smiled at Megan. "Do you play sport?"

Megan screwed her nose up. "I ran for a bus once."

"You've chosen well. You were hilarious up there tonight," said Taran. "Where do you get your ideas from?"

Megan shrugged. "Where do you get your ideas from when you paint?"

"Probably a similar place."

"Exactly. It's just we express them differently. It's all a creative process." She turned and looked at Simon, curious. "What do you do, Simon?"

Simon fumbled the menu. "Me? Oh … ah … I'm a – I work for Apsley Beer."

Megan pulled a face. "Oh shit, I hope you don't have to also drink it. Apsley Beer is worse than cow piss."

Simon's eyes nearly popped out of his head, and then he roared with laughter.

Megan continued to shove her foot in her mouth. "I've heard that whatshisface Apsley is a total cockhead to work for. What's his name again?"

"That would be Charles Apsley." Simon sipped his drink, and then added, as though it were an afterthought: "My father."

Megan went thirty-two shades of red. "Are you serious?"

"Yes, unfortunately."

"Oh shit … I'm so sorry."

"So am I. Regularly. Especially during family dinners. He really can be a … cockhead."

"The beer is okay."

"I'd prefer Guinness."

Taran, who had been in silent hysterics, couldn't hold back any more, and joined Simon in loud, raucous laughs. It didn't take long for Calypso, and finally Megan, to join them.

"I'm so sorry, Simon. I'm a total idiot."

"It's absolutely fine, Megan. I find you refreshing."

In fact, Simon was completely besotted. And as the evening progressed, he felt more and more at ease in her company. Normally, when he liked a woman, he clammed up. But tonight Simon shared a few choice stories of their college days that had the women in stitches. For once, he felt interesting.

By the time they left the restaurant, all four were well oiled with great wine and laughter. It was cool and Megan, dressed in nothing but jeans and a singlet top, faltered as the night air hit her.

"Shit, I left my jacket at the club."

Without a second thought, Simon whipped his off and handed it to her. It was a simple gesture that said so much about him.

"Thanks," she whispered. It was her turn to feel a bit tongue-tied.

He decided to take a leap. "Where do you live, Megan?"

"Finsbury Park," she said.

"That's on my way home," he lied. "You can ride in my cab and I'll drop you off."

Megan smiled. "Sure as hell beats the night bus."

Simon quickly flagged a cab, thrilled that it even stopped for him because quite often they didn't. His brothers didn't call him the Invisible Man for nothing. He ushered Megan into the backseat with a farewell wave at Taran and Calypso.

*

As soon as the taxi drove off, Taran turned to Calypso.

"Interesting."

"What is?"

"I'm staying with him, yet he didn't offer me a lift."

"Would you have taken it?"

"No. I'm a gentleman. I want to make sure you get home safely."

"Taran, I'm a big girl. I've been getting home safely for years."

"Okay, I want to get you home safely ... and make love to you all night long."

Calypso smiled. "That's more like it."

He held out his hand and she took it, surprised by how her fingers seemed to meld immediately into his. She had to concentrate to work out which were her own fingers and which were his. They walked for a while in a comfortable silence.

"Calypso?"

She sensed what was coming. "Yes?"

"Why did you leave New York without saying goodbye?"

"I remembered I left the iron on – in London."

"I've seen your clothes ... You don't own an iron." He pushed a lock of her hair back from her face and gently placed it behind her ear. "I really like you, Cal."

"You don't really know me."

"I'd like to."

Her eyes darted around. "We should get a cab."

He grabbed her shoulders and moved her back against a shop window. "I'm in London for three months."

"I can't guarantee I'll be here. I don't like to be pinned down."

"You liked it last night."

Calypso blushed at the memory. "You know what I mean, Taran. I'm not good with commitment."

"Don't use the C word. It doesn't suit us," said Taran. "But we suit each other."

His lips crushed down on hers and she immediately melted into his body. It was instinctual. She couldn't resist. She'd been desperately trying to remain aloof all night, but he'd matched her in every sense and it made her want him more than ever. Every tiny touch, every glance, every word he uttered to her set her alight. Her whole body hummed at the very thought of him.

Taran Dee was getting to her. It had to stop. And it would – tomorrow.

Chapter 9

Champagne is a diuretic

The next morning, Calypso asked Taran to leave. She waited until they'd made love, figuring she at least deserved one more for the road, and then she told him to hit it.

"I'm busy," she said as she tossed him his clothes.

Taran propped himself up on one elbow. "Wow ... déjà vu."

Calypso put her hands on her hips. "What are you waiting for? Breakfast in bed?"

"I've already worked out that I'm with the wrong woman if I want that sort of treatment."

"You're not *with* me."

"I would be if you stopped bitching and got back into bed."

She was tempted, but a steely resolve had settled overnight. "Come on, don't be an arse. You have to go."

He scanned her face. "Why? Scared?"

"Hardly. I'm going away," she said, way too quickly.

"Where to?"

Calypso stalled for a moment while she decided where to go. "Paris."

"Paris? Today?"

Calypso stalked over to her wardrobe and flung open the doors. The dramatic gesture was ruined when she realized none of her clothes were in the wardrobe, but scattered all over her floor. She began to gather them together. "Yes, didn't I tell you I was going to Paris today?"

Taran climbed out of bed and slowly dressed. "Nope. Didn't mention it."

Calypso, still naked, threw her half-packed suitcase on her bed and began to toss some final things into it. She didn't bother folding anything, and she didn't seem to be in a hurry to put anything on.

Taran pointed at a pile of jeans in the corner. "Don't forget those. Not that you seem overly attached to clothes." He finished dressing and gave her a peck on the cheek. "Paris is lovely at this time of year. I'm sure you'll have a wonderful time."

Calypso watched as he let himself out and then reached for her robe. She suddenly felt cold without him.

*

Later, as she sat on the Eurostar, Calypso felt a twinge of regret. Her mother certainly thought she was mad.

"What do you mean you're going to Paris? You've only just arrived home."

"And now I'm going again."

Batty put her hands on her hips and gave Calypso her "don't mess with me, young lady" look. "What are you running from?"

"You know better than to ask me something so ridiculous," snapped Calypso. "I'm never running *from* anything."

"Except when you left New York last year. And now, all of a sudden, Mr Sex-On-A-Stick arrives in town and you're off again."

Calypso's eyes narrowed and shot daggers at her mother. "I'm going to Paris for work."

"Look, darling, what happened with Scott was—"

"It has nothing to do with Scott." Calypso didn't want to go there – ever.

"You keep telling yourself that, Callie." Batty stormed out, leaving Calypso with the overwhelming urge to throw something after her.

The problem was, her mother was right. And Calypso *hated* it when her mother was right. She still wasn't completely over Scott, and felt the need to put some space between herself and Taran. Sure, a few days in his company would have been nice – he was great fun, addictively sexy and a phenomenal shag – but she'd ditched him a year earlier for those very reasons. He was way too dangerous. She had no intention of ever falling in love again, and she knew that falling for him was a very real possibility if she spent any more time with him. She simply couldn't risk getting hurt again. It had taken her years to piece herself back together after her last heartbreak.

Calypso's life was fine just as it was. She had her bar, her wonderful – if occasionally interfering – family and friends, and she loved being able to go wherever the wind took her. She'd never find a man who'd understand her need to keep moving. And even if she did, who's to say it would last? She'd met such a man once and had paid a very steep price for it.

Calypso met Scott at the Berlin Love Parade when they were both in their early twenties. She'd been dancing with friends when a gorgeous blond Aussie Adonis strolled up and stood in front of her.

"G'day," he grinned. "I'm Scott ... and I think I'm meant to meet you."

One look at him and she knew he was right.

Her eyes skimmed his body. He was shirtless, his T-shirt tucked into the back of his shorts. He was tall, and muscular, with smooth, deep olive skin. His stomach was flat and toned. Calypso had an overwhelming urge to run her hands across it. She wrenched her eyes upwards and looked him in the face, but that was worse. Boyish good looks; golden hair that curled in all the right places; clear blue eyes that looked achingly familiar. Calypso fell instantaneously and passionately in love.

They drank and danced and he met her friends. Later that night they made love under the stars. It was so right, so perfect.

"What now?" asked Calypso afterwards, petrified that he was about to announce his plans to go back to Australia.

"I don't know," he said. "Where are you going?"

"I was thinking about Rome," said Calypso tentatively. She'd change plans in a heartbeat for him.

Scott stretched lazily. "Cool."

Cool? Was that good-bye in Australian?

"Yeah, cool," he repeated, as if she should understand. "Rome. That's where we'll go next."

And so they did. Followed by Venice, Barcelona, and San Francisco. Apart from his guitar, Scott had no attachment to anything material. Their mutual passion for life and each other fed every moment they shared. Calypso adored him – totally.

The relationship wasn't perfect – what relationship is? – but it was close to it. The only thing that really marred her happiness with Scott was her fear that she'd lose him. Scott lived life on the edge. He needed to experience everything, no matter how crazy or dangerous it was. Filled with the naïve ignorance of youth, he thought he'd live forever, until one night in Thailand when he was robbed and nearly killed. It had been a horrible experience, but it had left Scott with the insatiable desire to live life to the fullest.

With wild abandon, he said.

Calypso realized then that he'd never change, and decided if she couldn't beat him, she'd join him. And join him she did: skydiving, scuba diving, sailing. They traveled around the world together for the next two years, supporting themselves with his busking and Calypso's tarot readings. They lived in Rome and Rio de Janeiro. They spent time on a commune in India and the ski fields in Canada. She truly and most joyously had discovered her soulmate, the man she thought she'd grow old with.

How wrong she was.

Calypso stared out the window at the ugly outskirts of Paris. It was a city famous for its cultured beauty, yet the reality could be a colorful mess of clashing cultures and grime. Paris kept her on her toes, which is why she adored it so. While she loved many places around the world, there weren't many that truly assaulted her senses and attacked her heart so simultaneously: Tokyo, Jo'burg ... and Paris. She loved this city and it was the perfect place to escape to for a few days, while she evicted Taran Dee from her system.

The train pulled into Gare Du Nord, and Calypso stood and collected her bag. She'd made a mistake loving Scott too much. She'd never make the same mistake again.

Chapter 10

Sloe wine settles stomach upsets

It was normally too early for La Barre Noir to be busy, but word had spread that Calypso was in town so it was filling up quickly. She came to Paris regularly and always worked here. She didn't offer the same assortment of cocktails and teas as she did in London, just a few of her more generic cocktails, using the base ingredients she carried with her everywhere. Anyone who wanted something more specific would eventually travel to London and her fully stocked Cauldron. But Parisians were easy to satisfy. On the whole, they came to her about love.

"My 'eart iz broken. She does not love me."

"'E iz a bastard ... he thinkz I do not know about 'er."

"I am filled with fervor for 'im, but 'e does not notice me."

Sure they were predictable, but passionately so, and Calypso loved them for it.

Tonight there had been no unusual requests or needs – thankfully, because Calypso still couldn't summon even the smallest spell. She had already prescribed a number of pre-mixed cocktails for lovelorn customers: a Sex on the Beach (vodka, peach schnapps, orange and cranberry juice); a couple of Orgasms (Cointreau, Bailey's Irish Cream, Grand Marnier); and a French Connection (cognac, Amaretto Liqueur, two drops of Earth Essence) for a German banker whose French girlfriend had dumped him.

Pierre, the bar's owner and Calypso's old friend, came over to her and hung his arm over her shoulder. "I 'ave missed you, my little gypsy."

"Oh Pierre, I was here two months ago."

"You should come more often. Every month. I'll pay you well."

"No money is worth the routine. You know that."

Pierre nodded, resigned to the fact that he'd forsaken his own freedom the minute he opened his bar. He wasn't able to juggle travel and the bar like Calypso did.

Pierre and Calypso had met on the road. Actually, it was more of an overgrown pass in Costa Rica. An immediate connection, a lot of rum, and the realization that they both loved Argentine men had led to the conclusion that they needed to move to Buenos Aires – together. A week later they were holed up in a flat in the capital, where they stayed for six months. Neither of them found true love, although they certainly gave it their best shot, but they did find true friendship with each other. They stayed in touch over the years, often joining each other in Prague or Nepal or wherever. Around the same time that Calypso met Scott, Pierre's father died and left him some money, which he used to open his bar. Before long, he too fell in love, but unlike Calypso's relationship, his was still going strong. Their friendship lasted through it all. Nowadays, Calypso envied Pierre's relationship, while he envied her freedom, which only served to strengthen their bond.

Pierre searched her face. "So, you 'ave a new lover, yes."

Calypso wasn't sure if it was a question or a statement. "No."

"You certain? You 'ave that look."

"What look?"

"The same one you 'ad after the Berlin Love Parade."

Calypso stepped back, as though she'd been slapped. She couldn't bear the comparison.

"Don't look so shocked, Callie. I see it in your eyes." Pierre reached out and touched her cheek. "You are all flushed, mon cherie."

Calypso turned and pretended to prepare some garnishes. "You know you're the only man for me," she teased.

"That's because I'm safe."

Calypso turned and met his stare. "Well, yes, I did have a fling last night with an old boyfriend," she admitted.

"I knew it!"

"Oh yes, Sherlock, aren't you clever!"

Pierre gave her a sly grin. "'E was good, no?"

Calypso giggled. "No – he was *great*."

Pierre clapped his hands. "You like this mystery man."

"Maybe, but that doesn't mean it's going anywhere."

Pierre looked affronted. He'd been known to walk over hot coals for love. Love was worth it. "Why not?"

How could she explain? Because Taran was too hot, too gorgeous, too funny, too smart? And because of that he was too dangerous? She picked up a glass and began shining it. "Well for starters, because I'm in Paris and he's not."

"Don't suppose you've got a drink for an old friend?"

Calypso looked up and dropped the glass she was holding. Taran was standing on the other side of the bar, a smug grin on his impossibly handsome face.

"Obviously you'll need another glass."

Calypso scrambled for a dustpan and brush, but Pierre snatched it off her.

"I'll do it," he hissed.

Calypso grabbed the dustpan back. "I dropped the bloody glass, I'll clean it up."

Pierre ripped the dustpan out of her hands. "If you touch the glass, I'll kick your ass. Now piss off." He crouched down and picked up the broken glass.

Calypso turned back toward Taran, seething with anger at both men. "What are you doing here?"

"I was kind of hoping for another one of those fantastic hellos."

Calypso hated herself for blushing. "How the hell did you find me?"

"You once mentioned where you work in Paris."

"My, what a good memory you have."

"God gave us memories so we can have roses in December."

"It's not December."

"No ... but you are my English rose."

Pierre choked back a laugh as he stood and emptied the broken glass into the bin.

Calypso glared at him and then turned back to Taran. "And you're obviously my thorn!"

Taran gave her a wink and thrust his hand across the bar to introduce himself to Pierre.

"You 'ave a difficult journey," said Pierre.

"No," said Taran. "I just came from London."

"I mean in front of you." Pierre chuckled, which sent both men into fits of laughter.

"Excuse me," snapped Calypso. "I have to work."

Taran shrugged and turned his attention back to Pierre. Before long the two were drinking wine and chatting about football, French politics and, of course, love.

"My boyfriend, 'e made me run after 'im like a dog for three years before 'e said yes," said Pierre. "There were other lovers ... many, many—"

"Humph! Many? What a bloody understatement!" Calypso mumbled.

Pierre raised one neatly waxed eyebrow. "You are 'ardly Mother Theresa, mon cherie." Pierre turned back to Taran. "Where was I? Ah yes, there is only one Adrien." He looked misty eyed for a moment and then howled with laughter. "And thank God! 'E is quite a 'andful."

Calypso pretended to ignore them both. She was dealing with a young man who had been offered the job of a lifetime in New York, but was nervous about leaving Paris.

She grabbed a cocktail glass and took a deep breath. She needed a clear head. Her intentions needed to be unambiguous, and her emotions couldn't get in the way. Calypso tried to tune into her customer, but Taran's voice, as he talked to Pierre, was distracting her.

Calypso was feeling somewhat defeated, but decided to make her customer a Manhattan – an obvious choice. She began to mix rye, red vermouth and Angostura bitters.

But Taran filled her head. What the hell was he doing here? Why couldn't he bugger off back to New York, where he belonged? He certainly didn't belong in Paris.

She shook her head. She had to stop thinking about Taran while she was mixing. She found it difficult to even summon up a small spell, so instead added a few drops of water collected during a lightning storm. It gave the drinker a big jolt and propelled them forward in life.

She decorated the Manhattan with a maraschino cherry and placed the glass in front of the customer.

"This should help you make the right decision," she said. "Toss it back quickly."

The guy swallowed his drink and stood still for a moment. Then he shook, as though a charge of light shot through him. The indecision had gone.

"What the hell am I doing here? I should *bugger* off back to New York where I belong. I don't belong in Paris … shit." He clapped a hand across his mouth. And then quietly, he mumbled, "Merci beaucoup, mademoiselle. My decision has been made." And bolted toward the door.

Calypso watched him go in horror. Damn. She'd somehow put her own energy into that drink, but not in a magical way. That was no spell. That was her thoughts, verbatim. What the hell was going on? That never happened. She couldn't cast spells, and now Taran was affecting her standard cocktails. It was yet another reason why he had to go. That poor customer didn't know what hit him. Still, he got a result and was off to New York. Perhaps she should make another one of those drinks for Taran.

She grabbed a cloth and wiped the bar down. She could hear Taran and Pierre talking in French now. So Taran was fluent in French? No doubt he played the saxophone, wrote poetry and could dance as well. Goddess damn him and his fluency!

And just how had he won Pierre over so easily? Normally Pierre was quite rude to strangers – unless he was drunk and trying to get laid – but they were getting on like a house on fire. At least, she presumed they were; her own French was a bit rusty. But Pierre regularly hooted with laugher and was hanging off Taran's every word. Taran had him eating out of the palm of his hand.

The Frenchman turned to Calypso and whispered: "You are one crazy *bitch* if you let this one get away."

Calypso had had enough. She couldn't concentrate and needed some fresh air. She gave Pierre a kiss. "I'm done for the day. We'll speak tomorrow." And then turned to Taran. "You coming?"

Taran gave the lazy, devil-may-care, impossibly sexy grin that never failed to wind her up. "That's a sweet offer, but I'm having a blast here."

Calypso shot Taran one last withering look and stormed out the door.

A moment later he followed and grabbed her arm. "Hey, I was kidding. I didn't come to Paris to hang out with Pierre … although he's a really great guy. Did you know he beat testicular cancer?"

Calypso shook her head in wonder. Pierre never spoke about that to anyone. Obviously Taran was his new best buddy.

They wandered along in silence for a moment until Taran heaved a sigh. "This is a beautiful city."

Calypso nodded. He was right. It was stupid to waste the opportunity to have some fun with him here. "Do you know Montmartre?"

"Not really. I've always stayed around the fifth when I'm here."

"And you call yourself an artist," she scolded. "Montmartre is my favorite area. Creative, free-spirited people have always been drawn to this area. The energy here is special. It's so lively … but with this underlying power that stems back centuries to the Gauls and Druids. This area was sacred to them." She took his hand and led him around a corner. "Come with me."

It was still early, and the streets were bustling. They wandered up rue Poulbot, past Espace, the Dali museum, and through to Place du Tertre, where they stopped to view canvases from the resident artists. Calypso relaxed and enjoyed watching Taran as he chatted to some of the artists about their work. He wasn't open and sunny like Scott, yet he was similar in that he took time to connect with strangers. There was nothing frivolous or superficial about Taran. His questions were deep, his compliments genuine. There was an intensity in his approach to everything, yet he balanced it with a sardonic sense of humor and she found herself laughing constantly.

"This is much more enjoyable than the last time I was here," said Taran.

"When was that?"

"Years ago. I was with my mother and grandmother. Both miserable bitches." He grinned. "Did I say that? I meant 'witches.'"

"Didn't they like Paris?"

"Sure. Separately. They just hated each other, so being here with the two of them was like traveling with Tom and Jerry."

"Do you get on with your mother?"

"Absolutely, as long as I do everything she asks." Taran was quiet for a moment. "Actually, both my siblings are so good that it takes a lot of the pressure off me. Her expectations of me aren't that high."

"What about your grandmother?"

"We get on really well now ... that she's dead."

Calypso laughed. "I have a feeling that would help me like my own grandmother more as well."

They wound their way around the cobblestone streets, past the small galleries and cafes, eventually emerging at the Sacre Coeur.

"What a view." Paris at night from the Sacre Coeur never failed to take her breath away. "Isn't she magnificent?"

"Yes, she is," said Taran, staring straight at Calypso. "You love to wander, don't you, Callie?"

"I'd be lost without my travels." She stared deep into his eyes. "But I think you understand that."

"I do. I'm the same. It's one of the many reasons I'm so drawn to you. I know that life with you would never be dull."

He reached for her and pulled her in. Her arms wrapped around him and she felt herself melt into his body. The kiss set off fireworks in Calypso's brain. The past vanished; the future was of no concern. Time slipped away while the kiss continued, uninterrupted.

Chapter 11

Catnip tea eases colic in children

Calypso stayed in Pierre's boyfriend's old apartment when she was in town. Adrien now lived with Pierre, but they kept the spacious studio in the rambling sandstone building for when friends and family came to visit.

Calypso led Taran through a large wooden door and a cobblestone courtyard. Montmartre's busy streets were immediately silenced. Light from neighboring windows lit the courtyard's wrought iron furniture, tubs of flowers and daisies sprouting between the uneven pavers with a soft glow. Unlike London, Paris was warm and spring was in full bloom.

Calypso took Taran's hand and led him up a flight of stone steps. "Welcome to my Parisian home," she announced as she flung open the door.

The apartment had sandstone walls, caramel-colored wooden floors and visible beams. There was a small eat-in kitchen, a bathroom and a large studio room, containing a queen-size bed – "What other size would a queen have?" said Adrien – a small sofa and a desk.

Calypso opened the French doors – wondering, as she always did, if they are called French doors in France – that opened onto a tiny terrace overflowing with flowerpots filled with lavender and roses. The perfume from both flowers immediately entered the apartment and settled in for the evening.

"This is great," said Taran. "Do you ever stay in hotels when you travel?"

"Not very often," said Calypso. "I have friends all over the place and they're always willing to put me up for a night or two. I do a lot of work in exchange for a place to stay."

"And you're never a tourist?"

"I'm a traveler. If there's a difference."

"Paul Theroux said, 'Tourists don't know where they've been, travelers don't know where they're going.'"

"I like that."

"I like you."

"I like you too."

"Is that why you keep running away from me?"

"I'm not in a position to get more involved."

"You think I am?" said Taran. "Do we ignore it because it's inconvenient, or simply seize it when it comes along?"

Calypso walked into the kitchen and grabbed two glasses and a bottle of wine. "This little number is from a vineyard right here in Montmartre. Unfortunately you can only buy the wine during the harvesting festival. Pierre got this for me last year."

Taran watched as she poured him a glass. "You didn't answer my question."

Calypso handed him his wine. "I have no answer."

Taran knew better than to push too far. Instead he said: "How long until you return to London?"

Calypso gave her famous shrug. "I'm not sure. I've got to be somewhere in three days."

"Here in France?"

"No."

She was as slippery as mercury. Taran realized he was going to have to start singing a very different tune. "Let's spend the next three days together, and then you can head off to wherever. I don't expect anything from you, Calypso. I'm really busy with this show coming up so I don't have time for complications either." Taran didn't admit that he found her far from being a complication, or that without her, Finn would continue to block his calls, which *was* a serious complication.

"Three days. No pressure, no strings?"

"None."

"We won't talk about the future?"

"What future?"

She sipped her wine quietly and then nodded. "I'll think about it."

Taran grinned and took a sip of wine, and immediately spat it back into his glass. "Holy shit!"

Calypso burst into peals of laughter. "I know. Some years it's good. This isn't one of them. It's bloody awful isn't it?"

"Are you trying to poison me?"

"It's the privilege of drinking this wine, rather than the drop itself."

"Okay, I feel privileged, but do you have anything else?"

Calypso poured them both a vodka and soda and added a slice of lime to each glass. "This vodka comes from the Czech Republic. The brewery has been working continuously since the fifteen hundreds, and the vodka itself is based on an old witch's recipe." She handed it to him and then returned to the window.

"You have stories for every drink."

"Every drink has a story."

"Yes, I've had a few drinks with stories attached." Taran laughed.

"That's different. People demonize alcohol, but it's not the booze that's the issue, it's the people who abuse it. Alcohol has been used medicinally for centuries." Calypso took a sip of her vodka and turned to look out the window. "Personally I think there's nothing better than a cold beer on a hot day, or a glass of good pinot after a long day. And nothing worse than the morning after too many of both."

Taran lifted his glass. "I'll drink to that." He made his way to the window and pressed his body to hers from behind.

Calypso didn't move. "Are you hungry?"

"Yes," he whispered, "but not for food."

He took the drink from her and placed it on the table. His hands began to roam her body. Her skin was like satin. He pulled at the flimsy straps on her dress and the whole garment fell to the floor. She wore nothing but white lace pants underneath. She moaned as his fingers slipped into them. Christ, she was wet. She shivered and he felt like he was about to detonate.

She grabbed at his pants and steered him toward her, begging. He pulled her hand away and pressed her up against the wall near the window, unzipping himself and sliding into her from behind. His hands locked her arms into place against the wall. She cried out and her fingers clawed at the sandstone. He thrust into her, again, again, controlled, fluid movements, and then just as she was about to come, he stopped.

"No Taran, please ..."

"You want more? So do I. Give me three days." His voice was ragged. He drove into her again – and stopped.

"Don't stop, Taran, please," she whimpered.

He lifted her hips slightly and plunged deeper. "Three days, Calypso. That's all I ask."

Calypso cried out as her whole body gave into him. "Three days ..."

Taran felt himself lift off. What was it she said? Did she agree to three days? He couldn't hold back a second longer. They exploded together, pressed tightly against a four hundred-year-old sandstone wall, adding to the stories it could tell.

Later, as she slept soundly, wrapped in his arms, Taran marveled at how good it felt. He had her. Three days would become four. He was sure of it.

But when Taran woke the next morning, the bed beside him was empty.

Chapter 12

Drink marigold tea to solve love problems

Batty pulled a pint of beer for Harry and then put her hand out for the money.

"Are you alright, Batty?"

"I'm just waiting for you to give me the money."

"But I asked for a beer. You've poured me a pint of Coke."

Batty stared at the glass and realized she had indeed filled it with cola. "Bugger." She grabbed a new glass and filled it with beer. "Sorry about that. My head's in the clouds today."

"You sure you're okay?"

"Sure ... fine, just a tad tired, that's all." But it wasn't all. She wasn't tired; she was worried, and hurt – and quite confused.

Being part of a powerful matrilineal line of clairvoyants meant others would always see her as an eccentric. And she was. But Batty was also quite practical and, at heart, a traditionalist. The King and Mistress prospered because of her prudent approach to business. It was one thing to be attached to the pub emotionally – it had been in her family for generations and she adored the place – but it still needed to make money. She was aware that other pubs were forsaking their traditional décor for more modern fittings, but after careful consideration she'd decided that the pub's character was its major drawcard, so swapping the worn wood for chrome would be a mistake. The King and Mistress had a history of hauntings, and a reputation for magic and mystery that drew people in. So she'd renovated to highlight the history, rather than erase it. The wood and slate shone. Cracked tiles and stained-glass panels had been replaced. The rooms upstairs had been completely renovated because while people loved history, they didn't want to sleep with dust mites. But downstairs tradition ruled. The various bars were filled with a mix of modern, antique replicas and lovingly restored antique furniture. Under her management the hotel had been rewired, allowing for bright daytime lighting, which dimmed as night fell. Small plaques were placed in each room, celebrating the many famous characters that had drunk too much, loved too many within the classic old tavern walls.

Oscar Fingal O'Flahertie Wills Wilde regularly slept in this corner.

Dickens drank too much here.

Dylan Thomas dropped by once. He still hasn't paid for this window he smashed.

It had become a very different pub to the one Batty grew up in without losing any of its charm. Batty's shrewd head for business made sure every single aspect of the hotel was running smoothly and making money. So yes, to an outsider Batty might appear to be quite flakey, but to those who knew her, she was the strong glue that bound the business together.

And her family.

It wasn't just the King and Mistress that was a success because of Batty, but also her marriage. She'd been married for nearly thirty years to a man she worshipped and adored. She'd known from the first moment she'd clapped eyes on Alf Patterson that he was the one and only man for her.

She remembered the moment she first saw him like it was yesterday. The memory still made her weak at the knees. She'd been serving customers behind the bar when she turned and looked straight into the big blue eyes of a huge, ginger-topped man. They both blushed and grinned, mutual attraction mingled with confusion. They knew they'd never met before, yet every cell in their bodies sang that they had.

"What would you like?" Batty had asked.

Alf had looked surprised at the forwardness of her question. "I ah … you …"

"I meant to drink." Batty giggled.

"Oh right." Alf's face was the same shade of red as his hair. "Sorry … a pint, please."

Batty poured him a pint, occasionally glancing at him as she did. She'd never seen such a handsome man. Sure, he was no Cary Grant, but then Batty had never been attracted to that type of man anyway. This lad in front of her, with his strapping shoulders, broad chest and twinkling eyes, was the type of man she wanted to wake up to … forever.

She slid the beer across the bar. "There's your drink." She leant toward him slightly and whispered, "I'm also available if you'd like."

Alf's whole life had changed that night. He'd walked into the pub with a group of friends and ended up staying with Batty, to the amusement of his three rather conservative pals. They'd congratulated him on scoring for the night, but he later admitted to Batty that he'd known he'd scored for life. They were married a month later – much to his mother's horror.

There had never been another man for Batty. Not even in thought. She was one hundred percent faithful … and because she was quite conventional about such things, expected him to be as well. It had never even crossed her mind that Alf could be unfaithful … until recently, as a number of things had come to her attention and began to add up.

There was the letter she'd walked in on him reading. He'd shoved it in his pocket and quickly left the room. And then the mysterious appointments he had. He'd always told her exactly where he was off to, but lately he simply "had an appointment" and would disappear for hours. They hadn't made love for at least a month, which may not seem that odd to many after thirty years together, but their marriage had always been a passionate one. He'd also lost weight, and if that wasn't a sign that there was someone else, then what was? Batty liked a bit of beef on her man, but whoever this other *hussy* was, well, she obviously liked her men a bit thinner.

Finally there was this morning. Batty couldn't bear to think about it. She walked into the bathroom while Alf was naked and he'd actually grabbed a towel and covered himself. It was like he didn't want her to see him naked, which was ridiculous. His body was as familiar as her own. They were virtually one person. At least that's what she'd always thought: that he loved her just as passionately as she loved him.

Surely she wasn't wrong. Not about *that*.

But all the signs added up. He seemed preoccupied, nervous, as though he was hiding something. What other conclusion could she come to? It was frustrating not knowing for sure. As a psychic, Batty had easy access to most answers, but she'd never been able to read her man. That was usually considered a blessing in her clan. But now – what she'd give to simply tune into him and know, *just know*, what the dirty old bugger was up to.

Batty glanced at the clock on the wall and realized she'd better pull herself together. Her monster-in-law, as she called Alf's mother, was due any minute and she was like a shark – one sniff of blood in the water and she'd attack. Eleanor had never really accepted Batty, and Batty had long since given up caring. But one snide swipe from Eleanor today, one caustic remark, would be enough to send Batty over the edge.

"Morning, Mum."

Nell gave her a peck on the cheek. Nell always simply appeared and disappeared. There was no grand entrance or exit like there was with Calypso. Not that Calypso ever meant to make an entrance or exit, it was just she was the type of person who filled a room when she entered it and left it feeling rather empty when she was gone. But Nell was more like a wisp of scented air. She'd drift in and the place was all the nicer for her being there, but only the truly observant missed her when she left.

"Are you okay, Mum? You look a bit pale."

Batty decided to blame her appearance on the pair of ghosts who lived in a front room and often quarreled. It had been one of their dreadful arguments that led to their death in 1894, when a neighbor, sick of their shouting, shot them both. "The lovers were fighting last night so I didn't get much sleep."

Nell nodded. "Why is it that our ghosts have no manners? Enid threw a bread roll at me in the kitchen the other night. She can be such a moody cow."

Batty laughed. She felt better already. Nell was a small ray of sunshine. Her appeal might not be immediately noticeable, but once discovered, you could bask in her warmth for hours.

"Is Gran here yet?"

Batty shook her head. "No. Could you be a pet and get her table ready?" Alf's mother didn't like to linger in the pub. She came once a week, to "support" her son – like he needed it – and had lunch in the restaurant. Nell sat with her while Alf and Batty took turns watching the bar and listening to Eleanor criticize everything from the government to the price of chicken to Nell's clothes.

Batty slipped out the back and ran a comb through her hair. Not that it helped. Unruly was a polite way to describe her curls. She occasionally considered getting it cut, but Alf always talked her out of it. He loved her mop of red, as he called it. Batty pinched her cheeks, quickly gave her lips a coat of lipstick and decided that if he was having an affair, the first thing to go was her hair. Followed quickly by him.

Chapter 13

A shot of rum and lime juice will ward off a cold

Eleanor Patterson paid the taxi driver and walked toward the pub. Her steps always felt slightly heavy as she did. You'd think after three decades she'd be used to the life her son chose for himself – but she wasn't. She'd never get used to it. His defection to this weirdness had, in her humble opinion (and she was his mother after all) not only destroyed his life, but also all her own dreams. Eleanor had spent her entire life planning her son's future, starting well before he was conceived. What she hadn't planned on was his fateful meeting with Bettina Shakespeare, an umpteenth-generation psychic and owner of a rather strange pub in Highgate.

It was by no means an obvious match. They were so different in every way. While Alf's family tree could be traced back to the fifteenth century to some minor English nobility and a prominent archbishop (not that one mentioned *that* nowadays), Bettina Shakespeare's bloodline included circus owners, several herbal women who had been burned at the stake, and a series of eccentric publicans. Alf attended reputable schools and went to church every Sunday, while Batty was raised in a pub by her Pagan mother and grandparents and their assorted crystal balls and eccentric friends. Alf followed his mother's advice and went to university to study law. Batty followed her mother's advice and lived on a commune in India straight out of school. Alf came from a good, upstanding family. Batty came from the Addams family. Admittedly, there were whispers that she was actually the illegitimate daughter of an earl, but in Eleanor's eyes, the illegitimacy aspect of that made her son's fate even worse.

It was inconceivable that two such different people would be drawn together so powerfully. But from the moment they laid eyes on each other, Alf and Batty had been pathetically and frustratingly inseparable. From the first kiss, a glazed look settled across his eyes, a fogginess that was bound to worry a mother. And every plan she had for her son had gone up in smoke.

In fact, that was her first thought. Pot! Within weeks of meeting Batty, Alf's behavior had completely changed. He said it was because he was finally free to be himself, but Eleanor was still certain it was drugs. How else could one explain the dramatic changes that took place? The way Alf quit university to become a chef, proclaiming that it was what he always wanted was ridiculous! Wouldn't Eleanor know what her own son wanted? His sudden habit of grinning like an idiot savant? And the constant laughter – what was he, a hyena? Not to mention that look in his eyes …

But after thirty years of marriage the glazed look had remained and, as far as Eleanor knew, her son had never strayed from Batty's side. That in itself was rather odd. Her own husband, Edward – God rest his evil manipulative soul – partook in numerous affairs. All men did. They couldn't help themselves. They hunted while women gathered. Men had affairs and women shopped. It was primal. So why the hell was her son the faithful type?

The thought had bothered Eleanor for close to three decades and the only explanation she could come up with was that he had been the unwilling victim of some sort of witchcraft. *A spell.* It was obvious, but she would never point a finger at Batty because she didn't want Batty to point a finger back. She didn't want to wake up with mottled skin, or bushy nasal hair, or a love for Lycra. Who knew what spells the woman had in her repertoire.

Eleanor entered the pub and looked over at her daughter-in-law and huffed, as she always did when she looked at Batty. There was no doubting the woman's beauty. At fifty-one she was as stunning as she had been at twenty-one – perhaps more so. She certainly wasn't a classic beauty, but with her mass of hair, her pale, freckled skin and slim curves, she exuded an air of earthy sensuality. She was a quirky beauty with an undeniable presence. It had taken Eleanor quite a while to put her finger on what it was about Batty Shakespeare that was so unusual – apart from the witchy psychic thing – and finally she realized it was that Batty drifted through life without that quality that afflicted others: the desire to impress. And by doing so, she normally impressed people more than if she'd tried.

Never once had Batty played the games most daughters-in-law play. It was as though it didn't bother her one way or the other if Eleanor liked her. Eleanor had secretly looked forward to a few intimidating mind games with her future daughter-in-law, but from the moment this urchin roared into her life she neither encouraged nor discouraged a friendship.

Behind the bar with Batty was the one thing that made it all bearable: Nell, Eleanor's favorite granddaughter. Nell was the third Confucian monkey. All three Shakespeare were gorgeous, with pale skin and flaming red hair. But while Calypso was tall and sexy and as restless as the wind, and Batty was freckled and wild with frizzy hair and a laugh that had actually curdled cream, Nell was neat and organized and blessed with a sense of normality that her mother and sister lacked. She never blurted out indiscretions at dinner parties, or read people's palms at weddings. In comparison to her mother and sister, Nell had her feet planted firmly on the ground. Given the right man, Nell would blossom and might even forget about all the eccentric hoo-ha that surrounded her. Unfortunately, she was extremely picky when it came to men, which, considering her background, Eleanor felt was a luxury Nell couldn't afford. Nell said there was no point getting serious until the right one came along. Eleanor had tried to explain that women rarely married the *right one*, just the best one on offer at the time. But Nell would smile and mention her parents and even Eleanor had to admit that they did stand out as two people who together made a whole, even if it was witchcraft that had made them that way.

Nell's behavior baffled Eleanor. Most young women were desperate to marry. They shopped for men like it was the Selfridges summer sale. They'd grab anything that looked like a half-decent fit, whack him on their Relationship Visa and worry about the debt he incurred later. As far as Eleanor was concerned, Nell took the dating process way too seriously. It was as though the girl lived in a world without divorce.

Eleanor had been fortunate that her husband had dropped dead at a reasonably young age. Divorce had not been an option back then, although she'd certainly envied those wild women who did dump their men. Edward – God rest his hideous soul – had been a pig of a man. He was mean, controlling and, after one too many drinks, violent. Not that anyone ever knew any of that. Some things were best swept under the carpet. Eleanor hated the way people aired their dirty family secrets; she preferred to cover her bruises and carry on. She pretended to mourn when he died, but privately she celebrated. She'd been resigned to a life of misery with Edward when he suffered a massive heart attack. She remembered thinking at the time how surprising it was that he even had a heart.

Of course, no one had ever known Edward's true colors, not even Alf. She clung to her widowhood tightly, and everyone thought it was because no one could compare to her good, solid, upstanding husband. But the reality was, Eleanor would never again forsake her freedom. She didn't need to. While she wasn't filthy rich, she was comfortably wealthy. Alone, she was able to enjoy the best of both worlds: her husband's solid name and money, and the freedom his death brought her.

Eleanor watched as Nell chatted to her mother. She had such a lovely nature. Not like the other one. Calypso was too wild for her own good. Yes, she'd been through some difficult times, but that didn't give her the right to behave like a sex-starved tinker. Eleanor had tried for years to turn Calypso into a lady. She'd bought her some lovely clothes, which Calypso swiftly rejected. Eleanor had set her up with a couple of young men from excellent families, but Calypso basically chewed the poor boys up and spat them out. She'd subtly suggested that perhaps Calypso shouldn't drink so much, to which Calypso responded by sculling a beer and promptly pouring a fresh one. She'd tried in vain to explain that worthwhile men simply didn't respond well to such independent women, but Calypso laughed at her. Eleanor finally accepted that her oldest grand-child never listened, and was a lost cause, so she'd given up trying to help her. But sweet little Nell *was* a lady, which was rare nowadays, and could have such a wonderful life if she simply tried a little harder. She was smart, and had chosen a lovely career path. There was nothing weird about working in a museum. And the men one met there were certainly of a higher caliber than those who frequented pubs. Which was why Nell had to break free from the insanity of the pub. It wasn't just her mother and sister, but also the clientele.

Batty noticed her mother-in-law hovering by the door. "Hello, Eleanor! Are you coming in?"

Eleanor entered, paused briefly so both Batty and Nell could give her a kiss, and then made her way toward the dining room. Nell and Batty followed, bracing themselves for the chore ahead.

"Where's my son?" Eleanor asked.

"He had an appointment," said Batty. "He'll be back soon."

"What sort of appointment?"

Batty's green eyes flashed angrily. "He had to meet with a toilet paper supplier. We need something softer on the bum." Batty took Eleanor's coat and handed her a menu. "There's a wonderful ricotta—"

Eleanor cut Batty off. "Just the usual dear."

"Good idea, Eleanor."

Batty headed into the kitchen.

Eleanor turned to Nell and smiled. "Let me look at you." And then she patted her pocket.

"You left your glasses at home. They slipped between the cushions on the lounge," said Nell.

"Right," said Eleanor tightly. "You'll just have to be a bit blurry today." She hated it when her granddaughter used her gift. For a while there it had looked like Nell had been born without any psychic abilities at all. While Calypso communicated with the dead from birth, Nell didn't display any signs whatsoever until she was four years old.

Eleanor remembered the heart-breaking day things changed as though it were yesterday. She'd been taking a rather embellished trip down memory lane, telling Nell a particularly touching tale of her and dear dead Grandpa Edward's first date. Nell was enthralled, listening intently, when suddenly she began to giggle and nod her head.

The more Eleanor elaborated, the louder Nell laughed, until finally Eleanor demanded to know what the joke was.

"Grandfather says you've just spun enough crap to fertilize a garden."

Eleanor froze mid-meanderings and stared at her grand-daughter in horror. Edward had said exactly the same thing to her too many times to count.

"And he said don't forget to mention the bit about the garden shed because that was the highlight of the night." Nell's red head bobbed up and down as she nodded to instructions inaudible to her grandmother.

Eleanor spilt her tea all over her shoes and cried. No one, *no one*, had ever known about the shed. That after seventeen miserable years of marriage and a son together *that* was the first thing her dead husband mentioned from the other side was enough to break her heart. Although it did confirm to her what a complete bastard he was, and that even death hadn't changed him.

So Nell had the gift as well. Although, why it was called a gift was beyond Eleanor. A gift was a Royal Doulton figurine or a cashmere scarf. Nell's ability to converse with the dead was a painful fact of life, not something to celebrate.

Eleanor sighed. Life had stopped playing by the rules the moment Batty Shakespeare first shook her hand and giggled how good it was to see her again. Again? Please! Reincarnation was for heathens. Yet it had unnerved her and every day since had been a roller-coaster ride.

Eleanor stared at Nell. She was incredibly pretty. Not dev-astatingly gorgeous like Calypso, who was way too sexy for her own good. Nell was "lovely," although she did need a makeover. Eleanor made a mental note to take her shopping for clothes soon. She wasn't a student any more. The retro Audrey Hepburn thing was all very well and good for Audrey Hepburn, but on Nell it simply looked quirky. And let's face it, classy would win over quirky any day in the eyes of a decent man.

"How's the job hunt?"

Nell folded her napkin. "Okay. I've had a couple of interviews."

"Are you still at Highgate Cemetery?"

"Only the weekend tours."

"You'll never get real work if you're spending all your time as a volunteer."

"It's only a few hours on a Sunday, Gran. Besides, I've had more hours at the BMR lately."

"Really, Nell, you can do so much better than that. All that education and you waste your time at a small museum that's full of overrated love stories."

"The British Museum of Romance is dedicated to educating everyone about Britain's greatest love stories. Byron and Lady Caroline Lamb, Shelley and Mary Godwin, Winston and Clementine Churchill ..."

"Who were all mostlikely miserable together. No point romanticizing them, Nell. The men were probably bastards and the women no doubt suffered them." Eleanor sighed. "I simply think you'd be better off in one of the more reputable museums."

"I love the BMR. I wish I could work there full time, but I don't think Percy can afford me."

"See, the fact that it's under funded proves my point. What type of man fills a prime piece of London real estate with relics from other people's marriages?"

"Underneath his dithering exterior, Percy is a true romantic."

"That place must be worth a fortune," said Eleanor, referring to the Hampstead house that Percival Smyth had converted into the museum. "Did he buy it?"

"He inherited it. And I think it's wonderful. Percy cares more about history and love than money."

"Obviously, if he can't afford to hire you full time. Honestly, Nell, Percy is an old fool who'll do your career no favors." Eleanor pretended to have an idea, even though she'd been plotting this introduction for months. "You know Marjorie DeHart's grandson is one of the curators at the

National Museum. He's in the Medieval department apparently. I could see if there are any job openings for you."

Nell shook her head. "No. I want to do this on my own. No pulling strings."

"You make me sound like a puppeteer." Eleanor patted Nell's hand. "What if I see if there's anything available? I won't *pull strings* to get you a job, just an interview. Could I do that for you?"

Nell thought about it for a minute. It would still be up to her to get the job *and* up to her if she took it. And if it got Eleanor off her back …

"Why not? That sounds great."

Eleanor relaxed in her chair and smiled. She felt better than she had in weeks. "So now that we are sorting out your life, how about I also see if Elizabeth Nelson's grandson is single again?"

*

Batty felt like screaming. Eleanor was organizing Nell's life and Nell was sitting there allowing it. Nell often said it was simply easier to let Gran think she was getting her own way, but she usually was. Batty adored and worshipped her daughter, but by Goddess she needed to develop some backbone. And to top it off, Alf still wasn't here to deal with his mother. Heads were going to roll when she got him alone tonight.

"Sorry I took so long, love. Got delayed at this meeting and—"

Alf's entrance couldn't be better timed.

"Where the hell have you been?" Batty snapped.

Alf looked guilty. "I told you, I had a meeting …"

"A meeting. A meeting? What sort of meeting, Alf Patterson?" Batty realized she was screeching and immediately lowered her voice. "Your mother is in the restaurant bulldozing our daughter. Deal with it." And she stormed back into the main bar.

She grabbed a cloth and wiped down the counter. "A meeting. I'll give him a bloody meeting," she mumbled as she took her frustration out on the lacquer.

Batty realized someone was watching her. She looked up and saw Taran standing by the door. They stared at each other for a moment, and all thoughts of Alf's betrayal vanished. "Is Calypso okay?"

"I was hoping you could tell me that." Taran approached the bar and sat. "She has a habit of disappearing."

Batty nodded, relieved. It was nothing new, but still a concern. "You make her nervous." She poured him a beer and placed it on the bar.

"Thanks," said Taran. He watched her over the rim of his pint glass as he took a sip. "Bad day? You were pretty aggressive with that cloth."

Batty was thrown. "I'd rather not talk about it."

Taran nodded.

Batty watched Taran with growing interest. He wasn't at all upset by her brush off. Unlike most people, silence didn't seem to bother him. And he was without a doubt the most beautiful man she'd ever seen. He was at ease in his own skin and the shadows that lurked around him added an air of mystery, but not ill intent. He seemed to be as comfortable with his own darkness as his light, which was a rare thing. Most people either ignored their shadows, or allowed them to rule. It was a rare man who lived comfortably with them. Batty had only ever met one person with such a compelling presence before, and that was Calypso.

"Would you like something to eat, Taran?"

"I wouldn't mind."

"I can get Alf to fix you something."

"I'll organize it. You have enough work to do." He stood and gave her a wink. "And judging by the way you were cleaning that bar, it's best if you steer clear of your husband."

"Was it that obvious?"

Taran shrugged as he walked off. "I wouldn't worry about it. My mother cleans like that on a regular basis."

*

Taran made his way through the lounge and into the kitchen. He could hear Alf talking to someone, so he entered. By the time he realized Alf was on the phone, it was too late to turn back.

Alf's voice echoed throughout the kitchen.

"I'd appreciate it if you called me on my mobile … I don't want my wife picking up."

Taran turned to leave, but Alf spotted him. His face fell. He finished the conversation, eyes locked on Taran as he did. As he hung the phone up Taran tried to backtrack out of the kitchen.

"No point asking if you heard all that," said Alf.

Taran wished the floor would open up and swallow him. "Sorry, Alf, I just wanted a sandwich."

"And instead you were handed a secret to keep." Alf smiled wryly.

"I know this is probably none of my business, Alf, but—"

"You're right, son, it's none of your business."

"You should tell Batty. Don't let her hear this from anyone else."

Alf turned away and started making Taran a sandwich. "I'll tell her in my own time."

"She'll work it out for herself."

"She won't. Gifted though she is, she can't read family."

Taran rocked back and forth on his heels.. "Do you mind if I ask how long this has been going on?"

"You ask too many questions." Alf handed Taran the plate. "Son, I need to work it out first. This will hurt her enough. I'll tell her when the time is right."

"Fair enough."

Taran returned to the bar and but could only pick at his lunch.

Batty watched him for a few moments, then asked, "Has Callie told you anything about why she's wary of getting too involved?"

"She's a locked vault."

Batty sighed. "Calypso was deeply in love with someone a few years ago, and it ended badly."

"I figured something like that had happened." Taran couldn't understand how any man could leave Calypso Shakespeare.

"She was devastated."

"Perhaps she's not ready to move on."

"It's been three years, Taran," Batty said. "She needs to move on. She's young. She has the right to love again. But my daughter is very loyal, and loves with great intensity. It was difficult for her to accept that the relationship wasn't … for life."

"I understand," said Taran, who didn't really. Who was this knucklehead who'd dumped Calypso, and why the hell couldn't she get over him?

Batty leant across the counter. "How far are you willing to go for her, Taran?"

"As far as she needs me to go."

"Try Vienna. There's a small bar called Birdland near the Kartner Strasse. Next to Stephansplatz. She often goes there to hide."

Taran finished his sandwich in silence. He glanced at his watch. If he managed to get a flight, he could be in Vienna by closing. He drained his beer and then smiled.

"Thanks. Shall I tell her you said hello?"

Batty laughed and the two shared a twinkling look of conspiracy. "Yes, that should be fun."

Taran reached across the bar and drew Batty into a hug. "Everything will be okay, Batty."

Batty looked embarrassed. "Goodness, do you mean with me, or with Calypso?"

"Everyone." With that, he strode from the pub.

Chapter 14

Rose petal wine heals the heart

Birdland was a stone's throw from Vienna's Stephansplatz Cathedral. Its patrons would leave the tavern and look straight up at the imposing house of worship and do one of two things: thank God they hadn't drunk too much, or ask forgiveness if they had.

The tavern itself was small and rustic, with tilted stone walls infused with four hundred years of history, roughly finished wood tables, a mosaic-tiled bar and dim lighting. Despite its proximity to Vienna's number one tourist attraction, or perhaps because of it, the tourists missed the bar completely. It was a locals' haunt only, and always busy.

Owners Franz and Gisella served delicious traditional meals. Franz was famous for his sauerkraut, wiener schnitzel, weiner backhendl, and eisbein, while Gisella had a gift with mehlspeisen: traditional deserts such as apfelstrudel and palatschinken, which she always topped with lashings of whipped cream and served with great coffee.

Birdland was Calyspo's favorite watering hole after her own Cauldron. She loved Vienna and over the years she'd grown to love many of the regulars. The Viennese were quite reserved in their requests. They came to her about family matters, or health issues. At first they were wary. The Viennese were very fond of tradition, and trust was built up over time. Over generations, Calypso often joked. But their cool exteriors belied warm hearts. Once a Viennese decided they liked you, they were loyal. Whereas Calypso dealt with many one-time customers in London, in Vienna she saw the same faces regularly.

"Hello, Michael! How's the family?"

"Gut, danke. But my health ... nicht so gut."

"Ah Wolfgang, did you propose to Amelie?"

"I did, Calypso, danke to you. But now I have problems with my business."

And so they returned, time and time again. Calypso loved it. She enjoyed forming these bonds. But mostly, she enjoyed seeing her friends Franz and Gisella. She had known the couple for years. In fact, it was one of her cocktails that gave Franz the nerve to propose to Gisella. Calypso had been bridesmaid at their wedding, and a regular visitor ever since. Theirs was a friendship that ran deep.

Franz placed a hand on Calypso's shoulder. "You are distracted."

Calypso had bottled everything up for the past few days – perhaps the past year – and needed to talk. It was why she chose Vienna when she left Taran asleep in Paris. She knew her friends would listen properly – and understand.

"I've met someone." She made it sound like she'd just caught the flu.

Gisella's eyes lit up. "But Callie, that's a good thing. Why are you so upset?"

Calypso was silent for a moment, gathering her thoughts. "I'm not ready."

"Callie, it's time you were," said Franz. They had both known Scott. They'd been with Calypso in Berlin the day she met him, and the four had often traveled together. "You've been alone a long time now."

"I know. And I do miss having someone in my life."

"Then what are you waiting for?" asked Gisella. "Enjoy it, grab hold."

"It's safer not to, Gisella. It's safer to be alone."

"Safer, yes," Gisella agreed. "But also lonely, and not nearly as interesting."

Franz pulled up a chair beside his friend. "Is this still about Scott?"

"No – yes. I don't know."

"Have you … heard from him?"

"Not a word."

"You'd planned your whole life with him. It takes time to recover from that," he pointed out.

Calypso smiled sadly. "Love hurts. I don't ever want to risk it again."

Gisella jumped in. "But it was worth it, wasn't it? To have it, even for a moment?"

"I guess."

"It was you who taught me the English saying, better to live one day as a lion than one hundred years as a sheep."

"I think it was an Italian saying, but yes."

"You live like that," Franz said softly.

"I try to."

"Why can't you love like that?"

Calypso felt a sole tear run down her cheek. "I wish I could." She wiped it away and stood up. "Martini time!"

Franz and Gisella glanced at each other; this conversation was over.

Calypso made her way behind the bar and stared at the spirits before her. "We should be celebrating," she said. "We haven't seen each other for three months." She grabbed a bottle of Turkish apple vodka in one hand and a bottle of

Pomme Verte in the other. "I know we usually drink them dry, but tonight we're drinking martinis with a twist."

"Martinis with a twist for twisted friends," Franz announced.

Calypso mixed the martinis, and rimmed each glass with orange blossom water. "Fill me in on your news."

"Everything is super," said Gisella, way too quickly.

Calypso carried the drink over to her friend. "I don't have to be psychic to know that is a lie."

Gisella looked down at the table, obviously willing herself not to cry.

Franz stroked his wife's hair. "We've been trying for so long, Callie."

Gisella shrugged his hand away. "We nothing. As the doctor said, there's nothing wrong with you."

"Or you, liebling." Franz looked over at Calypso, helpless. Calypso made her way back to the table and pulled up a chair beside Gisella, who glared back at her.

"I don't want your sympathy," Gisella snapped.

"Good, because you're not getting it. I've told you I see a child."

"Yes, and you also thought you'd spend your life with Scott." Gisella slapped a hand across her mouth, horrified. "I am so sorry, Callie. That was unforgivable."

Calypso shook her head. "No, it's true, I did. But that was because I hoped to. We Shakespeare women have never been able to read our men ... obviously." Dark shadows threatened to flood her eyes, but she pushed them back. "But I can read you. I know this is hard, but it will happen."

Gisella's face crumpled. "It's been nearly three years."

"I wish you'd let me mix a brew for you."

"No, you've done enough for us. We're together because of you. I can't ask for more."

"You're together because you're destined to be so. All I did was help Franz with his nerves. He was a complete bloody basketcase who kept putting off proposing because he was petrified he was going to throw up when he did."

"With nerves, Gisella," Franz teased. "Not because you make me sick."

Gisella smiled slightly. Franz could always make her smile.

"Besides," Calypso continued, "the universe doesn't mind how much you ask for, Gisella."

"We shouldn't ask for more."

Gisella had consistently refused Calypso's offers of help. Her strict Catholic upbringing had always made her a little wary of Calypso's gift. But tonight she didn't sound so resolute. There was a catch in her voice. Franz heard it and gently pushed his wife.

"Why shouldn't we, Gisella? We see how Callie's brews work for our customers. We never judge them for coming back."

"But that's business. Calypso is our friend."

"And friends help their friends," said Calypso. "Can't you see how relieved I'd be to do this for you? After all the support you've given me, you'd be doing me a favor."

Gisella looked up through her tears. She'd never thought of it like that. Part of her still wanted to do this alone, without Calypso's magical assistance, but she wanted a baby more. "Okay," she whispered.

"Okay?" Franz echoed.

"Okay," she said, more loudly this time. "I'll try."

Calypso took her friend's hand and squeezed it. "I need a few extra ingredients. We'll do it tomorrow night."

Gisella nodded, excitement rising. "I don't want to get my hopes up."

Calypso understood. "Then don't. We'll simply have dinner and drinks tomorrow night and if it works, it works. Stop putting so much pressure on yourself."

Gisella smiled and leaned toward Calypso. "Now that you've sorted me out, what about you? What about this guy?"

"Oh him … I left the poor bugger in Paris. He'll never find me."

"That's a shame," Gisella said. "Perhaps you could call him."

Calypso waved her hand, as though shooing away a pesky fly … or a very pesky issue. "I guess, yes."

"When?" Gisella asked, eyes suddenly alight.

Calypso paused for a moment and realized she actually missed Taran. Time to change the subject. "Soon, I promise."

Franz glanced at the door and smirked. "I hope you keep that promise, Callie."

"In my experience, she has a tendency to break promises," a familiar voice said from the doorway.

Calypso froze. Taran was leaning against the door, relaxed and obviously enjoying her confusion.

"The poor bugger found you," he drawled.

"What are you doing here?"

Taran shrugged. "Thought I'd drop by and teach you some manners. I'm not sure why you're so rude. Your mother is charming. Says hello by the way."

Franz and Gisella glanced from Taran to Calypso to each other, waiting, waiting. Taran and Calypso stared at each other … countless unsaid words thickened in the air between then. And then Calypso nodded.

"Two days."

"I said three."

"One has gone," Calypso pointed out.

Taran decided not to argue over a lost day, but simply try to pin her down for the two left. "How do I know you won't disappear?"

"You have my word."

"I thought I had it last night."

"No, last night I said I'd think about it," Calypso said. "Now I have. Two days."

"Shake to seal the deal?"

Calypso arched one perfectly shaped eyebrow. "I'd prefer a kiss."

Taran strode across the room, lifted her out of her chair and kissed her long and hard. Then they both laughed and Taran turned to the others.

"I'm Taran," he said, shaking Franz's hand. "I apologize for just barging in unannounced."

"Not at all," said Franz.

"I love surprises," said Gisella.

Calypso was swinging dangerously between elation and terror. "Would you like a martini, Taran?"

"Love one," he said.

Calypso escaped to the bar, grateful for a chance to restore her equilibrium. She couldn't believe he was here, but was thrilled he was. Although her mother would cop an earful anyway, simply because ... because – Calypso couldn't think of a reason right now, but one would come.

Franz and Gisella pulled up chairs and got to work getting to know this mysterious new man in Calypso's life.

"How did you meet, Calypso?" asked Franz.

"I was in New York," Calypso explained, uncomfortable with gushing details.

"I thought she was the most stunning woman I'd ever seen," said Taran, who didn't mind gushing details. "I dropped by Second Site—"

Franz interrupted. "Is that your cousins' bookshop?"

"Yes," said Calypso. "I took you there when we were in New York."

"Of course," said Gisella. "How are they all?"

"They're all well. Both Lilia and Rowie are married now, and Gwendolyn is apparently dating some poor fellow."

Calypso didn't mention that her cousin Rowie was pregnant. After the conversation she'd just had with Gisella, that news could wait until later.

Fortunately Taran was raring to continue his story. "So you know the shop I'm talking about? Well, I walked in and she was standing there with Rowie ..."

*

The Shakespeare family consisted of two small clans. There was the London-based clan of Batty and her girls, and the New York-based clan of Gwendolyn, Lilia and Rowie. The women spanned three generations, and the blood ties were actually quite distant and confusing, but they referred to each other as cousins because it made things simple. They all shared the same coloring, the same gift and the same surname, which was enough to forge a tight bond that their geographical and cultural differences did nothing to diminish.

While they rarely caught up, Calypso bridged the gap with regular visits. In fact, her first overseas trip at the age of fifteen had been to spend the summer with the New York Shakespeares. It was during that trip that Calypso and Rowie, who were only a year apart in age, promised to always, *always* stay in touch, no matter what. That usually meant Rowie would email regularly (Calypso never found time to write) and Calypso would visit (Rowie was a homebody). Consequently, they *were* always in touch, and Calypso would often turn up on Rowie's doorstep.

Rowie's doorstep was better known as the Grove, a rambling West Village brownstone she shared with her mother and grandmother. Next door was the family business, Second Site, a metaphysical bookshop and learning center. Gwendolyn, the family matriarch, was a sometimes difficult woman who made amends by having a wicked sense of humor. She loved her girls fiercely, and that included Calypso when she came to stay. Lilia, Rowie's mother, was an ethereal creature, never quite connecting with anyone, but always affecting everyone. Sweet, beautiful and kind, she didn't so much grab hold of life as float around it.

And then there was Rowie, caught between the magic of the Grove and the real world outside it, the infamous history of her ancestors and the future she so desperately wanted. She'd been assured from childhood that her path was clearly paved and that one day she'd take over the family business, yet secretly she yearned for more. How she'd get more, she was yet to discover, but she trusted she'd one day find a way. Until then, she worked at the shop, did psychic readings for clients, and spent her days making other people feel they'd be okay. In fact, that was why Calypso had recently arrived unannounced. She needed to feel okay again. Her boyfriend had left her without warning two years earlier. Her whole world fell apart. Just when she thought she was over it, and was ready to move forward with her life, something would happen and Calypso would be back to square one, missing Scott desperately and angry that he'd left. For someone whose whole life had revolved around moving on, Calypso was finding it extremely difficult to do so. She decided a change of scenery would do her the world of good. She needed to get out, have a few drinks, and a good flirt. And who better to do it with than Rowie – who'd always had problems finding lasting love herself?

The two girls spent the evenings taking Manhattan by storm, and the days behind the counter at Second Site. They talked and laughed and supported each other through all sorts of issues, and Calypso began to feel reborn. Until the fateful day she met Taran Dee.

Calypso and Rowie were perched behind the counter when the shop door jangled and in walked two of the most stunning men they'd ever seen, completely identical in all but hair coloring.

Dark-haired Taran and his blond twin, Finn, seemed equally surprised by the two redheads who bore an obvious resemblance to each other. The women were very different in build – Calypso was tall and willowy while Rowie was tiny – but they both had the same creamy skin, flashing green eyes and burgundy mane.

The four of them stared at each other for a moment and then burst into simultaneous laughter.

"I thought we looked alike," Rowie said.

"You have the same coloring," Taran pointed out.

"How do you explain yours?" Rowie asked, fascinated, as most people were when they saw the twins.

"No idea. Quirk of fate," Finn admitted. "We were both born with light brown hair and the doctor congratulated our parents and said, 'Identical twins.' Then around our first birthday Taran's hair went darker and mine went blond."

"Very bizarre," Rowie said, amazed.

Calypso glanced at Taran, feeling strangely faint. How long had it been since she'd experienced such an immediate and forceful attraction to someone? She decided the best way to deal with it was to act bored and ignore him.

What she didn't count on was his mutual attraction to her and his pig-headed ability to always get what he wanted in life.

"Our mother's theory is that our coloring goes with our in-dividual temperaments." Taran grinned at Calypso. "I'm the dark horse."

"Fascinating." Calypso concealed a sigh with a fake yawn. "Sorry, late night."

Finn stepped forward. "It's my girlfriend's birthday and she wants a unicorn crystal. I heard this is the only shop in town to stock them."

"You heard right." Rowie unlocked a cabinet and removed one of the pieces. The whole shop was immediately warmer, brighter, lighter, such was the crystal's power.

Taran gave Calypso a heated stare. "I feel like a moth being drawn into a light."

She ignored the innuendo and checked her manicure. "Careful, you might get burnt."

*

Taran couldn't keep his eyes off Calypso. He was mesmerized by the sheen of her skin, the tilt of her eyes, the way her hair curled at the nape of her neck. He tried to engage her in a private conversation, but she'd simply smile politely and ask the other two for their opinion as well. For someone who'd never had to even try to win a woman over, Calypso Shakespeare's indifference fascinated him.

He couldn't get her out of his mind, so the following day he returned to Second Site with a trumped up excuse about a gift for his mother. One hour later he left with three hundred dollars' worth of books and a massive crush on a woman who still hadn't noticed him. Oh sure, she was polite and helpful, but Taran was used to women throwing themselves at him. Calypso was so disinterested that she kept calling him Darren.

The following day it was his grandmother who needed some books, despite the fact that she'd been dead for ten years. He bought ol' Phyllis a book by Deepak Chopra, for no other reason than Calypso recommended it; the *Tibetan Book of the Dead,* which was probably right up Phyllis's alley; and John Edward's *Crossing Over* – which was the only way he'd get to deliver it.

Afterwards, Taran was furious with himself. He now had nearly four hundred dollars' worth of books he'd never read and the start of a huge inferiority complex. He'd tried everything. He'd made jokes, which she laughed at – it was like someone had let the sunshine in when she laughed. He threw in a few, in his opinion, intelligent remarks, which she politely responded to. But other than that she appeared to be completely disinterested.

On the fourth day he marched into the shop, and announced that he was taking her out for dinner that night. Calypso looked at him with an amused light in her eyes.

"Does that mean you'll be returning the books?"

"You knew? And you sold them to me anyway?"

"Business is business."

"Just for that, you'll also be having lunch with me tomorrow."

"I would've anyway, Darren."

"It's Taran."

Calypso grinned. "Yeah ..."

*

"Oh Calypso, you're wicked." Gisella laughed. "Did you like him?"

"I was hugely attracted to him," Calypso admitted. "But felt rather uncomfortable about it all. I certainly wasn't going to make the first move, but Rowie made me promise to go out with him if he finally found the courage to ask me."

"So we went for dinner," Taran said.

"Which turned into breakfast," Calypso added.

"We spent every night together for the following week."

"And then went away for the weekend."

It was like a tennis match. Gisella and Franz turned from Taran to Calypso and back again, occasionally exchanging gleeful glances as they did.

"Martha's Vineyard," Taran explained. "It was great."

"Taran painted me."

"That's right, I did."

"I ended up staying with him back in New York."

"And then to cut a long and lovely story short: I told her I had feelings for her, went and hopped in the shower, and when I got out ... she was gone." Taran looked around, smiling.

"Got to say, it was a blow to my ego." Slight pause. "But I'm getting used to it now."

Calypso looked guilty and then all four started to laugh.

"You owe Taran an apology," said Franz.

"Oh believe me, I'm getting one," Taran chuckled. "But I've only got two days apparently."

Calypso glanced at the clock. It was past three a.m. They'd had such a wonderful night lost in conversation that she hadn't noticed the time.

"One and a half." She giggled. "But I'll make it memorable."

Chapter 15

*Sprinkle periwinkle under your bed for wild
nights of passion*

Taran woke and immediately felt the bed beside him. She was still there. It was ridiculous how happy that made him feel. She stirred and turned to him, lifting her face slightly. He lowered his chin and their lips met. Their kisses were leisurely and sleepy. Unlike the urgent clawing of the night before, this morning they felt like they had all the time in the world, which they didn't. He was aware of that.

They spent time slowly exploring each other, an unhurried melding of two people totally in tune physically. Afterwards they showered and headed out for breakfast. Taran had been to Vienna once before, but didn't know the city well, unlike Calypso, who had spent a lot of time there. Experiencing Vienna through Calypso's eyes was like seeing the city for the first time. The city that Taran had always thought of as dull sprang to life in an explosion of delicious sights, sounds and tastes: the coffee houses and konditorei, side by side with elegant boutiques and glossy stores selling *objets d'art*. The pedestrianised streets were filled with outdoor cafes and buskers, and of course the Danube wound majestically around it all.

They headed to Naschmarkt, where they spent time walking the passageways filled with fresh produce. Small wasps danced around their faces. Flowers in pails and newly picked fruit laid out on stands scented the air. Calypso knew some of the vendors and was welcomed with warm hugs and strangely muddled conversations about herbs and plants, all carried out in a mix of English, German and sign language. Calypso sniffed flowers, rubbed leaves, and asked questions about when certain things had been harvested.

At one stall she bought some herbs: red clover blossoms, rosemary, nettle, red raspberry and peppermint. She followed her nose to another stand and found walnuts and asparagus. She bypassed stall upon stall of fruit until she found the freshest strawberries, the juiciest oranges, the finest raspberries and figs.

She led Taran through a maze of passages and into a small shop. It was a dark little cavern, and it took a moment for his eyes to adjust. The walls were lined with shelves, overflowing with jars and pots of herbs and potions difficult to find anywhere else in Europe.

Taran spotted a jar of eldercorn aspamatus. He didn't consider himself that well versed in herbal medicine, but all young witches were raised on stories of the powers of eldercorn roots and how the plant was now supposedly extinct.

Obviously not, thought Taran.

And then, out of the corner of his eye, he noticed a glowing jam jar, perched on the highest shelf. He moved closer, mesmerized.

"It can't be," he whispered.

Calypso smiled. "It is. A development company was building on top of a fairy mound in northern Austria. The woman who runs this shop met with the Fey folk and agreed to relocate them somewhere safe. It's amazing that that whole world fits in an old marmalade jar."

"Goes to show how time and space are relative."

"Exactly."

"But why move them? Can't they just shift onto a higher vibration?"

"Normally that's what happens. But more often than not now, these development companies come in quickly and completely destroy the energy in an area. The Fey folk didn't have time to alter the vibration they existed on."

The energy shifted as a third person entered the room. "Gruss gott, Fraulein Shakespeare. I vas expecting you."

Taran turned and saw a very old, rather hunched woman gazing warmly at Calypso. There was a sparkle to her that suggested faerie blood.

Calypso gave the old woman a kiss on each cheek. "Gruss gott, Madam Linzbichler. Are you well?"

"Yes, yes. My brews keep me healthy. They just can't keep me young."

"This is my friend, Taran Dee."

"Of course it is," she said, giving Taran a quick pat on the arm, before ambling toward her counter. "I have a gift for you, Calypso."

She handed Calypso something wrapped in faded newspaper. Calypso unwrapped it and found some wild yam and – very exciting – false unicorn root. It was quite a find considering that it was an endangered species.

"You always know exactly what I need."

"It is my job to do so."

Calypso rewrapped the herbs and tucked them into her bag.

Madame Linzbichler shuffled over to a small hotplate and placed a teapot on top. She lifted the lid and tossed in some water and a handful of mixed leaves and herbs. Then she placed some cups in front of her guests and a few minutes later poured them both a cup of tea.

"Delicious," sighed Calypso as she took a sip. "Quite a mix. Ginger, mint, jasmine, red rose, among other things." She savored her second sip and then grinned. "Aren't you naughty? Is that a hint of apple I detect?"

The old woman chuckled. "You are good, Calypso."

"Be careful, Taran, she's trying to bind us together in love," she said with a wink.

Madame Linzbichler gave a snort. "You don't need tea." She smiled at the two young lovers, before becoming serious again. "Did you speak to Adelein, Calypso?"

"I did, and he said he'd be more than happy to take them."

"Gut, good. I worry what will happen to them once I'm gone."

Calypso lightly touched the older woman's arm. "You'll be around for a long time yet, but at least they'll be safe now."

Madame Linzbichler stooped and found an old box and a small carry bag. Then she picked up a stool and carried it to the far corner, clumsily stepping up onto it and reaching for the jam jar. Taran went to help her, but she shooed him back.

She packed the faerie world into the box and cushioned it with tissue paper. And then, after placing it gently into the bag, she handed it to Calypso. "I know it is safe with you, child."

"I'm honored to be of help."

The two women said their goodbyes and Calypso made her way toward the door.

Taran held his hand out and Madam Linzbichler took it, but instead of shaking it, she pressed a small packet into his palm.

"Take this. Put it away safely," she whispered, out of Calypso's earshot. "You'll know when to use it."

"What is it?"

"Sylph dust."

Taran shoved the packet deep in his pocket. Christ almighty, what was this woman giving him Sylph dust for?

Sylph dust was only for the most experienced shamans to cross over to the Summerland, and often even they couldn't find their way back. And now he had some in his pocket? Was she mad? But one last glance in her milky grey eyes told him she wasn't – and that he *would* need it one day. It chilled him to think about it.

Calypso and Taran waved goodbye to Madam Linzbichler and headed back into the sunshine, although it did little to ease Taran's concern. He had a bag of Sylph dust in his pocket and Calypso had a whole faerie world in her bag. So much for shopping for some fruit.

"Hold on tight to that bag, Callie."

"It's safe with us, Taran." Calypso's secret cargo obviously didn't stress her out at all.

"What if we get mugged?"

"Then some poor thief will have the wrath of a displaced faerie community upon him."

Calypso slipped her hand into Taran's. "See that coffee house, Café Central? Trotsky plotted the revolution there." Calypso sighed sadly. "Full of tourists now."

Taran marveled at how easily she moved on. Pity she couldn't do the same when it came to her ex. But while he was still clutching tightly to his pocket, Calypso was quite blasé about what she was carrying in her bag. She was so courageous in all matters except of the heart.

They wandered for hours, hand in hand, Calypso pointing out local haunts on the way.

"That was Gustav Klimt's favorite watering hole. Oh look, Café Griensteidl. Arthur Schnitzler apparently came up with the idea for *La Ronde* in there," she said. Sometime later they passed Café Landtmann. "Freud and Jung were regulars."

They strolled Vienna's charming streets, talking and laughing. She was enchanting company: well traveled, well read and ... well, simply gorgeous to look at.

"Feel like some cake?" she asked.

"Sure." She could ask him to sell his soul to Santa and he'd say yes.

She led Taran toward Kartnerstrasse and into the Sacher Hotel. "You know when I said I never do touristy things? Well I lied. I love this place."

The Café Sacher was an opulent room filled with deep red lounges and crystal chandeliers. The musk-pink walls were plastered with gilt-framed sketches and paintings of long-dead Viennese.

Calypso ordered them some Sachertorte and coffee and they relaxed back into the sofas. "This is the original torte in Austria. The recipe is a secret."

Taran wasn't sure whether it was the cake or the company, but it was a mouthwatering experience. Lashings of cream accompanied one of the most delicious chocolate cakes ever to bless his taste buds. He was tempted to propose to Calypso immediately, simply for being the type of woman who knew where such a cake existed.

"I'm sold," he sighed. "I could die now, a happy man." He stared at her over his coffee cup. "You love Vienna."

"I love many places. This is one of them," she said. "What about you?"

Taran thought for a moment. "It's hard to choose. India is inspiring. South Africa. I have a soft spot for Bangkok. But my favorite place is Australia. Especially Sydney. Have you been to Australia?"

Calypso's eyes clouded over and he felt her tense.

"Yes," she admitted. "My last serious boyfriend was Australian. We spent a great deal of time there."

He searched her eyes, silently pleading for her to not close down again. "Your mother mentioned how wary you are of relationships. Your last relationship ended badly, and you were deeply hurt." Taran attacked the last of his cake with the fork.

"I see. What else did my mother say?" Calypso added an extra emphasis to "my mother" and it was obvious that poor Batty was going to get a verbal lashing over this later.

"She didn't say much else."

Calypso nodded, but remained silent.

Taran had had enough. "From where I'm sitting, this is an issue we need to confront. Whoever this idiot was, he left you and you're still not over it. I'm here. I want to be with you, which is more than I can say for this – what's his name?"

"Scott," said Calypso quietly.

"Scott, who's obviously a sandwich short of a picnic if he leaves a gorgeous woman like you. Don't you agree?"

Calypso was silent.

"What was so bloody special about him?"

"Does it matter, Taran? Why is anyone special? Others might have thought him quite ordinary, but to me he was extraordinary because he was destined to be so. He was my first real love. My only love … that's all."

"What type of man was he?"

"You really want to know?"

"Yes," Taran lied.

Calypso's eyes glazed over at the memory. "He was fearless," she whispered. Brave, bold … reckless at times. He was always trying the latest, greatest new thing. Abseiling, bungee jumping, riding rapids – he even base-jumped a few times until I begged him to stop. But he really grabbed hold of life. We'd walk into a bar and by the time we walked out, he knew everyone by name. Every country we went to, he'd stumble and struggle through the language, trying his heart out to speak to locals, despite the fact that English is so widely spoken. He said it was ignorant to expect people to speak it."

"I have to agree with him there," Taran grudgingly admitted.

"He had an incredible voice, a musical gift. He could play the guitar …" Calypso sighed, the weight of heartbreak still apparent on her beautiful features. "We were young," she said simply.

"Would you take him back?"

"No."

There was something so absolute about her answer, yet it didn't comfort him. The darkness that lingered behind her words did quite the opposite.

"I still think he's a complete nut-job for leaving you."

"There have been times when I couldn't agree with you more." Calypso motioned for the check. "Let's move on, shall we?"

Taran nodded, but wondered if she ever would.

Chapter 16

Apply yarrow leaves to alleviate a toothache

Taran watched from Birdland's door, beer in hand, as the sun set over Stephansplatz. In one day he'd fallen head-over-heels for Vienna. It helped that his tour guide was the woman he was falling head-over-heels for.

He felt closer to Calypso than ever before yet he knew she hadn't really told him anything. Admittedly, he now had a clear picture in his head of her ex-boyfriend: a blond, bronzed, Aussie Adonis with a sportsman's body and a cheery disposition. Oh yeah – he could also sing. But it was the things she didn't say that bothered Taran more: the dark veils that drew across her eyes when she mentioned her ex. The tightness around her mouth. Taran could only imagine the hatchet job this Scott had done on her heart.

The strains of a Strauss waltz drifted his way. Vienna's streets were filled with buskers. Mozart, Haydn, Beethoven, Schubert, Mahler, and Brahms were among the many musicians who'd made their home in Vienna. The city inspired some of the world's most famous music, and its streets had rung out with it ever since.

Taran smiled. He was enjoying himself. He wished he could share this with his brother. Up until their falling out they'd spoken daily, and Taran was used to giving Finn regular updates. He'd love to hear about Vienna ... and Calypso. But first Taran had to be certain that she wasn't going to do another runner. He pushed thoughts of Finn to the back of his mind. He missed his twin, but if things panned out like he intended, then Finn would be back in his life very soon.

He turned and wandered back into the tavern. Calypso was behind the bar, using a mortar and pestle to grind something. Gisella was perched on a stool beside her, chatting. Franz was in the kitchen cooking. Birdland was closed tonight, while the three friends whipped up a magical feast to help Gisella conceive. Taran understood the importance of the evening and Gisella's right to some privacy, so had offered to disappear.

"I could go to the opera," he suggested.

But Gisella wouldn't hear of it. "I don't want to take this too seriously," she assured him. "I just want an evening of fun. And it's such fun to see Calypso happy again, so you must stay, Taran."

He was touched to be included in the plans, and felt it boded well for the future. He intended to be included in many more of Calypso's future plans. He also couldn't believe he was actually thinking this way. It was a first.

Taran watched her now, her red mane pulled back into a ponytail, her green eyes flashing as they searched for ingredients. She seemed troubled, frustrated about something, yet trying to hide it.

She sprinkled dried rosemary, salt and cayenne pepper over some walnuts and passed them into Franz to bake them briefly. She brewed a tea of vitex and red clover blossoms, nettle, red raspberry, and peppermint leaves and poured it into glass containers, leaving a small jug of it out for Gisella to sip.

"Let the rest infuse overnight and then drink four cups a day for the next week."

Gisella looked a bit nervous. "Are there any negative side effects?"

Calypso placed her hand on her friend. "You can buy similar teas off a supermarket shelf. The only difference is this is fresher ... and made with love." She handed Gisella a small bottle. "This is a tincture made from false unicorn root. Admittedly, you won't find this one in a supermarket, but it's safe. And very powerful. I've written instructions on the bottle." Finally, Calypso grabbed a bottle of chilled Veuve Clicquot. "Now for the real magic."

She popped open the champagne and filled four flutes. Into each she dropped a vanilla bean, and passed the glasses to Gisella and Taran.

Taran held his glass high. "Here's to the French, for inventing this stuff."

"Actually, the English made sparkling wine at least thirty years before the French ... but here's to them for perfecting it." Calypso gave him a wink and then disappeared into the kitchen.

"Always has to have the last word. But you'd know that. You've been friends for a long time."

"Longer than a lady should admit."

"Did you know Scott?"

Surprise registered on Gisella's face. "Yes. Very well."

"He sounds like an interesting character."

"That's one way to describe him."

"I want you to know, I won't leave her like he did."

Gisella paled. "Taran, no one can predict the future. Not completely. Not even Callie."

"What happened? She won't tell me."

Gisella opened her mouth to speak but then slammed it shut again. Now was not the time.

Calypso entered carrying the tray of walnuts and the conversation ended. "Hey handsome, try some of these."

She shoved the tray at Taran and he grabbed a handful.

"Wow, they're delicious." He gave her a lopsided grin. "Are you trying to get me fat so you won't fall for me?"

Calypso gave his stomach a pat, ignoring the hard muscle she found there. "It's working, so keep eating."

Taran took the tray and placed it on the table and sat with Gisella. Calypso watched as they fell into an easy conversation about Viennese history, one of Gisella's favorite subjects. She left the other two chatting and drifted over to the bar to gaze at all her tools and concoctions. Only she knew they hadn't worked. Only she knew that she'd performed with great ceremony, rousing Gisella out of her depression – reassuring her that a child would come – but in fact given her nothing more than regular herbal remedies. Not a spell in sight, and bound to fail.

Not entirely true. Calypso comforted herself with that thought and a huge slug of champagne. Every ingredient she used contained healing energy, its own power, especially the false unicorn root. She'd combined all the elements to reap the maximum benefits. All were strong fertility herbs and foods in their own right. But Gisella and Franz were expecting more. They were expecting magic … and she had lost it.

Calypso watched Gisella now, telling Taran all about Elisabeth of Bavaria, better known in Austria as their beloved Sisi. She would tell her friends the truth, but not tonight. It had been a long time since she'd seen Gisella looking so relaxed, and that in itself was important. Perhaps it would be enough. There was always the hope that the experience itself would have a placebo effect.

"Dinner is served," Franz announced from the kitchen.

Taran, Franz and Gisella sat down to a feast of poached salmon with steamed asparagus spears, and baby chat potatoes, covered in a remoulade sauce. Calypso had stuffed zucchini flowers with fresh ricotta and salsa verde. Their main was followed by a chocolate fondue with strawberries, raspberries, orange segments and fresh figs.

Throughout the meal, the champagne, conversation and laughter flowed. Taran especially had the others in stitches with his stories and tales. He'd even managed to lift Calypso's spirits. She'd been watching him carefully all day and was yet to find even a small fault. Damn him! He was relaxed, and enjoyed going with the flow. He was interested in everything and everyone. She'd walked him around in circles all day, but he'd never once complained. He was, quite simply, wonderful company.

"Where did you three meet?" Taran asked.

"Corfu," said Calypso. "Gisella and I met first. We were working in a small hostel there when this new cook turned up."

"They both fell madly in love with me. It was extremely embarrassing," said Franz seriously.

"Actually we both thought him incredibly arrogant and annoying," Gisella added. "But we liked his food."

"I actually asked Calypso to marry me first," Franz joked.

"She was smart and said no." Gisella sniffed.

Calypso patted Gisella's arm in mock sympathy. "At least you'll never have to cook dinner again."

After dinner, as they nibbled on an array of cheeses, Gisella sighed and patted her tummy. "I'm full. What a lovely evening." She looked beautiful and relaxed as she snuggled close to Franz and whispered in his ear.

"Is your magic working?" Taran asked quietly.

"They don't need magic," she replied.

Taran reached across and took her hand and kissed the tips of her slender fingers. Calypso shivered and leant toward him.

"Speaking of magic," she said, "if you want to spend more time with me—"

"Oh God no, three days is my limit."

"We only had two."

"True … fine then. I'm available."

"I'd like to take you somewhere."

"Here in Vienna?"

Calypso gave him a mysterious smile. "No …"

"Do I at least get a country?"

"England."

Taran poured them both another drink. "Excellent. Love the place." He relaxed back in his chair and gave her a wicked grin. "The women are a nightmare, but sexy as all hell."

Chapter 17

Fennel tea increases the flow of milk in nursing mothers

Calypso and Taran flew into Bristol and rented a car.

"Do you get carsick?" asked Calypso.

"No."

"That means I can drive."

Taran didn't flinch, which impressed her no end. "Excellent idea, seeing as I have no idea where we're going."

They threw their gear into the back of the car and headed off. Calypso kept glancing at Taran waiting for the questions to begin. They didn't.

"It'll take us about two and a half hours to get where we're going."

Taran nodded and popped open a bottle of water. "Okay."

"Need anything before we head off?"

"Nope. Got everything I need right here."

Calypso maneuvered her way through the traffic. "Don't you have any questions?"

Taran thought for a moment. "Actually ... just wondering if ..."

I knew it, thought Calypso, as she watched him grab his backpack. No one could be this laid-back when traveling.

Taran rifled through a side pocket and pulled out his iPod and another gadget. "We need some music." He plugged it in, found a channel on the radio, and Michael Franti began to play.

Calypso couldn't help herself. "Aren't you even slightly interested in where we're going?"

"Where we're going is irrelevant. Where we're at is what's important."

"Well, thanks for that, Confucius, but I'm not buying it."

Taran relaxed back into the passenger seat. "I'll be interested when I get there. Until that moment, I'm just enjoying being here with you. Wherever we are."

Calypso pointed to a sign and laughed. "We'll be on the M5 soon."

"Great. Always wanted to see it."

"How's Finn?" asked Calypso. "You haven't mentioned him at all. I thought you two were inseparable."

"He's good – busy." Taran turned and stared out the window.

"Have you two had a falling out?"

"Finn lives north of Boston now. He's in a band and they've just released a CD and are planning a tour. And he's in love."

Calypso noted the slight edge to Taran's voice when he mentioned that last bit. "In love? Same girlfriend he bought the unicorn crystals for?"

"Oh God, no. They broke up ages ago." *Right after I slept with her.* "This woman is a friend of my sister's. Rhi opened a theatre in a small town called Hamlet and Tye runs a café there."

"You don't sound happy for your brother."

"I am. Tye is great. She's gorgeous, smart, a talented musician. And she's a witch."

Calypso laughed. "One of ours."

"Yep, our people." Taran was quiet for a moment. "I miss him. I'm not used to being apart from him."

"They say twins share an extra special bond."

"In my experience that's true." Taran decided now was a good time to change the subject – before he howled like a baby. "What about you and Nell? You're very different."

"We're chalk and cheese, and it works because of that. We've always been close."

"And how's Rowie doing?"

"Great. She married Drew Henderson—"

"The weatherman. Yeah, I read that. Big news in New York."

"They're expecting their first baby in a couple of months."

"We'll have to go visit them."

Calypso raised an eyebrow and shot him a look. "Will we now?"

"I'll go … and you can come if you want."

A couple of enjoyable hours later they pulled off the road and into a gravel driveway, just past the don't-blink-or-you'll-miss-it village of Trethevy.

"Okay," Taran said, "where are we?"

"Ha! Got you! I knew you'd eventually cave."

Taran almost looked offended. "I didn't realize I was expected to remain oblivious to my location even once I'd arrived."

"We're not far from Tintagel," said Calypso.

"Really? That's cool. I grew up on tales of King Arthur."

Before them stood a quirky looking cottage, wrapped in vines and hidden in trees.

"Not quite Camelot," Taran said. "More like the Addams's house."

"No. Ash Cottage," said Calypso. "My home."

Ash Cottage, a pretty little stone structure tucked away at the edge of a forest near Tintagel in Cornwall, had been in the Shakespeare family for four hundred years. It had been passed, in most cases, from grandmother to granddaughter. When Batty Shakespeare had done the unthinkable and had two daughters instead of the traditional one, her mother, Emma Shakespeare, had been faced with the problem of who to leave the cottage to. She chose Calypso, for reasons still baffling to the family, especially Nell, who was left with nothing but a cryptic letter and a rusty key. Everyone told her to contest the will, but she didn't. To be fair, Calypso had been especially close to Emma, while Nell had taken the role of nurturer with her paternal grandmother, Eleanor. And Calypso had a spiritual connection to the area. But still, as much as Nell assured Calypso that it was okay, it had hurt her deeply at the time, and reinforced her preference for Eleanor.

Emma had been the opposite of Eleanor. Emma was affectionate and playful and wise. She drank too much, her stories were saucy and peppered with mild obscenities and she told inappropriate jokes. She had a string of lovers, including her one true love, Duncan Althorp, earl of a now extinct peerage in Cornwall. Despite his regular proposals, Emma refused to marry Duncan. Even after Batty was born, she remained steadfast in her refusals. Marriage would not change her daughter's illegitimacy, or restore her rights to peerage, so she, quite rightly, remained independent of the man she loved. Or more to the point, independent of the stuffy, rigid world he inhabited.

Shakespeare women had always flitted between the pub and Ash Cottage, but Emma was particularly attached to her countryside home. Despite that, when Batty was still a baby, Emma returned with her to London to help her own parents run the pub. But she was never really happy there and handed the King and Mistress over to her Batty as soon as she was of age, and Emma went back home to Cornwall. For good.

Emma was, for her time, or for any time really, quite a woman. She often announced how grateful she was to be born in an era when witches were ignored rather than burned, because there surely would've been a pyre with her name on it. Instead, the locals pretended not to see her on the street, but in the dead of night they'd come to her for help. Calypso could clearly remember the quiet knocks after dark. The desperate whispers from the front room. The soothing clucks and chuckles her grandmother made.

Calypso had countless happy memories of wandering the fields near Ash Cottage, her grandmother by her side, teaching her about herbs and plants. Then, on the first full moon after her thirteenth birthday, Emma took her to the forest and handed her over to the Fey folk. It was quite a celebration. The Fey folk had been waiting since Calypso's birth. Calypso's connection to them had been prophesized generations earlier.

Calypso spent the next few days – or was it a few months? – being initiated into the ancient healing and herbal arts. She entered the world of Fey through a portal, and became immersed in a reality very different from her own. She was passed a knowledge few humans possess and given glimpses into a world protected by sturdy veils. She'd always been told that the faerie realms were drifting into the mists, but she discovered that that wasn't the case. The faerie realm was clear and vibrant and her senses burst to life while she was there. She realized that the human condition was draining her own world of life and it was *that* world that was drifting further into the mists as its vibrations became denser.

When Calypso emerged from her time with the Fey folk, she possessed the gift of healing more powerful than if she'd studied a lifetime alone. Her life was about fulfilling her destiny as a healer. Her connection to the Fey folk in the area remained strong, and she used her gift to help anyone who asked.

Or at least she used to. Perhaps some of the Fey folk could provide answers as to where her gift had gone recently. She felt she knew, but refused to dwell on it right now. She was simply too happy to be back. To say Ash Cottage and the area around it was special to Calypso was a massive understatement. It was, quite simply, the only place she would ever consider as home. It was where she brewed her mead, stored her wines, grew certain herbs and disappeared to reconnect with herself. It's also where she lived for eight months after Scott left, the longest period of time in her adult life ever spent in one place. She needed to visit now, to check her brews and harvest some herbs. But she also wanted to share it with Taran.

Calypso led Taran toward the house "The forest nearby is filled with magic. It's one of the only places in Europe you can still find moly ... and only under a full moon." She glanced up at the sky now. The sun hadn't yet set but already the waxing moon had appeared. "She should be full later tonight. I need to replenish my stock."

"Sounds like fun. I haven't seen moly since I was a child." Taran paused and looked around at the garden. "Is that Silphion under that bush?"

"I can tell you were raised by a witch."

"But it's extinct."

"I know lots of people who grow it. I've also got goldthread. I work by the threefold herbal law. If I find a plant that's endangered, I take some for my potions, and then replant the rest in three different spots. You wouldn't believe some of the stuff I've got growing here." Calypso flung open the front door. "Coming in?"

The cottage was a cozy little warren with stone walls and wood floors. While not much had changed in the house since Calypso's grandmother lived there, or her grandmother before her, there was a lightness to the rooms that sprang from centuries of laughter bouncing off the walls.

Calypso immediately yanked back the curtains, opened the windows, and let the cool afternoon air in. Downstairs was a lounge room, dining room, a kitchen and, at the very back, a rather antiquated bathroom. Up the higgledy-piggeldy stairs were two bedrooms and up a further set of stairs, an attic crammed full of family junk.

Below it all was an insulated cellar. It was filled with bottles of homemade wine, herbs and magical brews. One corner had been set up to brew mead, another beer. Barrels of the latest batch of both were fermenting side by side. She also had racks of homemade wines: elderberry, plum, apple and so on.

"This is my brewery."

Taran was impressed. "You should show this to Simon some time. Apsley Beer might be interested." Then, with a wink, "We'll get Megan to do a taste test first."

Everything was as it should be, so Calypso headed back upstairs and locked the cellar behind her.

"How do you like my little home?"

"It's strange, funny, slightly wild, and gorgeous ... just like its owner."

Taran was full of perfect comebacks. "I'll be taking you somewhere later tonight, so we should organize dinner now."

"I'm easy. And always hungry."

Calypso disappeared outside and returned with a handful of mushrooms, tomatoes and some basil. "I'll throw these into pasta."

"Sounds good." Taran glanced at the mushrooms. "They're not magic shrooms are they?"

"You're not much of a country boy are you?"

"I love the country – for weekends away."

"What is a Pagan without a patch of land?"

"I have a patch of land. It's called Central Park."

Calypso began to slice the mushrooms. "Do you like mushrooms?"

"I'm very fond of store-bought ones. Last time someone fed me handpicked mushrooms I spent ten hours sure I was melting."

Calypso burst out laughing. "That's awful. Don't worry, these are fine, I promise." She passed Taran a bottle of wine. "Can't be sure about this wine though. Will you open it for me?"

Taran read the label. "Plum wine, brewed by Calypso. Fabulous. I think I had this little drop last time I ate at Per Se." He popped the cork and poured them both a glass.

"All the good restaurants stock my wine."

"Hope it's not like the wine you gave me in Paris. That was right up there with some camel urine I drank in Turkey."

"I've kissed a mouth that has tasted camel urine?"

"The camel urine was mouthwatering compared to that."

Calypso swatted him with a tea towel. "Go on, drink it."

"I'm too scared." He began to laugh and laugh. The more he laughed, the harder Calypso laughed.

"You are so rude," Calypso squealed. "Only an American would be so bloody rude."

"And only a Brit would bottle her own plum wine." Taran took a sip. And then another. "Holy crap, this is amazing."

Calypso grinned. "You should try my apple wine."

Taran tossed back the rest of the glass. "You have a talent." He pulled her into his arms and gave her a kiss.

Calypso sighed. "You think that's going to make up for your lack of manners?"

"I have a feeling it will," he said, kissing her again.

Calypso turned the gas off. "I'll need more than a kiss." She laughed and ran upstairs, tossing her T-shirt off as she went.

Taran followed a trail of clothes up the sloping stairs, pausing at the bedroom door where Calypso's black lace knickers lay discarded.

"I'm waiting," she called.

Taran turned and stared at her, already under the covers in the old bed. She wasn't waiting for long. He tore his clothes off and joined her. The mattress sank, and they both rolled, laughing, into the middle.

"Oh shit! New bed?"

"Family heirloom. I doubt the mattress has been changed in over a hundred years."

"So it's not IKEA then?"

"No." Calypso was laughing again.

Taran stared down at her. "I love it when you laugh."

"I love that you make me laugh."

The tips of their noses touched briefly, and then they kissed. He slid into her, slow, sensuous strokes, as they stared deep into each other's eyes, and breathed in each other's sighs. The old bed creaked and squeaked as it had many times over the last century, when lovers met.

*

Afterwards, still naked, they returned to the kitchen and finished making dinner. Calypso pulled out a bottle of Captain Morgan's Coconut Rum and a couple of tall glasses, which she filled with ice. She poured an even mix of rum, orange juice and pineapple juice into each glass. "This is like a kick in the head."

Taran gave Calypso a quick pat on the backside. "I need one to wake me up. All I want to do is sleep after that little session." Taran took a swig of his drink. "Love it. What is it?"

"Called a Mike Tai. A friend of mine came up with it. It's his version of the Mai Tai."

Taran took another mouthful.

"Go easy there, big boy. It tastes harmless, but it can sneak up on you."

Calypso served up two heaped bowls of pasta and led Taran toward the dining room, but froze as she reached the door.

"What's up, sweetheart?" he asked.

"Look."

Taran followed Calypso's stare to the opposite doorway and nearly dropped his glass. Floating there, and still looking rather annoyed, was Enid.

"What are you doing here, Enid?" Calypso asked gently. "You've never left the pub before."

"I told you, I'm keeping an eye on you two." And with that, she vanished.

Taran and Calypso stared at each other in amazement.

"It's almost enough to put me off ever having sex with you again," Taran said in mock horror.

"Should we put some clothes on?"

"She's already seen it all now." Taran pulled out a chair for Calypso. "Drink your Mike Tai. From the sounds of it, a few more sips and we won't care about clothes anyway."

Chapter 18

Passionflower is an effective sleep aid

A few hours later, Calypso and Taran did get dressed and head outside. They wandered down a small lane and out onto the road. The night air was still and fresh. At first, Taran was overwhelmed by the eerie quiet. But as he relaxed, the countryside began to sing to him. Crickets chirped. The shriek of an unfamiliar bird occasionally broke the silence. Their footsteps crunched on gravel. They walked this way for a long time, at ease with each other, not needing to speak. Finally, Calypso climbed over a fence into a field. "Follow me."

"Like I have an option," Taran whispered. "I'd probably be attacked by werewolves or something if I went off alone."

"You're such a city boy." Calypso giggled.

"I've read about the English countryside."

"Oh please … there are no werewolves here. None have been spotted for at least five years."

"Don't suppose I can talk you into holding my hand?"

Calypso stopped and stared at him. "Listen, you big baby, go home if you're not enjoying yourself."

Taran gave her a wink. "So I guess a shag is out of the question."

Calypso gave him a lazy smile. "I'd say it could be arranged."

"Cool. I'm liking the country more each second."

Calypso turned and headed down the path. "But first I have some work to do."

Taran had grown up around magic so could feel the air thickening as they walked along the path.

Calypso pointed out some buildings. "That's the Hermitage. It's open to the public."

"Are we trespassing?" asked Taran.

"No. I've got permission to come and go as I need. I asked the owners out of respect, but really, it's the Fey folk who guard this place. And they know me."

Taran could just make out a small chapel, surrounded by trees.

"St. Nectan's," Calypso explained.

They walked deep into the woods.

"I can't see a thing. We should have brought a torch."

"Won't need one soon," Calypso called over her shoulder.

They continued farther into the woods. Ferns and flowers rustled around their feet. Echoed whispers chimed through the darkness.

"She's back."

"She's here."

"Welcome, Calypso."

Suddenly lights darted before them. Golden orbs floated around them, illuminating the way. Taran heard a symphony, and realized it was the sound of flowing water, melodic as it descended. Eventually they stepped into Tintagel's natural grail, St. Nectan's waterfall.

"This is one of the most powerful sites in Great Britain," whispered Calypso. "It's a sacred well, and guarded by the Fey folk … as you can see."

Taran would have to be blind to miss the hundreds of orbs that lit the sky. Some floated, some perched on branches, some came over for a closer look, allowing Taran a glimpse of the exquisite faces within the glowing orb.

"Hello, Taran," one said.

"You know my name?"

"Of course we know you," she sighed, and a thousand giggles tinkled through the air, making Taran feel that he'd just missed a joke.

"This is incredible, Cal."

The trees beside them rustled and parted and suddenly a handsome half man, half goat stood before them.

"Welcome, Calypso. We are honored to have you here again."

"The honor is always mine, Adelein," she said, bowing her head slightly. "This is my friend, Taran."

"Raised in magic. Yes, we know him and welcome him."

Taran and Calypso glanced at each other, but neither asked Adelein what he meant, as one never asked a faun, especially one of royal blood, personal questions. Any information they received would be offered freely, but without prodding.

Adelein's voice was deep and as smooth as treacle. "Did you bring them?"

Calypso pulled the jam jar from her backpack and handed it to Adelein, who tucked it protectively under his arm. Then he turned his attention back to Calypso. "Will you be harvesting tonight?"

"Yes. I'd like some moly."

"Certainly. Our supplies have picked up recently, so there's plenty for you, friend." Adelein's eyes narrowed slightly. "Tell me, how is your sister?"

"I haven't seen her all week ... so ah ... to my knowledge ... well – why?"

Adelein's nostrils flared slightly. "I need you to relay a message from the guardians."

"Of course," said Calypso.

"She wasn't forgotten. There is an inheritance. She is part of a lineage that will unfold but first she must find the missing piece."

"Missing piece?"

"Of the puzzle."

Calypso *looked* puzzled. Taran could tell she was desperate to ask more questions. But he also knew she wouldn't test the faun's patience. Calypso understood the forest codes.

"Cane Cata Juel."

Calypso repeated slowly. "Cane Cata Juel?"

"Correct." Adelein tilted his head slightly to one side. "There is another question you wish to ask." He looked slightly annoyed.

"You mean about my sister?"

"About your gift," he snapped.

Calypso glanced at Taran.

"It's temporary," Adelein assured her. "And hereditary. Consider when this has happened before." The faun stamped one of his hooves into the forest floor. He was done. "Take care, Calypso. And do not let the past ruin the future." With a curt nod to Taran, Adelein stepped behind a tree and vanished.

"'Do not let the past ruin the future'?" hissed Calypso. "What the hell does that mean?"

"Sounded pretty clear to me." Taran chuckled.

Calypso glared at him. "Come on, let's go pick some moly."

Taran watched as she climbed over some rocks. "What was he talking about before? What's 'temporary'?"

"No idea," said Calypso. Suddenly, her mood lifted. "Found it!"

The moly was located where most things magical and mythical are: right before their eyes. Using small clippers, Calypso harvested only as much as she needed, and then thanked the sentinels who watched over the precious herb – or holy moly as she fondly called it.

She made her way carefully around the rocks to the edge of the pool and snipped a piece of each of the *Jubula hutchinsaie* and *Trichocolea tromentallo* liverworts and removed small quantities of moss. Then she stored them all safely in her bag and returned to Taran, who'd been watching her from a comfy rock.

"I'm amazed you brought me here," he said.

"Why's that?"

"Because it's such an important place. Not the type of place you'd bring just anyone to."

"You're not just anyone, Taran."

"Then you need to listen to Adelein. If you trust me enough to bring to this place, you should trust me enough to allow me into other places."

Taran reached over and pulled her into him. They stared into each other's eyes, their breath mingling.

"Trust me," he whispered.

"I do trust you, Taran. It's love I don't trust."

"Surely one negative experience can't have scarred you that badly," he snapped, impatient. "Everyone is hurt by love at some stage. Kelly McManus was my first great love and she dumped me for Norman Normans. Imagine being dumped for a guy called Norman Normans?"

Calypso smiled grudgingly. "That's awful. How old were you?"

"Eight. But age is irrelevant in matters of the heart." Taran lifted her chin toward him. "What was so great about him that you can't let go? Tell me."

"Don't be silly. It's not the place to—"

"Actually this is the perfect place. Tell me."

Calypso's eyes flashed angrily. "Scott was special. He was funny and kind ... and despite the fact that he was really gorgeous, I never once saw him flirt with another woman. He was loyal. He was my best friend, and I trusted him."

"Until he dumped you."

Calypso sighed. "Scott didn't dump me, Taran. Scott died."

Chapter 19

Carry fresh borage blossoms for courage

Calypso found the Australian summer stifling. Normally heat didn't bother her, but the harsh sun was relentless and seemed to bite at her fair skin. Not that she held it against Australia; she was quite fond of the country that had produced the love of her life. Scott had taken her home to meet his parents soon after they met, and annually ever since. She adored the people, the landscape and the oddly lilting language. But the middle of summer could be cruel.

Scott didn't seem to notice. He romped around like an overgrown puppy, without a shirt or a hat. He caught up with friends and family, drank beer, played cricket, surfed and swam. He adored being home, but found it equally easy to leave. There was a great big world out there that Scott fully intended to explore. And once he was done, perhaps then he'd return home to Cronulla. With Calypso, of course. There was no future without Callie.

Scott reached over and wiped a trail of perspiration from Calypso's forehead. "My poor sweetie, all hot and bothered. Wilting away like an English rose."

"This is worse than Mumbai."

"That's because you refused to leave the air-conditioned hotel in Mumbai," Scott reminded her. "Come with me, baby."

He led her back inside his parents' house. They were both at work and not due home for hours. He drew the curtains and switched on the air conditioner, something his parents rarely did. Then he grabbed a cotton sheet and threw it on the lounge-room floor. Moments later, they were both naked, sprawled across the sheet, sipping ice-cold beers.

"That's better," sighed Calypso. "I was so hot."

"You're still hot." Scott grinned, placing his beer on the coffee table and reaching for her.

They lie on their sides for a while, staring into each other's eyes. Time passed, meaningless, as it had been since the first moment they met in Berlin. He reached out and ran a finger across her breast and she shivered. She'd never tire of his touch. And then he drew her toward him, the sweat on their skin dry now, cool.

He breathed her in, the faint smell of sunscreen lingering on her skin, her hair the scent of fresh vanilla. Their lips met, parted, and they dissolved into each other. Her hands slid around his back and she guided him to her, into her. Home. It was their home, the only one either of them needed.

Slow, languid strokes, loving words whispered, sighs that became more heated, faster, more urgent, her throaty moans as she climaxed and sent him toppling over the edge.

They clung to each other for a long time afterwards. Calypso sobbed, something she hadn't done for a long time. Scott held her tightly and stroked her hair, promising to always, always love her. The intensity of her emotions surprised her, but it wasn't until later that she wondered if she knew, on some level, that it would be the last time she made love to her beautiful man.

And then they heard the ice-cream truck in the distance. Scott jumped up and threw on his shorts.

"Great timing! What flavor do you want?"

"Strawberry."

"Of course. Strawberry for my strawberry mop-top." He grabbed his wallet and rushed out the door.

Calypso dressed slowly, in her shorts and singlet top, and followed him out the front. She watched from the driveway as he paid the ice-cream guy and took the ice creams. She saw the other car careen carelessly around the corner, too fast for the suburban street. She called out to Scott, but it was only later she realized the call never reached her lips. He stepped out. The car skidded – too late. A sickening thud echoed through the street; through her heart and soul and every move she'd made since. She ran, slow motion, stuck in a substance similar to hair gel, unable to move quickly or hear clearly. As much as she tried she couldn't speed up the movie she was watching. She reached for him, held him, begged him not to leave her, whispered words, meaningless words, pacts and bribes with the gods if only he'd stay.

He didn't.

He mumbled his last words ... and then she heard a scream, her own high-pitched, bloodcurdling scream that resonated throughout the universe. It wasn't until a doctor arrived and stuck a needle in her arm that the scream stopped.

*

Calypso sighed, back in the forest now, surrounded by the Fey folk who had helped her through her initial grief. They already knew the story, but were there once again while she shared it with Taran.

Taran's eyes were filled with horror and sadness. "I'm an ass, Calypso. Everything I said ..."

"You weren't to know."

"I'm so sorry ..."

"Taran, it's not your fault."

Taran stared at the waterfall, almost silent now, as though the forest sounds had been lessened, out of respect. "I can't imagine how tough it was."

She wiped a lone tear from her cheek. "On some level I'd always thought ... I never sensed his early death psychically, but the way he lived ... He'd had a close call once before, so he himself thought he was living on borrowed time." She shook her head. "But still, I think he expected to go out in a blaze of glory, not from a drunk driver when he was out buying ice cream."

"Was the driver charged?"

"Yes. Doesn't change what he did."

"Are you still in touch with Scott's family?"

"Sometimes ... I call around Scott's birthday. Other than that ... I feel like I'm a reminder."

"Do you still miss him?"

"Of course, but only ... moments. I'll see something that I think he'd like. Or pass a place we visited a lot together. Or whenever I see the ocean, and the waves are perfect, I think, what a waste. He should be out there, surfing." Calypso sighed. "I could never read the future with him, so even if he were alive, we might not be together. The grief I still feel stems from the senseless death of a wonderful person."

He reached out and took her hand. "I understand now. I do. I've never met anyone like you and would like nothing more than the opportunity to spend time with you. But if you're not ready, then I understand."

Calypso linked her fingers through Taran's. "I won't deny it, Taran, love petrifies me. It's such a fragile thing."

"Life is fragile, Callie ... love is the rock-solid foundation it clings to."

"I never thought I'd ever be ready again. What I had with Scott was special, and I'll never deny that, even if it hurts you."

"I wouldn't want you to. He sounds like quite a guy."

"He was. But so are you, Taran. And Scott would kick my butt from here to next week if I were foolish enough to miss a chance of happiness." She wrapped her arms around his neck and sank into him, completely and utterly certain that all was right in the world while she was there. "I'm ready to move on now, Taran. And I want to move on with you."

Chapter 20

Drink goldenrod tea for bladder and kidney
stones

Nell watched as her boss disappeared headfirst into the dumbwaiter shaft.

"Percy, please, let me look for it."

"It's fine, dear." His voice boomed from the small shaft.

She wondered if she should hold onto his feet. "It was on the right side, under a small ledge."

Percy stretched forward. "Oh, yes ... there *is* a ledge. Good God," he exclaimed "I see something."

Nell stood beside him, ready to grab his legs if necessary, just as he inched forward and disappeared a bit further into the shaft and then let out an echoing cheer. "It's here! Nell, I've got it."

There was a long silence and then:

"Do you think you could pull me back out, dear? I seem to be stuck."

Nell tugged Percy out of the elevator shaft and watched as he wriggled back to standing, adjusted his glasses, his waistcoat, and then his hair, before placing the package down on the table before them.

"Your gift is extraordinary, Nell."

"It came to me in a dream last night."

"I've been searching for this for years. It was one of the things my mother hid during the war. I never expected to find it again."

"Are you going to unwrap it?"

"Oh yes … of course." Percy unwound the string and cloth that covered his lost treasure. Beneath it was a medieval medallion covered in green patina. He turned it over, but it was impossible to make out the inscriptions. With great reverence, he placed it back on the table and the two friends, one old and male, one young and female, stood side by side, admiring it.

"Do you know anything about it?" Nell asked.

"My mother told me grand tales about this piece, Nell. Whether or not any of them are true remains to be seen."

Nell's psychic antenna was buzzing. There was something familiar about the disc.

Percy took his glasses off and cleaned them. The excitement was making them fog up. "Mother swore it had been given to her by a witch. I remember being quite frightened of that when I was young, but now that I've met you … I'm sure the witch was very nice."

"Most are, Percy." Nell patted Percy's arm. "So this piece was a gift?"

"Mother invested a lot of money buying pieces we now have on display, but this was given to her. It was her favorite. I'm not sure if it was a gift, or if it was given to her for safekeeping. I guess that's why she hid it so well."

"Can you remember what was on it, Percy?"

"Not really. There is an image on one side and an inscription on the other. My mother once said that translated it meant, *she who keeps secrets*." Percy turned it over. "I can't remember what language it is. One of the early Slavic languages, I think. I'll call a linguist I know at Oxford and get him to look at it."

"We'll need to take it to a conservator first, and have it cleaned properly."

"Any other insights, Nell?"

Nell's brow furrowed. "It's an unusual piece. I don't feel it stands alone. It's a part of something else." Nell shrugged at Percy. "Sorry, that's all I'm picking up. And who knows if I'm right?"

Percy gave her one of his slightly lopsided smiles. "I don't doubt you for a minute."

Nell smiled. She liked that Percy, who was in his seventies, had so much faith in her. Many men of his generation chose to ignore psychic phenomena, but Percy was always open to Nell's predictions.

Much of Percy's uniqueness came from his mother, Bea Smyth, an unusual woman for her time. Bea had been quite bohemian, something Percy's father, a wealthy, conservative man, never tried to quash. The family had lived in the Hampstead terrace, which was now the British Museum of Romance. Bea whispered grand tales of love and romance to her son. She collected romantic artifacts and the old house was full of things that had been owned by some of England's most famous lovers. She enthusiastically shared each new acquisition with her son.

"Look, Percy, Queen Victoria had this clock made for Albert."

"Geoffrey penned this poem for Philippa Chaucer. Isn't that romantic?"

"This medallion belonged to a witch. She was a keeper of secrets. She protected something of great importance, Percy."

Percy was six when Britain declared war on Germany. His father disappeared to fight and his mother became obsessed with saving their love – everyone's love, actually. With Percy's help she hid the pieces she'd collected in secret spots all over the house. She was determined that no one else would get their hands on them. All her beloved pieces remained safe, unlike her beloved husband, who was killed in France. She never remarried, despite a number of offers, and instead concentrated on raising her son.

Percy was in his fifties, teaching history at a boy's high school, when his mother passed away, leaving him a number of properties around London, including the family's Hampstead home. Percy's wife, Nancy, was ecstatic. They'd hit the jackpot. At last, she'd have the life she'd always dreamt of.

But Nancy's plan to move to Hampstead and live off Percy's inheritance was thwarted by a condition in the will. Percy's mother stipulated that the home be turned into a museum, otherwise everything would be left to charity.

Nancy screamed and cried and cursed her dead mother-in-law. Percy pretended to comfort his wife, but behind his act of unity, Percy was ecstatic. It was his dear old mother's final act of love for her only child. They'd always had a secret dream of opening a museum, but then he'd married Nancy and he felt it best not to test her patience. She didn't have much at the best of times.

Of course, Bea had been bitterly disappointed when her son fell in love with the cold, disinterested Nancy. She never voiced her disapproval, but she secretly vowed that not even over her own dead body would that icy bitch strip her son of his chance at romance – even if it were only in a museum.

And so she changed her will and by doing so, Percy's life.

Percy sold some of the real estate to fund the museum. He and Nancy did move to Hampstead, but to an apartment near the big house. Despite her moaning, they were actually quite well off. Percy was certainly happier than ever once he opened the museum, and tried to include his wife in all his grand plans.

But Nancy never showed the slightest bit of interest. Her bitterness finally manifested physically, and three years after her mother-in-law passed away, so did she.

Percy mourned his wife, but he had to admit that it was much easier without her around. That was nearly fifteen years ago, and while the British Museum of Romance had never reached the potential he dreamed of, it stayed afloat and was appreciated by thousands of romantics annually. And Percy rose each day excited to be doing something he found so completely fulfilling. He honestly felt blessed, and not a week went by when he didn't drop by his mother's grave and thank her.

And now, the final hidden piece belonging to his mother had been found. He felt like her vision was complete. It was quite an emotional moment. It called for a celebration really.

"Would you like a cup of tea, Nell?"

"I'd love one, Percy."

He made a pot of Earl Grey and they sat and admired their find.

"There's more to this piece than meets the eye?"

Something about that statement made Nell uncomfortable. "It's certainly a mystery." Her phone rang. She checked it and groaned. "Sorry, Percy, it's my grandmother."

Percy's eyes lit up at the mention of Eleanor, who he thought was a handsome woman, if slightly uptight. "Go ahead, dear. I need to catalogue this piece and register it with the antiquities scheme."

He took the medallion and headed out the back while Nell answered the phone.

"Hello, Gran."

"Where are you, Nell?"

"At work."

Slight pause. "Oh, you got a job?"

"At the BMR."

"Well, that's hardly work, seeing as he hardly pays you."
Eleanor sniffed. "Good news, dear. I've got you an interview
for a *real* job."

Nell was tempted to argue that the BMR was a real job,
but knew she'd never win. Eleanor continued anyway.

"Julian DeHart is expecting you in his office at two p.m.
today."

"But I'm working until four."

Eleanor's frustration was building. "So leave early. Percy
probably won't even notice." She gave Nell all the details and
a few extra instructions on what to wear and how to act that
left Nell wondering if she was going on a job interview or a
blind date. She hung up and wandered into Percy's office.

"Everything alright with your grandmother?" Percy asked.

"Yes, apart from her being a meddling old busybody."

To Nell's surprise, Percy defended Eleanor. "Now, now,
she's simply concerned for you. It's a delight to see such an involved grandmother. It warms my heart."

Nell stared at him, surprised by his fervor. "She's set up
a job interview for me this afternoon. Her friend's grandson
works for the National Museum, and he has agreed to meet
me. The poor guy probably had no choice, just like I don't."

"That's wonderful. What department?"

"Prehistory and Europe. Her friend's grandson specializes
in early medieval Europe."

"Nell, it sounds perfect for you. I think you should take
the rest of the day off to prepare for it."

"No, no, Percy, I don't need—"

"I won't hear another word. The National Museum is the
most important institution in Britain," Percy said. "It would
be an incredible honor to work there, Nell."

Nell gathered her things. There was no point arguing with
Percy – he was very much like her grandmother in that respect. She didn't mention that she'd rather work full time for

the BMR. She didn't want to pressure him, but she needed a job. She couldn't survive forever on what she was earning, and that meant looking for work elsewhere. And the National was an amazing museum. But she left the British Museum of Romance that afternoon with a heavy heart.

Chapter 21

Hot elderberry on a cold morning wards off colds

Batty tried to concentrate on the accounts, but it was an impossible task. Nearby, Alf was preparing the menu for the coming week. Normally he'd interrupt her regularly with a stream of questions:

"Steak and kidney pie?"

"Sounds good, Alf."

"How about soft-shell crab lasagna?"

"That didn't sell so well last time. Not sure why. What about a new chicken dish?"

"Good idea. Lemon and pink peppercorn chicken?"

And so it would go until Batty eventually lost her patience and snapped, "Alf, I'm trying to do the books. Can't you just be quiet for five minutes?"

But today he was silent. Not a question, not a suggestion, not a word sprang from his mouth. And that silence bothered Batty more than his endless chatter ever could. Finally, she'd had enough.

"Everything alright, Alf?"

"Sure love, all good."

"Need any help with the menu?"

"No, it's taking shape."

"Got something on your mind you'd like to talk about?"

A nervous pause. "No, Bettina ... everything is fine."

"Have you added the linguini primavera?"

"Yes, I added that."

"Are you having an affair, Alf?" There, she'd said it.

Alf stared at her in complete horror. His mouth opened and closed like a gasping fish. "Good God, woman, what on earth ...? How could you ever think ...?"

Batty knew immediately how wrong she'd been. Every cell in her body knew the truth just by looking at him. Her husband definitely wasn't having an affair. But still, all the signs were there.

"It's just you're not present at the moment. And you have a lot of mysterious appointments. You're distant, closed off from me, Alf." Tears welled in her eyes. "Little things have added up recently ... and you are a handsome man. I thought perhaps someone had caught your eye ..."

"Oh, love, how can anyone else catch my eye when my eyes are still glued to you?"

"Then what is it, Alf? Something is up. I just know it is."

Alf made his way over to her and pulled up a stool. "Yes, Batty. Something is up."

*

Nell waited nervously in Julian DeHart's office. She hated job interviews, or anything else that took her out of her comfort zone. She glanced around the room. By most people's standards, it was cluttered, but to one who had a passion for history, the books and papers and artifacts waiting to be studied or numbered were fascinating. Julian's tiny, cramped, partitioned office in the Prehistory and Europe department was a small slice of heaven to a bookworm and history nut like Nell.

A tall, goofy-looking man with a pleasant, if rather craggy, face loped into the room.

"Nell, so sorry to keep you waiting." Julian stretched out a hand. "Just had a collection arrive from Hallstatt. On loan for an exhibition we're doing. So thrilling." Julian's eyes were alight and she almost expected his bow tie to start spinning through sheer excitement.

Julian motioned for her to sit again, and he squeezed his long frame behind his desk. Nell took a moment to check him out. Her grandmother had raved about how handsome he was, but she obviously still hadn't found her glasses. She'd mentioned stylish, but the bow tie blew that theory out the window. He was also supposedly a genius, but it was too soon to tell. One thing was clear: Julian DeHart was nice. Nell was immediately drawn to him and was glad she'd agreed to the interview.

"So, Nell, let me tell you a bit about the job. It's assistant curator, here with me. It's a twelve-month contract while my current assistant is on maternity leave, but I'm sure we'd be able to create something for you afterwards. The National Museum, as you know, is the largest museum in the UK. And the most prestigious."

Nell nodded, trying not to feel too overwhelmed, just as Julian leant forward and gave her a conspiratorial grin.

"But what the tour guides don't tell you is how fun it is. This is Disneyland for history geeks like us."

Normally, Nell would've been offended to be called a geek, but in this instance she felt quite honored to be included. To her, having access to some of the world's most important historical artifacts *was* the ultimate fun.

"Over one thousand people work here," he continued. "And it would be a rare employee who didn't feel privileged to be a part of such a great institution."

Nell was tempted to ask whether the people who cleaned the toilets felt that way, but kept her mouth shut.

"Your key responsibilities would include record keeping and handling of all incoming and outgoing pieces. You'd be involved in installation, both the permanent collection and special exhibitions, and new media projects. The list goes on. The job certainly never gets boring." Julian gave Nell a sweeping stare and she wasn't sure whether he was checking out her potential as a coworker or a date. "Normally we hire people with a minimum of two years' experience, but your grandmother said you've just finished your degree."

"My masters, yes. But I've also been working part time at a museum for nearly three years."

Julian's face lit up. "That's great. Where?"

Nell steeled herself for his inevitable disappointment. "The British Museum of Romance."

To her surprise, Julian clapped his hands together in delight. "I know it well. Wonderful little place. Wasn't it called the London Love Museum?"

"Yes, we changed the name a couple of years ago." Nell didn't mention how she'd pressured Percy into the name change because she was sick of dealing with people who arrived expecting a sex tour. Percy had originally resisted the change, but was now grateful. He'd been wondering how to get rid of all the hookers who dropped by.

"The BMR offers wonderful information on some of this country's grandest love stories." Julian actually seemed impressed by the museum. "Dreadfully under funded though. Such a pity." He glanced down at the application form she'd quickly filled in when she arrived. "Says here you also volunteer at Highgate."

Nell nodded. "I do tours in the West Cemetery." Nell paused and realized Julian was waiting for more information. "I have a thing about graves," she explained.

"You start the newspaper at the obituaries."

"Is that on my resume?"

"I'm also obsessed with old cemeteries," Julian explained, "and would never consider reading the news before the obituaries."

"Where does the sport rate?"

"Very low, I'm afraid. I'm not particularly athletic."

"I've never owned a pair of sneakers," Nell admitted.

"I bought a pair in the mid-nineties. Was arrested soon after. The police said it was a crime against fashion. The case is still pending ... New charges have been laid – the bow tie apparently."

Nell laughed. She liked him a lot. He had a rare and admirable passion for history, and a self-deprecating sense of humor, so while she had absolutely no interest in dating him, which was obviously her grandmother's main motive for setting up the interview, she decided then and there that she'd really like to work for him. Nell turned on her considerable charm and set about winning Julian over.

"I'll be honest with you, Julian. I was hesitant about coming here today."

"Would that be because our grandmothers set this up, or because your heart lies at the BMR?"

She was amazed he'd pegged her so easily. "Both. But now that I've met you, I think I'd learn a lot working with you. And I'd enjoy it, which would be a bonus."

Julian stretched a skinny arm across the desk and extended his hand. "I think we'll work well together."

Nell noticed the emphasis he placed on *work*. "Does that mean I've got the job?"

"Of course you've got the job. You could've arrived here covered in tattoos and speaking in tongues and I'd still give it to you. My grandmother is like yours: not a woman one argues with." Julian gave Nell a friendly wink. "I'm just lucky you're also perfect." He looked horrified. "For the job, I mean. Perfect for the job."

They stared at each other for a moment, and then began to laugh. Whatever the future held, Nell was certain she'd just made a new friend.

Chapter 22

Carry comfrey for protection when traveling

Calypso and Taran pulled up in front of the King and Mistress just as Nell was hopping off the bus. The two sisters flew into each other's arms. They hadn't seen each other for days and had lots to catch up on.

"I've missed you," Calypso squealed.

"You too, Callie. And guess what? I got a job!"

"It's not with that guy Gran was raving about, is it?"

"Yes, and he's lovely."

"Really." Calypso's eyebrows shot up. "Lovely-to-shag lovely?"

"Callie! Lovely-to-work-with lovely." Nell stepped back and stared at her sister. She looked from her sister to Taran and then her hand flew to her mouth. "Oh …!"

Calypso shrugged nonchalantly, but was obviously thrilled. "He's under my skin. Like a rash."

Taran nodded in agreement. "She's like a boil – I can't stop squeezing her."

Nell wrapped her arms around Taran. "Do you have any idea what you're in for?"

"I'm a masochist."

"Don't ever say I didn't try to warn you."

They made their way to the entrance, excited about sharing their news with their parents. Instead, they found the pub shut, with a scrawled note stuck to the door apologizing for any inconvenience and promising to reopen soon.

"Okay, weird," Calypso said, immediately worried. "They never close. This'll be on *Ripley's Believe It or Not*."

"Perhaps they've decided to take the afternoon off," said Taran.

"There's more chance of a comet hitting London tonight," Calypso said.

Nell took her sister's hand. "Let's go around the side."

They used Calypso's key on the side door and walked through the dining rooms and into the bar. All the lights were off and it was deathly quiet. Then they heard someone crying.

Calypso tilted her head to one side. "It's upstairs."

"It could be Enid," said Nell.

But as they reached the bottom of the stairs it became clear that the sobs belonged to Batty. Calypso charged up the stairs two at a time, Taran and Nell were right behind her. She ran along the third floor landing and flung open the door to her parents' sitting room. There, curled up on her husband's lap, completely inconsolable, was Batty. Alf looked both relieved and horrified as his daughters and Taran stormed into the room.

"What's going on?" Calypso demanded.

Batty was roused from her hysteria and tried to smile, but it only made her look like a meerkat that was about to attack. "Oh hello, dears. Nothing. Everything is fine. I'm a bit hormonal, that's all."

"Bullshit! Why are you crying? And why is the pub shut?" Both rare events.

Nell looked frightened. "Has something happened to Eleanor?"

"No, no," Batty assured her. "I'd hardly be this hysterical over Eleanor, would I?"

The sisters watched as their mother tried to put on a brave face, but her chin continued to wobble. It was incredibly disconcerting as Batty rarely cried, and certainly not in front of other people. Then Calypso noticed that her father had been sitting in stony silence since they entered, his usual cheerful demeanor completely absent.

"Is something wrong, Dad?"

She knew by the look on his face that it was.

"Now, it's nothing to get worked up about," said Alf.

"Mum obviously thinks it is."

"Well, I'm telling you it's not," snapped Alf.

Nell sat on the lounge beside him and slipped her small hand into his large one. It gave him the courage to continue.

"I was diagnosed with a melanoma ... Nasty bastard of a thing on my leg."

Batty began to cry again. Calypso slumped into a chair opposite her father. This wasn't good and she knew it. She'd heard hideous stories about melanoma, especially during her time in Australia.

Nell looked confused. "That's not very common here, is it?"

"Thirteen thousand cases a year apparently," Alf said. "I spent a lot of time in the sun when I was in Spain."

"I told you to wear a hat," Batty wailed.

"He can't wear a hat on his leg, can he?" Calypso snapped.

"Can't they just cut the melanoma off?" Nell asked.

"They already have," Alf said. "Didn't quite get it all so I had to go back again. Carved the thing out."

"Twice," Batty cried. "And he didn't tell me. I thought he was having an affair."

Calypso shook her head. "How did you make that leap?"

"We hadn't made love for a month."

"Glad I asked."

"We're all adults here." Batty sniffed.

Alf ignored his wife and continued, "They got it all from the leg. That's the good news."

"And the bad news?"

"There are some spots on my liver …"

Calypso paled. "What sort of spots?"

"He owns a pub … of course he has spots on his liver," Batty interrupted.

"I had a biopsy. It's melanoma."

Calypso felt like she was having an out of body experience. "I don't understand. How does it get there?"

"It's a secondary cancer, Callie. It spread from my leg."

Nell clutched her father's hand. "What are your options?"

"I've decided on surgery. They'll remove three-quarters of the liver." He gave his daughters a cheery smile that did nothing to hide his fear. "Apparently it rejuvenates …"

"We should post that on the wall of the pub," Calypso said. "'The liver rejuvenates, so drink up.'"

"Are there risks?"

"Of course there are risks. But there are more if I don't do it, Nell."

"Why didn't you tell us earlier, Dad?" Calypso was beside herself with fear. "I can't believe you waited until now."

"I wasn't going to worry you until I knew everything," Alf said.

Taran shuffled uncomfortably. "If I could say something."

Alf locked eyes with him, protesting with a stern shake of the head.

Taran stood firm. "I believe honesty is the best policy."

Alf waved his hand in front of his mouth – universal speak for "Zip it."

"I understand why Alf wanted to keep this to himself until he knew more."

Alf cut him off. "Because that's what men do ... keep things to themselves. Right, Taran?"

"Yes, Alf, and sometimes that might hurt the people they love."

"Not if they don't know."

"Well, we know now," snapped Calypso.

"Good God, son, first rule of survival for men in this family is to know when to quit: while you're ahead."

Taran backed off a bit. "I just want to clear the air—"

"Excellent idea." Alf stood abruptly and marched over to the window. "I need air." He yanked open a window and stuck his head out. "There's too much talking. We just need to get on with it."

Taran knew when he was defeated. He retreated to his chair in the corner.

There was a moment of silence and then Nell quietly encouraged everyone to make some decisions. Under her guidance they quickly decided that he would have surgery as soon as possible, that Megan would run the pub for a few weeks and that the restaurant would be closed until further notice.

"Who wants to tell Eleanor?" Nell asked.

Silence.

"Fine, I'll let her know tomorrow."

"Does she need to know?" Calypso asked.

Nell looked appalled. "Of course she needs to know."

"Perhaps we can tell her at Christmas, when it's all over and done with and your father is in the clear," Batty suggested.

"I'm happy if we don't say anything at all," Alf said. "Unless I die ... then she'll need to know."

Calypso shrugged. "If we tell her now she'll make it all about her."

Nell glared at them all in disbelief. "This *is* about her, as much as any of us. I'll deal with Gran."

Nell continued to make a list of people who needed to be contacted. Then she called the doctor while everyone listened, and confirmed her father's date for surgery.

At that point the past came back to haunt Calypso with a vengeance. She watched her mother's face, twisted with grief and fear, and it was like looking into a mirror. She'd been there. She'd looked like that. She'd experienced both grief and fear, and of course loss. And all she could think was how would she survive, how would any of them survive, if her father died?

Calypso felt ill. She looked at Taran, sitting in the corner, his impossibly handsome face etched with concern. Yes, she'd fallen for him, but it wasn't too late. She could get out now.

The whole situation was so surreal. Was it only an hour ago that she was ecstatically happy? It's absurd how quickly life can snatch that away. It was happening again. And all she could feel was herself sinking, sinking, sinking ...

Chapter 23

Use alcohol to sterilize a wound

Calypso sat in the front pew with Scott's family during his funeral. She remained stony-faced as his parents and sisters cried. Behind them sat two hundred family and friends, some she knew, many she didn't. Sobs and sniffles filled the room. But Calypso refused to cry. If she let go now she would never survive. She had to keep it together and get out of there.

Afterwards, everyone went back to Scott's parents' home for tea and lamingtons. Scott's friends drank beers and told hilarious stories about their mate. Calypso was somewhat comforted to see how much support Scott's family had. She'd grown to love them over the years, and knew they'd survive this.

Unlike her. She was alone now. Yes, she had her own family in London, and good friends scattered around the world, but Scott was her anchor, her home, and her soulmate. *Was.* Now he was nothing but ash.

Scott's family circled Calypso warily. They weren't sure how to comfort her. They didn't really know her without Scott attached to her side. But mostly, she was a glaring reminder of what they'd lost. Calypso only existed in their lives because Scott had fallen in love and morphed into the entity that was "Scott and Callie." All they could do was watch the beautiful redhead as she seemed to sink deeper and deeper into her silent grief.

A few days after the funeral, when Scott's ashes were returned to the family, Calypso perched on a stool in the kitchen, staring first at the urn and then at a big bowl of Nutri-Grain sitting beside it. She was sure Scott would approve. She had decided on Nutri-Grain for a number of reasons. It was, so the commercials said, the breakfast cereal for real men, iron men, sporty men: men like Scott. But it also had a hint of sweetness, just like Scott. And, because Scott would appreciate the humor, it tasted fabulous in the morning ...

Scott's mother, Patricia, appeared and placed a hand on her shoulder. She was pleased to see Calypso with food in front of her. She hadn't eaten a thing since Scott died.

"Are you hungry, Calypso?"

"No." Callie stared at the cereal. She was certain he wanted this. He'd said so on numerous occasions after he'd been mugged in Thailand. She'd laughed at the time, but he'd been adamant. "This is Scott's wish."

"That you eat some cereal?"

"Yes ... with his ashes sprinkled on it. Just so he can be inside me one last time."

Patricia held the counter to steady herself and watched Calypso for a moment.

"I don't think he really meant it, Callie," she said finally

"How can we be sure? If he meant it, I have to do it." Calypso had always said she'd do anything for him. "I can't let him down."

Patricia took Callie's hand. "You couldn't let him down if you tried."

Calypso finally voiced what had been haunting her for days. None of her spells, her powers, her connections to the other side had helped one iota when it really counted. "I already have let him down. I couldn't save him."

"You need to concentrate on what you did for him, not what you couldn't do."

"What did I do for him?"

"I've never seen someone so young love so well," Pat said gently. "Or so deeply."

It was true. Calypso loved Scott, exposed her soul to him, placed her trust in him, all in a way the average person is incapable of doing. Most people aren't even aware such a level of surrender exists, yet Calypso reached deep inside until she found the edge and then she took herself there, over it, and stayed there. All for him. And in return, he also did the same for her. Theirs was an intense and deep love.

Patricia sighed, a sigh filled with heartbreak only a mother can feel. "And really, Callie, he's gone. So it doesn't matter."

Calypso looked at her with all the wisdom of one who sees beyond the veils. "But he'll be back. And I'll have to explain why I didn't do as he'd asked …"

She stopped short. Patricia had never been entirely comfortable with her psychic abilities, and certainly wasn't ready to talk about them now. Calypso tipped the Nutri-Grain into the sink. She couldn't bear the thought of placing a spoonful of the fine gray dust in her mouth. She couldn't stomach the idea that the man she adored would enter her in this manner. That their love had come to this: that he, in their final physical experience, would be the weaker one, so weak that a simple breeze could whisk him away.

"You're right. Even if he knew, he wouldn't care." It was true. It no longer mattered. Scott was but a pile of dust and nothing, not even the return of his spirit, would ever change that.

They stood in silence for a long time, staring at the urn, both aware that they, Scott's mother and his soulmate, were the two suffering the greatest loss. Despite this, they still couldn't help each other. How could either of them help? Could Calypso bring the dead back to life? Could Patricia turn back time? Could they wake each other from this nightmare? No. They felt for each other and shared a common pain, but grief was a relative thing. The greatest tragedy was always one's own and their personal loss was so great neither felt they'd survive it. They were, and always would be, two islands alone in the same sea of despair.

Patricia finally spoke. "Would you like some of his ... ashes? To take with you?"

Calypso nodded.

"I'm not suggesting you leave. You're welcome to stay, for as long as you want."

"I have to go, Patricia."

"I thought so. Will you be okay?"

"No."

Patricia gave Calypso's arm an affectionate squeeze. "Nor will I."

The following morning, clutching a small portion of her beloved's ashes, and leaving only a note for Scott's family, Calypso left for the airport. She was headed for Ash Cottage, where she would stay for eight months.

It was there that she finally cried.

Chapter 24

Jagermeister is an excellent digestif

Taran reached for Calypso the minute she closed her bedroom door, but she placed a hand on his chest, and put some distance between them.

Taran stepped back and sat on the bed. "Not quite the night we expected."

"I've had worse."

"I know tonight has been tough—"

"That's one way to describe it."

"—but I'm here for you. We're in this together."

Calypso looked at him with complete calm. "I appreciate the support, Taran, I really do. But I don't want to be in this or anything else *together*."

Taran was completely blindsided. "What do you mean by that?"

Calypso spoke as though he didn't understand English. "I feel that ... it's best if we don't see each other for a while."

"How long's *a while*?"

"Pretty long."

"You're in shock, Calypso."

"Perhaps, but the fact is my family needs me. I need them. We have to concentrate on each other now."

Taran totally agreed. "And I'd never stand in the way of that."

"Not intentionally," Calypso conceded. "But relationships take a lot of work, and I won't have the time or energy."

"Ever?"

"For a while."

Taran held out his hands like he was haggling at Istanbul's Grand Bazaar. "I can wait. We're in no hurry. How about we take a break, until your father is well."

"What if he dies?"

"Geez, Cal—"

"I'm in no position to make any promises."

"I'm not asking you to."

"Taran, I don't want a relationship."

"But everything that happened between us at Tintagel …?"

"It was fun."

Taran stared at her in disbelief. "But you're in love with me."

"Define 'love'," Calypso stuttered. It was the first time she'd cracked.

"Define it? To me it's the way you looked at me when we last made love. The way you smiled at me this morning. And honestly, the way you're looking at me now."

Calypso was annoyed. "Okay, so I kinda love you."

"Kinda? What are you, five?"

"It's not enough."

"You won't know that unless you try."

"I don't have time to try. My father has cancer."

"I know, I was there. Let me be here for you."

"Quite honestly, you seemed to annoy Dad earlier. I don't know why, but he just wanted you to shut up."

"Your dad just needed some air."

"I'm sorry, Taran, but it's best if you go."

"Just like that – it's over? The end?"

"In my experience endings are usually unexpected and quick."

"You know what, Cal? You are a goddamn pain in the ass." Enraged, he moved forward and grabbed her. She tried to pull back but he held on. "You're crazy if you throw this away."

His lips slammed down on hers. It was a kiss that exploded in every cell of her body. She wanted to fight ... knew she should ... but instead her arms slipped around his neck and she tore at his hair. She bit down on his lip, so angry she couldn't say no to him. With all the force she could muster she began to push him back toward the wall. Her fingers tore at the buttons of his shirt. She could taste blood from his lip. Her whole body screamed for him as she slammed him into the wall. But the moment was shattered into a million pieces when something smashed beside them.

It took them a moment to realize it was a framed photo that had fallen from the wall.

Calypso gave a cry. "Scott." She bent down and began to collect the broken pieces from the floor.

"Calypso, you'll cut yourself. Let me help."

Calypso thrust an arm out to stop him. "Don't touch it. It's Scott."

"What's Scott?"

"His picture." Calypso was crying silent tears now, as she removed the photo from the broken frame.

"It's okay, Cal. We'll get a new frame for it."

"No, it's a sign. Please go."

"It's not a sign, babe. We knocked it off the wall. You need to settle down."

Now there was life inside her eyes again. She stood, and in the calmest voice she could muster, said, "Don't tell me what I need. I know what I need. I need you to go."

Taran paused for a moment and then he turned and left, shutting the door quietly behind him.

Chapter 25

What butter and whiskey cannot cure, there is
no cure for

Taran made his way back to Simon's house, wondering what the hell he would do next. Leaving Calypso clutching that broken frame had torn his heart out, but she'd given him no choice. She didn't want him. He'd fought hard, and done a damn fine job for someone who'd never had to compete for anything before. Especially not a woman. Normally it was a piece of cake. Turn on the charm, the humor, toss in some romance. Most women were like putty. Hell, sometimes all he had to do was turn up.

But Calypso was made of sturdier stuff and he had no idea how one competed with the ghost of genuine love. Common sense told him not to compete at all, but simply be himself. That they were meant to be together and that would win her in the end. But he hadn't won her over. She'd declared it over.

He let himself into the darkened apartment, made a stiff drink at Simon's bar and, with the glass in one hand and the bottle of scotch in the other, wandered into his studio. He shuffled some of his paintings around and waited for inspiration to hit, but it felt like inspiration had just thrown him out of her family's pub.

He took another slug of scotch and refilled his glass. It was a cliché, but the artist intended to get roaring drunk and drown his sorrows. Not that, in his experience, sorrows ever drowned. Sorrow was the Michael Phelps of emotions and would be treading water long after he'd sunk to the bottom. But he'd have another drink anyway.

Taran sank back into the couch and stared at the painting of Calypso. It was good. He'd captured qualities on canvas that he hadn't even seen before tonight. There was the grief, the fear, not obvious, but definitely clouding those amazing green eyes.

He shook his glass slightly and the ice tinkled. For a moment he thought it echoed right down the hallway and up the stairs, but then he realized it wasn't the ice he could hear, but a woman's laugh.

There it was again. A woman laughing.

He was hardly Sherlock Holmes, but there were a few things he did know. Firstly, Simon lived the life of a monk, so whoever was laughing wasn't with Simon. Secondly, Simon had mentioned he'd be away for a couple of days, which once again pointed to the fact that whoever was laughing wasn't with Simon.

"Damn it!" Taran was furious. He'd had a hell day and the last thing he needed was a confrontation with a burglar. Especially a happy one. He was tempted to call the police and hide in the closet, but by the time the cops arrived the thief (or *thieves*, as there was obviously also a witty burglar who was making his accomplice laugh) could be long gone. Simon had a lot of expensive gear in his apartment so if he was being robbed, Taran really ought to do something about it. Immediately.

"Damn, fuckeddy damn!"

He noticed a set of golf clubs in the corner. He dithered between a putter and a wedge for a moment before berating himself for being such an idiot. He was using it as a weapon, not to play eighteen holes.

He grabbed an iron – and then a wedge – and made his way up the stairs and along the corridor toward one of the guest bedrooms. Fear prickled his skin. Was he crazy? He should just call the police. And then he heard a strangled moan and realized someone was being attacked. He flung open the door and barreled into the room, only to find Simon and Megan buck naked in bed together, going at it like a pair of teenagers.

"Holy shit … oh shit!"

Megan and Simon grabbed for the bedcovers, but not before Taran got a full view of Simon's bare ass.

"What the hell are you doing?" Simon knocked a box of Durex off the dresser. Taran noticed it was nearly empty.

"Looks like he's playing golf." Megan burst into giggles and hid further under the duvet.

Taran shielded his eyes with his hand. "I thought you were being burgled."

"If this is being burgled then bring it on." Simon laughed.

Taran slunk toward the door. "You did say you were going away."

"Our flights were cancelled. Bad weather in Spain."

"And it's not your room …"

"Well, technically I own the whole apartment, but no, I don't sleep here."

"We decided to give every room in the house a go," Megan explained.

"Right." Taran marched out the door and slammed it behind him.

Simon followed him out, grasping a sheet around his waist. "You okay?"

"Yeah, yeah, sure." Taran looked at his friend for a moment. "Are you?"

"Never better. Madly in love."

Taran was surprised. "Oh, that's great, Sime." And it was. Simon deserved some happiness. And Megan was a real cracker. Taran noticed something on Simon's arm. "Is that a tattoo?"

Simon looked embarrassed. "Yes, ah ... small one. Hurt like buggery but I'm quite pleased with the result. Makes me feel quite ... foxy." He admired the small image of a fox for a moment, and then turned back to Taran. "How's Calypso?"

Taran was tempted to tell his friend everything, but now wasn't the time, especially with Megan in the other room. She was going to be devastated and would have to take on extra work at the pub. He decided to let them have the night together, trouble free. They'd find out the truth soon enough. "Calypso's at home. Needed a rest. See you in the morning, Sime."

Simon headed back into the spare bedroom, but paused at the door. "By the way, thanks. I know how much of a wimp you are at heart. So charging in here with the golf club took some balls." Simon let out a whoop as he shut the door. "Of course, you didn't have balls. Only clubs."

Taran made his way into his own room. He briefly wondered if they'd given his room "a go", but then decided he didn't care either way and threw himself on the bed. He was restless and a bottle of scotch wasn't the answer. He needed his twin. He reached for the phone, dialed the number and Finn answered on the third ring, with his usual greeting.

"Hello, Taran."

"Hey ... how's it going?"

"Not bad." A pause. "You've called me with good news?"

Taran knew his twin. Finn was a softie. He'd yield. "Yes, well, not quite what you initially stipulated—"

"Then I've got to go, Taran."

Christ it was unlike his twin to be this tough.

"I'm sorry, Finn. I understand how much I hurt you now, and I'm so sorry."

"Sounds like you've been burnt." Finn almost sounded worried.

"I have been – torched."

"That makes you more dangerous than ever," Finn said. "Tye is the love of my life and seeing as you have a habit of hitting on women I love, I don't want you around."

"Finn, you're being unreasonable ..."

"Fuck off, Taran. I caught you with her."

"It takes two to tango."

"She thought you were me, you ass. You're lucky I'm giving you a chance at all."

"I know, Finn, but I can assure you—"

Finn cut him off. "I don't want your assurances or your promises. I want to see you in love. Only then will it be safe to let you back in my life. Don't call until you're really, truly, deeply in love."

"But Finn ... I am—" The phone went dead in Taran's hand.

*

Finn placed the phone back on the receiver. It took every ounce of his strength to not immediately call Taran back. He sensed his brother's agony and his role had always been to nurture his often frustrating twin. He'd never hurt Taran before.

"Was he okay?"

Finn turned and gave Tye a pained smile. "No, he's not okay."

"You don't need to go through with this, Finn."

"Yes, I do. It's the right thing to do."

"Are you sure you're not secretly jealous?" Tye tilted her head to one side, her perfectly shaped lips curving slightly upwards, teasing him.

"He acted like an asshole, but I can hardly blame him for wanting you." Finn chuckled. "And it's not like you're the first woman of mine he's hit on."

Tye pretended to be offended. "So now I'm just one of a long list?"

Finn pulled Tye into his arms. "Afraid so, but you're at number one."

"That's okay then." She nuzzled his neck. "I just want you to be happy, and you're not happy without Taran in your life."

"He'll be back. For once, he's trying to solve things between us, rather than just expecting me to forgive and forget."

Finn watched his girlfriend for a moment. He wanted Taran to love someone as much as he loved Tye. To experience what that meant. Finn knew, without a doubt, that happiness would come to Taran when he worked things out with Calypso Shakespeare. If he ever did. His brother could be a stubborn bastard, and Finn's few experiences with the British redhead gave him the impression that she could be too.

They were a perfect match.

Tye seemed to read his mind. "You really think she's the one for him?"

"I do. I've never seen him so bowled over by a woman. But he needed a bit of a kick to look her up again."

"And he has, so your plan worked. Now call him back and tell him everything is okay."

Finn gave Tye a playful grin. "Nah ... I'll wait a little longer. If their past is anything to go on, Calypso will be giving him the run around right about now."

"And you don't mind seeing your twin have his heart broken."

"Well, he did hit on you ..."

Tye gave Finn a playful slap. "You are shocking ... come here. I think you should be punished."

What followed was hardly a punishment, but Finn had no intention of pointing that out.

Chapter 26

Ingest watercress at daybreak to increase dreams
the following evening

Calypso was ecstatic. She was back in Australia ... with him.

She could see him perched on his surfboard, chatting to some of the other surfers. It was an achingly familiar and incredibly sexy sight. Over the years, she'd spent countless hours lying on the beach reading while he surfed. Every few pages she'd look up from her book and gaze out to sea ... to Scott. She'd watch the waves carry him, work with him and occasionally pound him. Her stomach would twist each time he went under a wave. She'd wait endless seconds disguised as hours until he reemerged, only to pull himself back on his board and paddle back out for more. His muscular arms cut through the water at a determined pace; he was always certain the next wave he caught would be the perfect ride.

Calypso's memories of those times were wonderful, pure, free and magical, but being back now, she remembered that she also hated waiting in the midday sun. She enjoyed the beach in the late afternoons, but was uncomfortable during the warmer hours and counted the minutes until he returned to her side. The sand was hot and her skin burnt easily. She grabbed her sunscreen and slathered it onto her legs, which were already pink, but still the sun clawed at her. She took a sarong and threw it over her tingling shoulders and pulled her hat right down over her head. She'd forgotten how unpleasant she'd found these long hours waiting for his perfect wave. She was annoyed and realized she'd felt annoyed a lot when Scott was alive. She'd spent a great deal of time waiting for him to finish his surf, or ski, or skydive.

"Hungry?"

A shower of cool water drops rained over her. She could almost hear them sizzle as they hit her skin. She shielded her eyes with her hand and looked up at Scott. He always shook his hair over her, like a big old wet dog. He undid his wetsuit, yanked himself free from the top half, and left it hanging at the waist. The sun was positioned behind him and blasted down on his lean, brown body. The bright light and relentless heat never bothered him – he seemed to thrive on it. He tilted his head to one side and smiled, and Calypso fell, positively tumbled, in love with him all over again.

"I'm starving," he said.

No surprise. He was always starving.

"You eat like a horse."

He held his hand out and helped her up. "I'm also hung like a horse."

Calypso gave him a slap. "In your dreams, buster."

Scott stopped smiling. "In my dreams ... or yours?"

Fear clutched Calypso's gut. "Is this a dream?" She grabbed him, wrapped her arms around him. He was real. She could feel him. She kissed his neck, his shoulders. Her fingers clutched at his firm flesh. She could taste the salt on his skin, for God's sake. He had to be real.

"If this is a dream then I don't want to wake up. I can't lose you again."

He kissed her, softly, gentle kisses that started on the lips and wound their way around to her ear, where he whispered, "What are you doing, Callie?"

Calypso woke with his voice ringing in her ear. She could still feel his kisses on her neck and smell the ocean air. Loneliness washed over her like a wave on the beach where she wished she still stood. Would she ever stop missing him?

She threw back the covers and stared at the sheets in horror. They were, for the third night running, covered in sand. She'd experienced some major weirdness in her life (by most people's standards anyway), but these recent dreams took the cake.

She crawled out of bed and slipped into some jeans. The clock said midnight, which meant the pub would be closed now. She'd gone to bed early, desperate to escape the depression that was settling in her limbs. Even in the darkest days just after Scott's death, she'd never been depressed. Distraught, yes, angry, scared and totally grief stricken, but never depressed. It was an entirely new experience and she didn't wear it well. Depression came with its companion, lethargy, and she hated them both.

She made her way downstairs and unlocked her bar. She shuffled around the counter looking for a hair band, found one, and scraped her hair off her face. And then she turned on the grinder, and set to work. She couldn't bring Scott back, but she was determined to get her powers back. At least her insomnia meant she had time to work on that.

She started with marigold flowers, which she soaked in lemon juice and sugar. She grabbed bottles of Boudier Saffron gin, Tanqueray gin, Liquore Strega and Licor 43, and began to mix and strain. The routine of it helped. She hated the way the dream lingered, but would give anything to return to it … with him. She missed Scott again … yet as she settled back into her body and shook the dream free from her brain, it was

Taran who filled the space, who filled her thoughts. There was a crossover period where the two men were almost one in her mind. She had to concentrate to separate them, to remember which one was gone and which one remained.

And then came the awful realization that they were both gone now. She missed Taran, she wanted him, but she couldn't call him. It was better this way. She paused and stared at the cocktail.

"Please work," she whispered.

She summoned the force that had always coursed through her so easily, but now nothing happened. She took a sip. It was delicious, crisp and layered. There was nothing wrong with the cocktail. It was her magic that needed fixing. She tried again. Nothing. The gift she'd always taken for granted now required major concentration and effort. She centered herself, focused ... acknowledged the guardians of the gates she was about to enter ... and then attempted to pass through. And again. And again. And again.

"Damn it!"

Calypso smashed the glass and its contents into the sink.

"Not having a good night?"

Calypso gave a start and noticed Megan standing in the doorway. "It's right up there with the night you played in Bristol."

Megan chuckled. She'd dragged Calypso to her first gig in Bristol, only to have her hold her hand in the local ER instead, while she got twelve stitches in the side of her head. The guy who threw the beer glass obviously didn't appreciate her routine. She fingered the scar, still noticeable under her hairline. "I always think back fondly on that night. It was my initiation into stand-up." She made her way into the room and pulled out a stool. "What's up?"

"Oh, you mean apart from the fact that Dad could die and the love of my life already did?"

"Yeah, life sucks." Megan thought for a moment. "Out of interest … how do you know Scott was the love of your life?"

Calypso gave Megan a look of total disdain, and refused to answer.

Megan, unperturbed, carried on talking. "Seriously. Are you carking it today, or do you think that if you're going to be around for a few more years, then it is entirely possible that the best is still to come?"

"Not going to happen."

"No, it won't. Not if you keep disappearing on him." Megan shrugged. "Oh, stop looking at me like that. Simon told me what's been going on. Taran is devastated. And honestly, Callie, I think you're crazy not to give it a shot with him. He's a great guy."

"So was Scott."

Megan jumped off the stool, stormed over to the bar, and held the side of it as she hissed at her best friend. "You think I don't know that. I fucking loved Scott. He was like a brother to me. You're not the only one who lost him. We all lost Scott. Losing him was right up there with losing Mum. But he's dead, you stupid cow, and you're not. And your use-by date on the grief is just about up."

The two friends eyeballed each other for a moment. To an innocent observer, it was the point of no return. In any other relationship it would be, but to Calypso and Megan, who had been through everything together, and argued all the way, it was simply what was expected. They demanded complete honesty from each other.

But that didn't mean they had to like it.

"If my parents didn't need you to run the pub, I'd toss you out."

"You couldn't toss lettuce." Megan matched Callie's withering stare and one-upped it. "We're in this together. Your parents raised me too. You're not the only one suffering. Have you asked after Nell? She can't wallow. She's too busy mak-ing *all* the decisions. And as much as I'd love to spend the day crying over Alf, I don't have time. I have to learn how to run the pub, so he can go into bloody hospital and not worry about it. So let's not fight and just concentrate on being there for everyone." Megan paused briefly as she pulled herself to-gether, and then added, "… and each other."

Calypso nodded. She'd been so caught up in her own grief that she hadn't taken Megan's feelings into consideration. Of course Megan was having a rough time. She'd grown up around the pub, especially once she'd hit puberty. Her baffled father simply couldn't face conversations about periods and boys. He left all that to Batty. He wasn't sure how to express his love for his daughter, so left that to Calypso's parents too. Most of Calypso's childhood memories had Megan in them, so of course Megan's own memories, own identity, had been formed around and by Callie's parents.

Calypso watched her friend carefully and a thousand images flashed through her mind: Alf hugging Megan; Alf teaching Megan how to play poker, how to fish, how to ride a bike, how to pull a beer; yelling at her for running away once, and then hugging her tightly because he'd been scared something had happened to her; rolling his eyes at each new tattoo, but totally accepting of her all the same. And the day Megan's mother died … it was Alf who held her while she sobbed. A wave of shame engulfed Calypso for not taking Megan's feelings into consideration. She smiled at her friend, who looked so incredibly vulnerable behind the punk-pixie camouflage.

"I'm an arse," Calypso conceded.

"Yes, you are," Megan agreed. "Anything else bothering you?"

Her friend knew her so well. "Having some weird dreams … about Scott. Nothing major." Calypso didn't know how to put her dreams into words, or considering the sand in her bed, even if they *were* dreams.

"He'd want you to be happy, Callie. I think he'd like Taran."

"That's not saying much. Scott liked everyone."

Megan laughed. "True."

"I feel like I never got to say goodbye. There's always this feeling of Scott and I being … unfinished."

"Honey, he's dead. It's finished."

Calypso and Megan looked at each other for a moment and then cracked up.

"You're vile," Calypso said.

"I do understand, Callie. But that's what happens when people die suddenly. It's why you've got to take this chance to spend time with Alf. Just in case. And it's why you can't blow what you have with Taran." Megan ran her fingers through her hair. "What else is wrong?"

"Nothing."

"Bullshit. I know I'm not psychic like you, but something else is up."

"Well, I'm not psychic either." There. She'd finally admitted it out loud.

Megan looked confused. "What do you mean?"

"I haven't been able to brew for a while."

A thousand thoughts clearly crossed Megan's face. "You're serious?"

"Yep."

Megan knew what that meant. "Callie, that changes everything."

Calypso waved her hand for her friend to stop. "I can't, Megan. Let's not go there now. Not tonight."

The two friends stared at each other. Megan knew not to speak. They'd discuss it in time.

Calypso changed the subject. "Want a vodka tonic?"

"Does the Pope wear a dress?"

Megan watched as Calypso poured her a drink. "So the pub is busy. Harry has been holding up the bar most nights. He's worried about Alf."

Calypso sliced a lime and dropped a piece into Megan's drink, then slid it across the bar. "When did you run into Simon?"

Megan sipped her drink. "When we had sex."

Calypso's eyes widened. "You slept with Simon?"

"We hardly slept."

"When?"

"Every night since we met." Megan laughed. "Close your mouth. You look like a goldfish gaping at me like that."

Calypso was suddenly in a much better mood than she'd been all week. "You shagged Simon? Bloody hell! What's he like?"

"Quite a surprise package ... package and all."

Calypso clapped a hand across her mouth. "I had no idea."

"You've been busy." Megan fiddled with her straw and then quietly added, "And I wasn't ready to share it with anyone yet. Even you."

"Holy shit ... You're in love!"

Megan grinned. "Yeah, I am, Callie."

Calypso slipped through the gate and embraced her friend. "I am so happy for you, Meg." She pulled back and stared at her friend. Megan's eyes shone, her skin glowed.

Megan blinked back tears. "I never believed all that stuff about soulmates, but I don't know how else to explain what I feel for him."

"And he feels the same?" Calypso had seen Megan get hurt too many times over the years, by men who didn't value the huge heart underneath the tough exterior.

"He does. He's introducing me to his family tomorrow night. Batty said she'd cover the bar for a few hours." Megan pulled a face. "Fuck, I hope they like me."

Calypso threw her arms around Megan. "Like you? They'll love you. How could they not?"

*

Simon and Taran were halfway through a six-pack each and a game of pool.

"My parents are going to hate her."

Taran nodded. "I know. But it's time you stand up to them."

They stared at the pool table silence for a moment, before Taran added, "Or you could run away and live in Fiji."

Simon's eyes lit up. "Now there's an idea."

"You've never introduced anyone to them before, have you?"

"No, they usually introduce women to me." Simon slugged back some beer. "Remember Ashley Sherringstone?"

"Was that the horsy looking one?"

"No, that was Rebecca Jones."

"Oh yes, so it was. Ashley … oh, the one with the …?"

"Yes, gammy leg."

The two men laughed.

"Excellent pedigree, though," said Simon.

"Didn't make up for the stutter."

"Yes, that was unfortunate. Especially seeing as she already had the leg thing."

The two men were pissing themselves laughing now.

"That is the type of woman my parents expect me to marry." Simon sunk three balls in a row in protest.

"Oh man, your poor kids."

"Actually, my mother was vile enough to point out that the gammy leg was the result of an accident and therefore not genetic, and the stutter first showed up after Ashley was caught in the middle of a fox hunt as a child. Once again—"

"… not hereditary," they finished together.

"When are you taking Megan over?"

"Tomorrow."

Taran could barely contain his glee. He thought Simon's family were the biggest bunch of tossers in London. "I'd love to come, just to see how the evening pans out, but I think you should turn up alone with Megan."

"Why's that?"

"It will put an end to your father telling your brothers that he thinks you're gay."

Simon nodded. "Good point." He paused for a moment. "I'd better get Megan to wear a dress … just to drive that point home."

Chapter 27

Sage enhances the memory

Megan didn't wear a dress, because Simon didn't ask her to. He liked her just the way she was, and that included the rather inappropriate outfit she wore to meet his parents: tatty jeans and tight black T-shirt with the words *One Martini, Two Martini, Three Martini, Floor!* plastered across the front.

Megan chatted all the way to the six-bedroom Mayfair mansion with no awareness of what was about to hit her. Yes, she desperately wanted Simon's family to like her, but love had made her even more fearless than usual, and she sincerely believed everything was going to go well.

How wrong she was.

Her first mistake – apart from her appearance, her inability to bottle her exuberance, her obvious lack of breeding, and the fact that she existed at all – was to hug the butler when he opened the door to them. Simon cringed, only because he realized then and there that he'd failed to properly prepare the love of his life for the onslaught of his family.

"Simon has told me so much about you," she lied. Simon rarely talked about his father.

Fitzpatrick calmly peeled the strange creature from around his neck and raised one judgmental eyebrow. "How kind of Master Simon to mention me."

"Actually, Meg, this is Fitzpatrick ... our butler." Simon kicked himself when he saw Megan's face flood with embarrassment. And then, without thinking, he too threw himself into Fitzpatrick's arms. "But yes, good ol' Fitzpatrick is like family and deserves a hug."

A startled Fitzpatrick shrugged Simon off and took his coat. "Your parents will receive you in the sitting room."

"Thank you, Fitzpatrick."

Simon slipped his hand into Megan's and led her up the hall. Her palms were suddenly sweaty and she was unusually quiet. He'd already discovered that when she was nervous she talked incessantly and made a lot of jokes. But this was a first – total silence. Finally, as she reached the end of the hallway, she whispered: "Your parents receive you?"

"I know. Dreadfully fucked up, isn't it." Simon turned to her and gave a snort that reminded her to not take it too seriously. "Sometimes they even ... tolerate me."

Megan giggled. "Oh shit, they're going to hate me aren't they?"

Simon decided to be very honest. "Probably. But it doesn't matter. I love you, and that's all that counts."

Megan noticed the painting behind Simon. "Is that a Monet?"

"Yes."

"Original?"

"Yes – one of three."

"Oh shit, I'm screwed."

Five seconds later, Megan was standing in the middle of the Coliseum and the lions had just been released.

"Mother, Father, this is Megan."

Penelope and Charles Apsley did nothing to hide their absolute horror. Penelope did at least have the grace, as she later told her friends, to rise and make her way across the room. In her mind, she did so with regal bearing. To anyone watching, especially Simon, she looked like a well-dressed barracuda swimming toward a minnow.

"Megan, is it?" she asked as she grabbed Megan's hand a touch too tightly. There was an audible crack of bones.

"Yes, lovely to meet you, Mrs Apsley."

"Yes," Penelope drawled. The feeling obviously wasn't mutual.

Simon forged on: "Over there is my brother David, and his lovely wife, Annabelle."

David and Annabelle glanced at each other in unmasked glee. Dinner here was always a dull affair, but tonight was going to be quite different.

"Lovely to meet you," said Annabelle, genuinely thrilled.

Simon knew that Annabelle really was happy to meet Megan. She'd been trying to please Penelope and Charles for years, to no avail. The answer to her problems had arrived, piercings and all. Next to Megan, Annabelle looked like Princess bloody Diana.

"Goodness, is that a piercing in your lip?" Annabelle exclaimed, just in case her in-laws had missed it.

Megan shuffled uncomfortably from foot to foot. "Yes."

Annabelle's hand flew to her mouth dramatically. "Didn't it hurt?"

"No," Megan admitted. "I was off my trolley when I had it done."

Simon took a deep breath and continued. "And this is Richard."

Richard took one look at Megan and made a face like someone had crapped under his nose. Simon felt like punching him, but instead politely added, "Those who know him well call him Dick."

Simon regretted the evening already. "Slumped in that chair is the one we all look up to, Thomas ... At least we do on the rare occasion that he's upright."

Thomas was obviously slaughtered and stared straight at Megan's chest. "Nice tit – T-shirt."

Finally, Simon turned to an old gentleman, whose wheelchair had been placed in the corner, facing the wall, with him still in it.

"And that's ... ah ... my grandfather."

GeeGee, as everyone called him, stirred. "Turn this bloody thing around."

Penelope jumped to attention and turned her father around to face everyone else. GeeGee looked up at Megan. She nodded her greeting, too petrified to talk now.

"Who's the boy?"

"This is Megan, my new *girlfriend*."

"That's a girl?"

"Yes, GeeGee."

"So you're not a fag?"

Megan jumped to her beloved's defense. "I can assure you he's not."

"What the fuck is wrong with your lip?"

"Megan has a piercing," Annabelle explained loudly.

"What sort of weirdo would get her lip pierced? Are you on drugs?"

Megan's eyes narrowed. "No ... but if you're offering ..."

And so the evening went from bad to worse. Megan couldn't do anything right. Her elbows on the table raised eyebrows, as did her obvious ignorance when it came to which piece of cutlery to use. And there were some audible gasps when she asked for a top-up of beer. As she explained to Simon later, "I thought they'd be impressed, but instead I had to put up with their negativity as well as that crap your family passes off as beer. Although now I know why Thomas is such a drunk. It's the only way to get through dinner with your parents."

Penelope bored everyone senseless with updates on her various charities, and Charles could barely string a sentence together.

Or perhaps he simply didn't want to. Annabelle didn't shut up. She was as transparent as glass and Simon knew exactly what she was up to. She was like an archeologist and Megan was the dig. She kept chipping away for any little piece of history that could be put on show for all to see.

Thomas fell asleep in his soup, although everyone pretended not to notice. David kept leaving the table to make phone calls and returning with white powder around his nose. And Richard lived up to the shortened version of his name every time he opened his mouth.

"I see that artist friend of yours is in town, Simon."

"Taran? Yes, he's staying with me."

"You two were always rather cozy."

"I don't know why you let these people take advantage of you," Penelope snapped. "He's not really the type of person you should associate with."

Simon chewed his roast slowly, uncertain how he'd ever swallow it … or one more thing any member of his family said.

"All that occult hoo-ha." Penelope sniffed. "Witches and the dark arts. It chills me to the bone, Simon."

"I've known Taran for years and he's never discussed that part of his life with me. It's simply his faith. Unlike a lot of Christians, he doesn't push it on people … Mother."

"There are subtle ways to brainwash those around you."

Simon sighed and pushed his plate away. His mother should know. She'd been practicing her subtle brainwashing methods for years.

Penelope turned to Megan. "Do you go to church, Megan?"

"Oh yes." Megan nodded and smiled sweetly. "I went once." She squeezed Simon's hand under the table.

Penelope waited until dessert arrived to ask Megan what she did for work.

"I do stand-up."

"What's that dear?"

"I'm a comedian."

Penelope actually chuckled. "No, really, what do you do?"

"I really am a stand-up comedian ... and I also work part time at a pub. We have Apsley on tap." Blank stares all round. "But for some reason it doesn't sell well."

"You get paid to ... tell jokes?" Penelope looked as though she was asking if Megan got paid to strip for lepers.

"Paid? Hardly. I'm trying to crack it."

Simon knew if looks could kill, Megan would be dead. He jumped in. "That's how we met. I saw Meg do a routine at a club, and honestly thought I'd die laughing."

Penelope looked at Simon as though she wished he had.

"Tell us a joke then," said Richard.

"Oh no ... now's not the time ..."

"Oh, please do," Penelope insisted. "Especially if Simon thinks you're so funny. Tell us a joke."

Simon felt like a cricket ball gliding through the air toward Brian Lara's bat. He sighed, the calm before the storm ...

*

Megan glanced at the deer head mounted on the wall in front of her and felt nothing but sympathy. Probably an old girlfriend of Simon's. How he'd emerged from this family so unscathed was beyond her and made her admire him all the more. They were vile, every single one of them, but the vilest by far was GeeGee. All through dinner he raged on about the Jews and blacks and that fucker Mr Pataki from the Indian place up the road. He bitched about women, and children and everyone who supported homosexuality, especially Simon, who he obviously thought was gay. Megan quickly surmised that he'd always been a right bastard, and that no one had ever had the courage to stand up to him, even now when he was obviously quite feeble and in a wheelchair. While her initial reaction had been a sympathetic one, she now realized why the family had a tendency to push him into a far corner and leave him there. Over the entrée alone, she fantasized about pushing him down a long flight of stairs ... into a vat of acid.

"Come on, boy, tell us a joke," growled GeeGee.

Megan's eyes narrowed as she stared at the old man. She wasn't stupid. She knew it was a trap. She knew she had no choice, but that any joke she told would be the height of distaste. So she decided then and there to choose one that was.

"If you insist." A steely look settled in her eyes. It was the same determined stare that allowed her to cope with hecklers and drunks and appalling work conditions. "There's this man at a bar ..." She shifted in her seat, more confident than she'd been all night. "He's so drunk that he's sprawled out across the floor. Some of the other clientele, three guys, decide to be good Samaritans and get him home. They help him up, but he falls down again. They figure he must be really drunk, so pick him up off the floor again, and drag him out to the car. On the way he falls down again and again. They toss him into the car, slam the door shut and drive him home. They get to his house and help him out of the car but he falls into the gutter. They pick him up and carry him to the door and ring the bell. A woman answers and one of the guys says, 'Here's your husband!' Megan glanced at GeeGee, preparing for the kill. "The man's wife looks at her husband, looks at the guys and says, 'Where the fuck is his wheelchair?'"

Complete silence.

And then Simon doubled over with laughter. His family snapped their attention away from Megan and stared at him in total disbelief.

"Are you on drugs?" Charles had barely said a word to his son all night, but enough was enough.

Simon was still laughing. "No! But if you're offering."

"Why would you laugh at such a distasteful joke, when poor Grandpa George is in a wheelchair."

Simon laughed even more. "GeeGee doesn't know what day it is, so the joke means nothing to him."

"It's Thursday," said GeeGee.

It was Sunday.

"Nineteen Forty-three."

"And the joke was funny," Simon continued.

Megan squeezed his hand under the table.

Penelope looked apoplectic. "It was offensive."

"Most jokes are, Mother, and you insisted she give you one. If you weren't so bloody uptight, you would have enjoyed it too."

"You owe mother an apology," said Richard. "I think—"

Simon cut his brother off. "Save your breath, Dick. You'll need it to blow up your girlfriend later."

"I have no idea what's come over you." Penelope's icy tone sliced through everyone except Simon, who was immune now. "Although I have a fair idea."

"You know what's come over me, mother? Love! And it's wonderful. You should give it a go." Simon stood and looked down at Megan with love shining in his eyes. "Let's go home, Meg."

Megan stood. "Thank you for dinner. It was … enlightening."

Penelope rose before her. "You won't get a cent. We'll cut him off."

Megan shrugged. "If that means I don't have to suffer through dinner here again, then I'm all for it."

Charles turned to his son. "For God's sake, don't blow everything over the first piece of pussy you get."

Simon shook his head in amazement. "Blow everything? By loving Megan I gain everything."

And with that, they walked hand in hand from the house.

"He's obviously on drugs," said Penelope.

"I thought it was quite romantic," sighed Annabelle, but then quickly added, "And I agree, Penelope, definitely drugs."

"At least he's not gay," Charles said, then thought for a moment. "But I think she might be."

Chapter 28

Alcohol's medicinal properties are mentioned
191 times in the Old and New Testaments

Batty was dealing with the final few stragglers. It had been an easy night – not too busy, and much more enjoyable than she'd expected. As much as she'd wanted to run upstairs constantly and check on Alf, she didn't. He needed some space. He'd started fasting for his operation in the morning, so couldn't go near the pub. He was already climbing the walls, annoyed at both the hunger pangs and the confinement. So escaping that to work her bar had lifted Batty's spirits – slightly. Only Alf's full recovery would lift them back to normal.

The front door opened and she called out: "Sorry, we're closing up."

"Just me, Batty."

A teary Megan entered with a young man. Batty knew straight away that this was the boy Megan had fallen in love with – and that his family hadn't fallen for her.

"Oh dear, pull up a stool." Batty poured them both a beer. "They didn't warm to you, Meg?"

Megan looked completely mournful. "Colder than the farm house in *Dr Zhivago* by the time we left."

"I wouldn't take it personally, darling," Simon said. "My mother has been known to wake with icicles hanging from her face."

Megan blew her nose, but did manage to smile slightly.

"Don't take it to heart, love. It doesn't matter," Batty assured her. Although deep down she knew that it did, very much, to Megan. Batty wanted to march over to Simon's parents' house and beat them with a broom. A big one. Megan was family and it pained Batty to see her hurting.

"That's what I keep telling Meg. I'm Simon, by the way."

"It's a pleasure to finally meet you, Simon." Batty shook his outstretched hand. "So are they cutting you out of the will?"

Simon looked surprised.

Batty laughed. "I'm not reading that in your future. I lived it in my past. Eleanor did the same to Alf."

Megan's eyes widened. "But she still hates you."

"I know." Batty sighed. "Although hate is probably the wrong word. I'm different, which upsets her. But here's the thing: I don't care what she thinks. I only care what Alf thinks. I've had my moments over the years, but none of her negativity has ever come between us."

Simon turned to Megan. "That's exactly how I feel. I don't care what that family thinks. I want to build a new family with you."

Tears rolled down Megan's cheeks. "Family is important."

"True," Batty said. "But family is not always bound by blood. You should know that, Megan. What you mean to me – to all of us – that's family."

Megan nodded. "I know. I just feel so bad about tonight."

"They're the ones who should feel bad." A steely resolve settled in Simon's eyes.

"What about your job? They'll fire you, Simon."

"God, I hope so. I hate the job anyway." Simon grinned. "Now I can follow my dreams."

"And what are your dreams?" Batty asked.

"No idea ... I've never been allowed to have any. I'll find out now."

"But you've lost your—"

"I've lost nothing and gained everything!" Simon insisted, turning to Megan. "I don't give a toss about the money. I've invested. I own my home. I'm fine. I'm excited. I've always been aware that this day might come, but I never had the balls to break free myself. I should be thanking you, Meg. I'm glad to be rid of the bunch of them."

"Good for you," Batty said.

"All those years of tip-toeing around their psycho mood swings and manipulative behavior ... I feel rather daft really. But no more." Simon held his glass high. "Fudge me, I'm free! Here's to a new start. A new life – with you Meg."

Megan held her own glass out. "Okay, I'll drink to that. Even though you said 'fudge' which freaks me out a bit."

"I'm in the company of ladies."

Batty pretended to search the room. "Where are they? I've said the pub is closed."

They laughed, then Batty added, "Speaking of the pub, Simon, perhaps you can help Megan run it for the next couple of weeks. If you want a job."

Simon nodded. "I'd like that, Batty. We'll look after it."

Batty patted his arm affectionately. She already liked him immensely and wanted to get to know him better, but right now she needed to get back to Alf. She glanced toward the stairs that led up to their rooms.

"I'll finish locking up," Megan offered.

"Thanks, love." She stared at Simon and Megan for a moment. "You'll never regret this ... either of you. Make no mistake, you were born to be together, and nothing else matters. And that *is* me reading your future."

*

Two floors above the bar, Batty slid into bed beside Alf. He was awake, but sleepy as he rolled toward her and enveloped her in his huge arms. She breathed in his scent. Thirty years and still his smell made her dizzy. A wave of fear washed over her. She didn't see how she could continue breathing if Alf's scent wasn't a daily part of that.

He slipped her nightgown over her head and kissed her. His flesh was as familiar as her own, and three decades after she'd first touched it, she still couldn't get enough.

Alf was no psychic but he could read his wife. "It'll be alright, Red."

She smiled. "Yes, Alf, it has to be."

Chapter 29

Apply whiskey directly to varicose ulcers

The hospital waiting room had recently been renovated in soft blue and beige hues. The chairs and sofa were comfortable, there were piles of well-read magazines, and the painting that adorned the wall was of a sunny, foreign landscape.

Batty refused to look at the painting. It just reminded her of Spain.

Alf had been in surgery for three hours and counting. A nurse occasionally emerged from the operating theater to provide a vague update, but mostly the women paced, flicked restlessly through magazines, or stared at the wall. Batty felt physically ill. From the moment the anesthetic took hold of Alf she could sense each incision and stitch. She was going through the whole procedure herself, without the relief of drugs.

"Do you realize this will be the first night your father and I have spent apart in thirty-five years?"

The girls both nodded.

Batty continued. "We've never needed a break. Or space. We've never argued much. He still makes me laugh every day. After all these years, he still surprises me. Like yesterday, when I packed his yellow pajamas. He said, 'Love, not the yellow ones. I'm not fond of yellow and if I cark it in hospital I don't want to be dressed in it.' I never knew he didn't like yellow."

"He has lots of yellow clothes," Calypso said.

Batty nodded. "I like yellow and I buy them. He wears them because he loves me." Batty shook her head, as though shaking off a million memories. "I put them back in the drawer and asked which pajamas he wanted, and he said, 'The red ones – now that's a color I love.'"

A woman in a hospital gown walked into the waiting room and stared at the Shakespeares.

Batty wiped a stray tear from her cheek, and waved the woman away. "Not now, dear … This is family time." She wanted the hospital ghosts to leave them alone. This woman was the third today.

"You've passed over, sorry to say," Nell said.

"Why are you sorry? You didn't kill her." Calypso sighed.

"Callie!" Nell looked at her sister in frustration and turned back to the ghost. "Look for the light. You'll see people you know there."

The woman nodded and drifted out of the room. Her bare bottom could be seen through the gap in the gown.

Batty gave a stifled sob. "That's why I packed pajamas for your father."

*

It was another two hours before Alf was wheeled out of theatre. Alf's doctor assured them that the resection was a success and the liver was rejuvenating.

"Can we see him?" Nell asked.

"Yes, but he might take a while to respond. The anesthetist had some trouble putting him under." The doctor cleared his throat a little before continuing, almost apologetically. "Redheads always need more anesthetic."

"We're used to rolling with more punches, doctor, so it takes more to knock us out." Batty sniffed.

Finally, they crowded around Alf's bed. Seeing her larger-than-life father hooked up to a drip and oxygen mask was almost more than Calypso could bear, but she held it together, just, for her mother's sake.

"I've read that people in comas can hear the conversations around them," Nell said.

"He's not in a coma," Calypso said.

"We should talk to him."

"Fine." Calypso perched herself on the edge of a chair. "Then this would be the perfect time to tell you, Dad – I did put that dent in the car. I was perving on one of the builders when we were doing renovations. I started the car, and accidentally put it in reverse. Ran into an empty keg."

Batty put her hands on her hips. "Your father almost fired that young apprentice over that. Swore it was him."

Calypso gave her an innocent smile. "Any guilt I felt over that dissolved when I caught him with his hand in the till."

"True," Batty said. "Well, I should 'fess up too then. Alf, darling … your cat didn't run off – I gave him away."

Calypso and Nell looked at their mother in horror.

"He loved that cat," Calypso said.

Batty shrugged. "The cat didn't like me. I tried to get your father to see it but he'd just say, 'Rubbish, Red, all witches need a cat.' Well, I didn't need one who ate everything in sight and liked peeing on my shoes. So I gave him to Saffron Didding."

"The Highgate cat lady?"

"Don't look at me like that, Callie. Admittedly she's a little odd, but you can't deny her love of cats." Batty turned to Nell. "Your turn. What have you been hiding from your father?"

Nell blushed. "There is one thing ..." She shuffled closer to her father.

Batty leant in slightly, while Calypso braced herself for whatever Nell thought was a worthy confession. Knowing Nell, she was about to confess to breaking a glass in the kitchen, or failing to order some supplies.

"Remember that teenage boy you caught robbing the pub?"

"The one who swore he hadn't taken anything so Dad agreed to not call the police?" Calypso asked.

"He wasn't a burglar," Nell admitted. "He was my boyfriend."

Batty and Calypso stared at Nell, dumbfounded.

She gave them a naughty wink. "Wouldn't life be dull if you knew everything about me?"

*

During her father's time in hospital, Calypso watched her mother carefully: her original hysteria had been replaced by an unsettling listlessness. When Alf opened his eyes, Batty would smile and whisper loving words, but the minute his eyes closed, the black cloak would descend. And there wasn't anything Calypso could do about it. Not when she felt the same way.

Calypso hated herself for being so weak, but knew she was teetering on the edge of a very large precipice. She spent all day, every day at the hospital. Then at night, when insomnia took hold, she'd lock herself away in her Cauldron and make infusions and decoctions and tinctures for everyone around her. But no matter how hard she worked at it, nothing brought her powers back.

Still, she refused to lose faith. Herbs and plants hold their own powers, so she placed her fragile trust in that and continued to mix. There was nothing to be gained from any of them getting run down when Alf so obviously needed their support. She tried to not dwell on her father. There was no point worrying until his test results came back. And she did her best to block out all thoughts of Taran. He'd tried to contact her a couple of times, but she didn't respond. She couldn't. She simply focused on supporting her family in the best way she knew how.

Calypso prescribed a tonic of bitter herbs for her mother. Depression often originates in the liver, so it was no coincidence that Batty was depressed. She was so connected to her husband that everything he was going through was manifesting in her as well. The tonic set about healing the organ where the condition was based. For extra support, she also mixed her a tincture of oat straw and vervain. She wished she could reach out and truly help her mother by talking to her, or making her laugh, but she couldn't.

Her family was famous for its unwavering and occasionally suffocating support. They were well known for their laughter and ability to bounce back from anything. So Calypso was just as surprised as everyone else that when it came to the crunch it was each redheaded woman for herself. Perhaps they'd never truly been tested as a unit before. Scott's death had torn away *her* foundations, but while her family certainly grieved, they had been removed enough to offer support and stop her from completely falling. But this time they were all equally vested in the grief.

Nell's levelheaded calm surprised Calypso, although she knew it shouldn't. Nell wasn't displaying any new traits. It was just – for once – her more forceful family members weren't overshadowing her. While her mother and sister crumbled, Nell coped by keeping busy and organizing everyone else. She had, in her own gentle way, taken charge. Calypso made Nell a tincture of astragulus to boost her immune system and advised her to also drop some in her bath water each night to help clear her energy.

For Eleanor, who was suffering regular migraines and quite often passing them on to everyone else, Calypso made a marjoram compress and feverfew tincture. She also sent her grandmother a small bottle of brandy, infused with the healing powers of quartz and the color blue. A nip of that at bedtime would help her sleep and alleviate her worries. But Eleanor, being Eleanor, refused to take it and continued to suffer migraines, insomnia and worries, which therefore meant everyone else continued to suffer them as well.

The one person Calypso wished she could heal, needed to heal, was her father, but that was impossible. Even if her gift were working she would be unable to change the course he was on. While her gift helped remove blockages, or guide someone onto the right path, it never cured a disease or mended a situation that was fated. It could help a person cope and alleviate stress and symptoms, but it could not alter destiny. Calypso had learned that the hard way. She had called upon the forces of the universe to save Scott as he lay dying in her arms, but the line had been heartbreakingly busy.

Calypso knew she couldn't change the path her father was on. Or that any of them were on. And that frightened her. She was scared of living, of losing people, and of loving people. There were moments when she despised her weakness. It was now obvious to her that despite her often bold approach to life, she wasn't actually brave at all.

And at night, locked in her Cauldron, that was the thing that bothered her most.

Not the thought of her father dying, or the fact that Scott had. Not that she had sent Taran packing. The thing that troubled her most was her weakness. She was terrified of everything – and only just realizing it.

*

The whole family was together when the doctor gave Alf his test results. Batty and Nell sat either side of Alf, while Calypso stood near the door, wishing she could exit it and never come back.

"It was melanoma, but it was confined to one small area."

"That's good, isn't it?" Batty needed some reassurance.

"Very good."

"Will I need chemo, doc?"

"There are a number of new treatments we can discuss if it returns, but at this stage it's not necessary."

"What about alternative therapies?" Calypso asked.

The doctor turned to Calypso. "Meaning?"

"I'm a healer and would like to work on my father." Calypso braced herself for the ridicule that usually followed when she admitted this.

It didn't come.

"What type of healing?"

"Herbs ... medicinal drinks."

"I don't see a problem with that." The doctor looked down at his notes. "All I ask is that you consult me on what medication your father is on, as we don't want any adverse reactions."

"Of course."

Alf asked the big question that had been haunting everyone. "Can I still drink?"

The doctor chuckled. "Once your liver has regenerated, then absolutely. As long as you take it easy, there's nothing like a medicinal wine or beer."

Alf's face lit up. "Ya hear that Callie?"

Calypso winked at her father. She was liking his doctor more and more.

Batty gave Alf's hand a squeeze. "What now?"

"His prognosis looks good, Mrs Shakespeare. I'm extremely optimistic and I think you should be too.

"I googled and—"

The doctor cut Batty of with a kind smile. "Google can be the most frightening place on earth. The fact is, surgical resection can and does achieve long-term survival in many patients. If he reaches the five-year mark without a reoccurrence, then his chances are excellent."

"Five years?" It sounded like a thousand to Calypso. "What do we do until then?"

"My advice would be to enjoy life."

"Sounds good to me," Alf said.

The Shakespeare women nodded. The doctor turned to leave, but Batty stopped him. "One more question. When can I take my husband home?"

"He'll need another week to recover."

"Very good, thank you."

The doctor disappeared out the door and the family looked at each other.

Alf was the first to speak. "It's a good outcome."

Calypso plonked herself into the chair. She had no intention of entering into this.

"Five years, Alf!"

"Listen, misery guts, I could be hit by a bus before this bloody cancer gets me, right? I say we just get on with it."

Nell gave her father a hug. "I agree, Dad." She grabbed her phone from her bag and headed for the door. "I'll call Gran and let her know."

"You do that, Nell," Alf called after her. "At least someone will be happy for me."

Chapter 30

Horse chestnut alleviates arthritic pain

"Man, she's got big balls," Taran said as he watched Megan confront a drunken heckler.

"Only a very brave, or incredibly stupid, man would take her on." Simon was obviously proud of his girlfriend.

The C Spot was a small, shabby club that still smelt of cigarette smoke, despite a ban. Megan wore black jeans, a vintage Sex Pistols T-shirt and a black flat cap. She owned the stage, legs slightly apart, hands on her hips, and a scowl on her pretty face. Simon knew she'd cut back on her performance schedule while she was running the pub, and was in no mood to have her precious stand-up time interrupted by a sexist drunk.

"Are you gonna strip for us or what?" yelled the drunk.

Simon wanted to crack a stool over the guy's head, but knew the knight in shining armor routine wouldn't go down well with Megan.

"Listen Richard-face," Megan snapped back, "have some respect. This is my job. I don't go into KFC and yell at you while you're working."

"Tell us a frigging joke."

"Oh great! An alcoholic who won't remain anonymous."

A number of people in the audience laughed uncomfortably, unsure how the slip of a girl onstage would handle the large drunk.

"You've got no tits and look like a boy," the drunk slurred.

Megan just nodded sympathetically and in a voice dripping with disdain said, "You've got no manners and look like a cockhead. Difference between us is that I can buy boobs and put on a dress. What the fuck can you do?"

She was rewarded with a huge cheer from the audience and continued her set uninterrupted.

Simon gave Taran a wink. The woman was a complete pocket rocket and he adored her. She was the smartest, sweetest, funniest creature ever born. Her short hair, piercings and tattoos only emphasized her femininity and beauty as far as he was concerned. There had not been one single moment where he'd regretted choosing Megan over his family, despite the furor it had caused.

His father's lawyers had contacted him immediately and informed him of his new status. Basically, he no longer existed. He'd been removed from the will, fired from the job and uninvited from his brother's upcoming fortieth birthday. None of it fazed Simon. If anything, he finally felt free. He took stock of his own financial situation and knew that his cautious nature had in many ways prepared him for this. He was fine, certainly better than most. And he had Megan.

To her credit, his mother had called and wished him luck. She acknowledged that insanity ran through both family lines and that perhaps he was displaying similar symptoms to her own Great Uncle Earnest, who had turned his back on his family and married a Greek olive farmer's daughter. Family legend had it that Great Uncle Earnest eventually went insane and ended his days in an asylum, thinking he was a goat, but Simon had once intercepted a Christmas card from Ernie who was, at the time, still living very happily on a farm outside Athens.

The last act of the night wound up and the lights came on. Simon and Taran finished their beers while they waited for Megan.

"Have you decided what you're going to do for work?"

Simon shook his head. "I'm too busy helping run the King and Mistress at the moment. One thing I know for sure, I have no intention of going back into the corporate world."

"Are you sure? Perhaps with a different company—"

"Never. I never liked it."

"Really? I never knew that."

"Nor did I." Simon looked intently around the C Spot. It had once been the hottest comedy venue in London, but bad management had run it into the ground. He took in the character of the small club, the craftsmanship of the ceiling, the dull brass and wood details, the quirky tables and bar. "I like this place."

Taran nodded. "I saw Eddie Izzard perform here, years ago."

"They used to have all the big names play. I wonder what happened?"

Megan bounded over to them and threw her arms around Simon. "I missed you."

"Next time aim better." Simon grinned. He no longer felt like a bumbling fool. Meeting Megan and stepping back from his family had done wonders for his confidence.

She gave Taran a peck on the cheek. "How are you?"

"Good … really … you know."

"Yeah, that's believable."

"Any chance someone misses me?"

"Oh, someone misses you alright, but that doesn't mean the stubborn cow is going to give in."

Taran stood and jammed his hands into his jeans pockets. "How's Alf?"

"He's recovering well. It's just they're all so gloomy."

"They've been through a lot."

"True, but no more than many people," Megan pointed out. "And they have each other. They should grab hold of that, and really appreciate it." Her eyes glazed slightly. "I'd give anything to have my mother back for one day. They've been given another chance and they're wasting it."

"Is there anything I can do?" Taran asked.

Megan slipped her hand into Simon's and they all made their way toward the exit. "I'm on it. I have a plan." The two men waited for more information, but she simply grinned and led them outside. "Not one I'm sharing yet."

"You'll keep me updated, won't you?" Taran knew he was bordering on pathetic now, but couldn't help himself.

Megan gave him a friendly hug. "Of course I will."

Simon watched as Megan comforted Taran. It meant everything to him that his best friend and the woman he loved got on so well. He turned his head away from them, slightly emotional – God, he was a sop lately – and noticed a "For Sale" sign attached to the front of the club.

"Is the C Spot for sale?"

Megan shrugged. "There was some talk backstage tonight that they've declared bankruptcy. Can't work out why – not like they pay any of their acts, and they have enough drunks buying booze in the audience." Megan stalked over to the curb and flagged a cab. "What I'd give to find a club in London that pays well and isn't the last stop of the night for London's obnoxious." She shook her head. "Come on, you two. Let's go home."

Later, as he lay awake, safe in the arms of the best woman in the world, Simon devised a plan of his own.

Chapter 31

Oregano oil can be used as a cough remedy

Nell stared at the porcelain brooch in front of her and tried to muster up some enthusiasm. Normally such an exquisite piece would have her in raptures, but today she really didn't give two hoots that Mary Sidney Herbert had worn it.

"Eighteenth-century penny for your thoughts," said Julian, placing a copper cartwheel on the desk beside her.

Nell smiled. "I thought you'd left for the day."

"Just going." He ran his long fingers through his floppy hair "Hungry?"

"Not really."

"Pity, I was going to take you out." A broad grin spread across his face. "In fact, I think I'll take you out anyway."

Nell began to argue that she didn't have time, but Julian cut her off.

"I'm your boss, so you've got no choice. Get your coat, or bag, or whatever you women lug around."

"As you said, Julian, you're my boss. An excellent reason why I can't go out with you."

Julian laughed. Nothing ever fazed him. "I'm not asking you to sleep with me, Nell. If I were, I certainly wouldn't try it on straight after work. That's more of a … morning tea thing, don't you agree? Coffee, scone and a quickie in the mop closet?" He grabbed her bag for her. "Come on. A quick bite and perhaps one beer."

"I don't drink."

"You're about to start."

He took her to a Japanese restaurant nearby. It was empty, still too early for most people to be out. They were seated in a corner table and Julian immediately grabbed the menu.

"I come here all the time, so I'll order for both of us. If you don't mind?"

Normally, Nell would've. But today she was simply grateful that it was one less decision she had to make. And she had a feeling that's exactly why Julian did it.

He ordered sushi, sashimi, agedashi tofu, tempura, wakame salad and a beer each. Nell was too exhausted to argue, and when the Asahi arrived, she had a sip and was surprised to find she liked it. It was the perfect drink for such a warm evening.

Julian watched her carefully. "Enjoying work?"

"Very much," Nell lied. She desperately missed Percy and the British Museum of Romance, although she liked working with Julian.

"How's your father?"

Julian knew all about her father, mainly because their grandmothers were close. He'd even postponed Nell's starting date at National Museum until after her father's operation.

"He's doing well." She stared up at his big brown eyes. They were so kind and genuinely concerned. She felt like she knew him well, even though she didn't. Most of all, she trusted him. She had no idea why, but she did, and he sensed this. "It has been a dreadful few weeks," she admitted. "Dad's not entirely out of the woods. It might come back. But I don't think so."

"It's important to believe that."

"I never once thought we would lose Dad. I'm not sure if that was my intuition, or because I'm pathetically Panglossian." Nell sipped her beer and considered this for a moment. "Probably the latter."

"I think it's the best way to be, Nell. I'm an optimist. The other option isn't that appealing to me at all."

"What has been really upsetting is the way everyone else handled it."

"Apparently Eleanor is a basket case."

Nell couldn't help but roll her eyes. "Eleanor is always a basket case."

Eleanor had been reduced to a blubbering mess at the sight of her only child after surgery. She hyperventilated so badly that the nurse had to grab the oxygen mask from Alf to help Eleanor breathe. Batty had used the opportunity to her advantage. While Eleanor was muzzled with the oxygen mask, Batty showed her Alf's surgery wounds, mentioned the pictures of livers she'd seen on the internet, and finally checked his catheter. Once the mask was removed, Eleanor bolted and had refused to set foot back inside the hospital since – much to everyone's relief. Nell visited her as often as she could and put a positive spin on all the doctor's updates, which helped ease Eleanor's stress, but only added to Nell's. She was already juggling hospital visits, meetings with Megan and Simon and finalizing things with Percy, while starting full time at the museum.

She took another large swig of her beer. "I've always been surrounded by these tough women. Eleanor can reduce a grown man to pulp with one withering look. My mother is the backbone of the family and the business. And my sister ... she spends most of her life traipsing around the world, going through boyfriends like I go through Kleenex during allergy season. I've always been different. Nell the quiet one. Nell the shy one. Never Nell the strong one."

"It's funny how a reserved nature can be perceived as a weakness, when in my experience, the opposite is true."

"I've even been guilty of seeing myself that way, Julian. They're all loud and colorful and therefore stronger than me, right? And yet, when I really expected them all to pull together for my father, they fell apart." Nell finished her beer. "I'd like another one, please."

Julian motioned for more drinks. "Perhaps they're not as tough as you think."

"They're tough. Calypso's boyfriend was killed a few years ago." Nell paused for a moment. "Obviously she was devastated, but she bounced back ... quite quickly in my opinion."

"Anyone serious?"

"What do you mean?"

"Any serious relationships since her boyfriend was killed?"

"No." Nell thought for a moment. "There was someone recently but she ended that."

"She's not over her boyfriend's death. She's running around using brief relationships as a band-aid over a very large wound."

"I suppose you're right. I love Callie, but I've always been a little uncomfortable with how she grieved for a few months and then started dating again."

"Were you close to her boyfriend?"

Tears stung Nell's eyes. "Yes, I was. Very. It made me angry that she moved on while I continued to grieve. I guess everyone grieves differently. I just thought I wasn't as strong as her."

Julian watched Nell toss back another beer. "Have you ever considered that the lesson in all of this is that you're just as tough as these women? Tougher? It sounds like you've been living in their shadows, and never realized you are just as impressive."

Nell thought about this for a moment. "You could be right, Julian. The quiet one could be stronger than expected. The tough women might need some extra support." She finished her second beer. "And perhaps the conservative one who never drinks actually doesn't mind a few beers."

Julian laughed. "People change."

"What if I'm only getting drunk now because I'm bloody petrified of everything?"

"That's fine too, Nell. You have every right to feel overwhelmed at the moment. You've been a tower of support for those around you – but received no support yourself."

Nell leaned toward him, amazed. "How on earth can you know me so well, Julian?"

"Honestly, Nell – I have no idea. Usually I'm quite oblivious to people. I'm more caught up in things and events. People baffle me. But you … I see you so clearly."

Nell sat back in her chair, more relaxed than she could ever remember being. "I wish I could say I see you clearly, but I do think those two beers have made me quite tipsy."

"Good. You need it. Shall we have a third and then go dancing?"

"I don't dance."

"You didn't drink until two hours ago, but already you've got the hang of that."

Nell watched as he ordered another round of beer and smiled. Julian DeHart might not be Brad Pitt, but he was a truly lovely man.

Chapter 32

Red Clover helps reduce the symptoms of
menopause

Batty flicked through the channels on the small hospital television. "Want to watch *The Bill*, Alf?"

Alf closed his eyes. "I don't want to watch anything, Batty."

"How about a magazine, Dad," Calypso said, offering him a choice between *Natural Health Weekly* and *Publican's Monthly.*

"No thanks, Callie."

"I have some more cards here to read, Dad." Nell waved a pile in front of him. "This one's from the Sweeney family. 'Sorry to hear about the accident'." Nell quickly grabbed the next card. "Okay, that was weird ... here's one from Harry. 'Miss you carrying me out to a cab when I've had one too many'."

"That's kind of him," Batty said.

Alf gave her a half-smile, but secretly wished all three of them would bugger off and leave him to heal in peace. He didn't want to be fussed over. And the tension! What he'd give for something, anything, to not only break the tension in the room, but to smash it to pieces.

The door swung open and in marched Megan. She stalled for a moment – Alf could tell it threw her to see him outside his normal terrain. He belonged behind a bar or in his kitchen, not attached to a drip. Then Megan placed her hands on her hips and opened her mouth.

"Bloody hell, Alf. If you wanted time off you could've just asked. This is a bit extreme, just so you can lie around in bed all day, don't you think?"

Calypso and Batty stared at her with open-mouthed horror while Nell and Alf simply looked confused.

"When I first heard you were sick, I thought, oh no, his hypochondria is playing up again. And then Calypso told me you had cancer and I thought ... that's not right. Alf's Taurean."

"That's enough, Megan—"

A slight glimmer of amusement lit Alf's eyes as he cut his wife off. "Let Little Miss Big Mouth continue, Batty."

Megan took a deep breath. "Melanoma! I had no idea what it was ... sounds like a new dessert for the restaurant. 'Ah yes, I'll have the pumpkin soup ... the lamb ... and for dessert I'll have ... oh yum, the melanoma please ... with cream.' I googled melanoma, did a bit of research. Apparently redheads have the highest risk of getting it, and I thought, 'Fuck, Alf must feel ripped off, being bald.'"

Alf snorted – a slight laugh, but noticeable. Calypso, Batty and Nell all turned to him in surprise.

Megan noticed his untouched meal tray and lifted some of the stainless steel lids. "Oh wow, hospital food. Custard ... nice, especially if they removed your teeth with your liver ... Oh and speaking of liver ..." Megan stared warily at the main course. "There it is! I didn't realize hospitals were into recycling. They go through it all in the new nurse training sessions. 'The empty bottles, old bedpans, and any plastics go here ... The old magazines and newspapers are put into this box ... And all the organs and tumors are sent to the hospital chef.'"

Alf let out a gruff chuckle. Batty grabbed his hand and turned her attention back to Megan.

Megan shoved her hands deep into the pockets of her ratty denim shorts. "Did you hear about the bee and the ant who had moles removed? The bee's was *bee*nign. The ant wasn't so lucky. His tests came back and his mole was malign*ant*."

With that, Calypso caved. She groaned and rated the joke. It was something she'd done since they were ten years old. "Oh gawd, Meg, that's a four."

"What about the beaver and the mole who got married? Soon after, the beaver walked into the skin clinic and said to the doctor, "I'm a bit concerned … I've got this rather strange mole.""

Alf and his girls all burst out laughing.

"I like that one. Excellent," he roared.

"Very funny," Batty agreed.

Nell perched herself on the other side of her father's bed and giggled. Calypso sank back into her chair and took a deep breath.

Alf could feel the bars of the cage crumbling, the oppressive energy of the past three weeks already lifting. All it took were a few jokes and shared laughter, yet they'd been unable to manage it until now. He understood that his girls were focusing on the fear, and ignoring the hope and humor of the situation. Not for the first time, Alf admired the feisty little moppet now in front of him. She'd known some tough times yet had always been able to make the people around her laugh. It was vital to laugh in the face of adversity. It was the only way adversity would eventually back off.

Megan was on a roll now, enjoying every second of the routine. "My advice, Alf, is always get the news from the doctor yourself. Don't trust Batty to do it. I know a couple – the husband had been admitted to hospital and after a series of tests, the doctor went to speak to the wife who was in the waiting room. The doctor told the wife that her husband had cancer. 'Can he be cured?' she asked. The doctor said, 'There's a chance we can cure him with chemotherapy, but you will need to take care of him every day for the next year. You'll need to cook all the meals, clean up the vomit, change the bed pan, drive him to the hospital for daily treatments, and so on.' The wife thanked the doctor and went to her husband's bedside. He looked at her and weakly asked, 'What did the doctor say?' The wife sighed sadly and answered, 'He said you're going to die.'"

The room filled with howling laughter. It was slightly rusty, but genuine and welcome.

"Look, Alf, I know cancer is no laughing matter. Just ask anyone who died from it."

More laughter.

"And I know it's been tough on the girls. Nell has been upset because you're the nicest medieval artifact she knows. Calypso hasn't coped well. Being vegetarian, she'd prefer your liver was kept in your body, not in a jar. And Batty is obviously devastated ... probably because she knows that if you die she'll have to learn to cook. On the bright side, all the regulars at the pub have been so depressed about you that they've been drinking like fish. Profits are soaring." Megan grinned. "I'll just wait for the laughter to *die* down. It's the only thing in this room that will *die*! You're going to *liver*!"

"I'll drink to that!" Alf's voice was still weak but his spirit had just gained strength.

"Of course you will. You'll drink to anything." Megan pulled two bottles of Alf's favorite beer out of her bag and passed him one. Then she held hers high in the air. "To Alf, who will die like my grandfather did: peacefully, in his sleep, a very old man." And then with a cheeky wink: "Not screaming in fear like the passengers in his car." She gave Alf a gentle kiss.

"Now get off your big, beer-loving arse and get back to work. I'm getting married and need a week off."

And then, before they could stop her, Megan grabbed her bag and bolted from the room.

*

A few minutes later she slid into the passenger seat of Simon's car.

"How did it go?"

Her heart still hammered against her chest, but she was elated. "It worked. They laughed and laughed. It really worked."

Simon kissed her. "I love you, Megan."

Megan turned a bright shade of red and smiled. "I love you too, Simon. So much so that I was wondering … will you marry me?"

*

Back in room 124, Alf and his three redheads were still in shock. Finally Alf spoke.

"Married?"

"Good for her." Batty chuckled. "Lovely boy."

Alf glared at Calypso. "Why didn't you tell me?"

"That's the first I've heard of it." Although she wasn't at all surprised.

"Have I met him?"

"Simon Apsley," Batty explained.

"Of Apsley Beer? But they're a bunch of nutters. And the beer is shit!"

"He's been disowned by them." Calypso filled in the gaps. "Plus, he's Taran's best friend."

Alf's face lit up. "Then I like him already." Alf stared at his daughter. "How is Taran?"

"No idea." Calypso casually flicked her hair. "But perhaps I should find out – one of these days."

Batty and Alf glanced at each other. Alf linked his fingers through Batty's. "We should throw her a wedding party."

"Absolutely." Batty removed the beer from Alf's free hand. "You don't need that." She handed it to Nell. "And you do."

Nell looked surprised. "What's that for?"

Batty gave her daughter a wicked grin. "Hair of the dog, my little teetotaller."

Nell gave her mother a wink and took a sip.

Calypso stood and yanked the curtains back, and the afternoon sun poured in. "Beautiful day," she whispered, and for the first time in weeks, they all agreed.

Chapter 33

Mix brandy, milk and sugar to fix a fever

"Gisella is what?" Calypso pushed her way through the crowd of shoppers at Topshop as she yelled into the phone. "Franz, I can barely hear you. The music is too loud. Hold on a second." She made her way out of the store and onto Oxford Street. "Did you say what I think you said?"

"Yes, Callie, she's pregnant. We found out a couple of weeks ago."

"A couple of weeks ago and you've only just called?"

There was a long, uncomfortable pause. "You've had enough going on, with your father's operation. I figured our news could wait."

Calypso was unconvinced. "Your news would have been a bright spot in a really crappy few weeks and you know it. What's up?"

"Gisella has been inconsolable ever since we found out. She spends all day everyday in bed, crying."

Calypso felt uneasy. "With ... joy?"

A slight pause. "Ah ... nein."

"Has she seen a doctor?"

"Of course. He said the baby is fine, but that Gisella is depressed." Franz took a deep breath. "She believes this child was created because of your magic, and therefore it can't really be hers. I've tried to get her to see reason, but she feels it's ... unnatural."

Calypso stepped over to the curb and flagged a cab. "I'll be there as soon as I can."

"No, Callie, don't come over. Just talk to her."

"I will, face to face. I'll let you know what flight I'm on."

She slid into the taxi and turned her attention to the driver. "Highgate please ... and then if you could wait ten minutes, I'll need a lift to the airport."

The next call she made was to the airline.

*

"You're a very naughty boy. In London, but you haven't called me!"

Taran paused just long enough for the owner of the sexy voice to realize he had no idea who she was.

"It's Laura, you utter bastard." The voice wasn't so sexy any more.

"Laura! Of course I recognized your voice." And the unnerving bipolar mood swing, he thought.

"Did not," she sulked. "I only left New York two months ago and you've already forgotten me."

"How could I forget you? Laura ... Laura ..." *Dance at your grandfather's graveside Laura.* "How did you know I was in town?"

"Everyone knows you're here, Taran. You can't have a show opening at the Gate and go by unnoticed. Congratulations by the way."

"Thanks. And I was going to call," he lied. "I've been busy getting everything ready."

"I forgive you."

"Sorry to hear about your grandfather."

"Who? Oh, Grandpapa." She didn't sound particularly upset, but then sighed in faux grief. "He'll be missed."

They chatted about some mutual friends, followed by an embarrassing lull in conversation, a riveting discussion about English weather, and an enlightening chat about why Laura never gave money to homeless people. Apparently it encourages them to remain unemployed and on the streets. And then finally …

"The reason I called, Taran, was to see if you're free tonight."

"Tonight?" Taran tried to think of a good excuse to get out of meeting her. He stalled and stuttered slightly … but was stumped. "I'm not sure."

"You have plans?"

"I'm painting. It's impossible to commit to anything at the moment." Now he sounded like Calypso.

"I'm going to the Crow Bar with some friends. Come down if you need a break."

"Thanks, Laura. I'll see how I go."

Laura donned her sexy voice again. "I look forward to catching up again, Taran. If not tonight, then soon."

"So do I." *Right up there with my next prostate examination.*

Taran switched off his phone and poured himself a large scotch. "Shit … shit, shittedy, shit!"

"Hey mate, are you going to be here later today?" Simon stuck his head in the room and saw the glass in Taran's hand. "What the hell are you doing? It's not even lunch."

Taran glanced at his watch. "It's eleven o'clock. Early lunch."

"Oh, well that's fine then. Drink yourself into oblivion."

"I will." Taran placed the empty glass on the table. "Laura just called and asked me out."

"*Laura*, Laura? Dance at My Grandfather's Graveside Laura?"

"That's the one."

"If I were you I'd change my number."

"I can't really think of a good reason not to go," Taran admitted.

"I can give you twenty."

"One would do."

"You're in love," Simon said.

"Am I?"

"Oh come on, Taran, why else would you even consider a date with Laura when there are so many other women out there?"

Taran folded his arms across his chest. "I don't freaking know, but you obviously do."

"Because you don't want to move on. You can't forget Calypso, so you've decided to choose a woman who will definitely magnify that fact and feed your misery. Go out, get laid by all means, but don't punish yourself."

"Excellent, you finally get a bit and now you're Dr Phil?"

"I do feel like I have smug-man syndrome."

"I'm happy for you. You deserve it. Sounds like Megan could be the one for you."

Simon chuckled. "She'd better be because we're getting married and I've bought her the C Spot as a wedding gift."

The room crackled with shock, which made Simon laugh more.

"Close your mouth, Taran. You'll catch flies."

Taran snapped back to life. "Wow, Sime, sorry ... congratulations ... that's just a helluva lot to absorb in one hit." He stared at his friend for a moment. "This is good. Real good."

Simon nodded. "It is, isn't it? Feels right. No point mucking around. We want a life together, so why not start it now? There's nothing I'd rather do than marry Megan. And I really like the idea of turning that club into a profitable venture. It excites me. Way more than pushing crap beer at people."

"I take it you won't serve Apsley on tap."

"Only when hell freezes over."

"Who'll run it? You'll run it? What about Megan?"

"I'll run it. Megan will be the MC and entertainment booker." Simon was actually jiggling up and down on the spot. "I'm bloody inspired, Taran. Beats the hell out of pushing papers at Apsley." He glanced at his watch. "I've got to dash. Megan expects me at the pub. You sure you're okay?"

"I will be once tonight's done and dusted."

Simon looked embarrassed for a moment. "You will be my best man, won't you?"

"Of course, buddy. I'd be honored."

"Thank Christ for that. I don't have any other family to ask." Simon gave Taran a rough slap on the back and headed for the door.

Chapter 34

A shot of Jagermeister will soothe a cough and sore throat.

Gisella was furious with Franz for calling Calypso and even more upset that her friend had flown to Vienna.

"You are completely insane, Calypso."

"Rubbish, it's what friends do."

"Friends email, they call. They don't *fly over*."

"Don't be ridiculous. It's a couple of hours on a plane. You live in Vienna, not Vanuatu."

"I might move to Vanuatu if you two don't leave me alone!" Gisella shouted.

Calypso placed her hands on her hips and looked down at Gisela, sprawled out in bed. She was pale, her hair hadn't been washed in days, and her eyes were red from crying. Calypso needed to be careful. She could sense that Gisella was close to completely cracking.

"I hear congratulations are in order."

"You should know," Gisella snapped.

"I didn't know, because you didn't tell me." Calypso sat on the edge of the bed. "But that's okay, because you've been busy ... getting yourself all worked up over nothing."

"Nothing? Nothing? I'm pregnant because of one of your spells. Witchcraft! God knows what's growing inside me."

Franz saw the look of distress on Calypso's face and jumped to her defense. "We asked Callie to help, Gisella."

"I would never have asked for her help if I knew I'd feel like this." Gisella turned to Calypso. "I'm sorry, Callie, I am, I'm sorry. I love you, but I can't help how I feel. I wish you'd never done it."

"I didn't," Calypso said quietly.

A deathly hush fell over the room for a moment and then Gisella sat up. "You didn't? What does that mean?"

"I didn't cast a spell. You fell pregnant naturally."

"You're lying, to make me feel better."

"I wish I was." Calypso stood. "Get up, have a shower and clean your bloody teeth. You stink. Then we'll talk about it over dinner. I owe you an explanation."

*

Calypso sat opposite her friends and poured her heart out. She explained that she'd lost her ability to read people and mix cocktails to cure.

She picked at the varnish on the table. "I was hoping my powers would work when I made that dinner for you, but they didn't."

"Not at all?" Gisella asked.

"Not at all. Every ingredient I used has power. We shouldn't underestimate the energies in those foods. They were strong fertility foods, but there was no spell. I wanted to tell you that night, but you were so happy and relaxed ... I was hoping that alone would be enough."

"Obviously it was," said Franz, staring at Gisella.

She nodded. She looked tired, but like a weight had been lifted from her shoulders.

Calypso reached out to her. She needed to make something very clear. "I apologize for not telling you, Gisella, but I'll never apologize for my gift. The spells and potions do nothing but good. They help people. It's not dark, or manipulative, or anything you should be scared of."

"But if I'd fallen pregnant because of that—"

"It would have been the same as if you'd fallen pregnant after a course of IVF. Women use whatever they can to conceive."

"That's science," Gisella snapped. "It's nothing like what you did – what I *thought* you did. It's cloaked in mystery. The unknown aspect of it is frightening."

"No more so than lighting a candle at Stephansplatz and praying to God. It's simply putting it out there and asking for help from a higher power." Calypso looked her friend deep in the eye. "My faith is filled with as much light as yours."

Gisella nodded. "I'm sorry, Calypso. My reaction must seem so disrespectful to you. And I know you do help. I see our customers returning time and time again."

"But you realized that it's not for you," Calypso said gently. "And that's fine."

"And irrelevant," Franz added. "Seeing as no magic was used."

"No magic," said Gisella. "Fancy that."

Franz and Gisella nodded slowly for a moment but then couldn't contain it a moment longer and their display of concern turned to chuckles.

Calypso rolled her eyes. "I'm glad you're happy, but I happen to be quite upset that I've lost my magic."

"I know … It's not that, Callie—" Gisella could no longer hide her laughter.

"It's just we're so happy for you." Franz was now grinning from ear to ear.

"I thought you would be."

"You get another chance," Gisella said.

"I'm not sure I want one," Calypso said.

"Whether you want one or not, it's here," Franz pointed out.

Calypso felt like she was tied to a roulette wheel. The whole room began to spin. She'd spent the past couple of months barely admitting to herself what the loss of her magic meant. But now, with her friends, there was no escape. They knew exactly what it meant.

Franz prodded. "Aren't you happy?"

Calypso blinked a few times. Everything was blurry. Oh hell, she felt quite faint.

Gisella reached out and took her friend's hand. "It's okay, Calypso."

"It's not okay. Sixteen generations of Shakespeare women have had one … one true love …"

Franz shrugged. "Looks like you have two."

*

Calypso had never been so happy. Each day, each minute with Scott was an incredible adventure. They were roaring through life as only the young can.

They were in Rome with Franz and Gisella. It had only been three weeks since Scott had joined the group, yet they all felt like they'd known each other for much longer. Perhaps forever.

Calypso, Franz and Gisella had already spent a lot of time in Rome together, and were having a blast introducing Scott to each and every one of their regular watering holes. They took Scott to their favorite restaurant where they were treated to pasta and lashings of cheap house wine. Guido, the owner, loved it when Calypso visited and they were treated like royalty. As the evening wore on, the bar was cleared for her to mix her magical cocktails behind.

Calypso had always loved this particular bar. It was filled with bottles of booze most people would never dream of buying. She doused some sugar cubes in cinnamon bitters, mixed them with Pomme Verte and topped it with rum and lots of rock ice. All the while, she spoke and gazed around the restaurant at the remaining patrons: some wary tourists, a few regulars who'd seen her work before, two horrified nuns, the staff, who all adored her, and her expectant friends.

"Who will be my first victim?"

"You've done us so many times." Gisella had never been comfortable with her friend's gift.

"True," Calypso agreed.

She poured the drinks and passed them over the bar to Franz, who handed them out.

"Some starters," Calypso explained. And then her green eyes rested on Scott. "Step up to the bar, handsome. I'm doing you first."

"You've already done me," Scott said with a wink. "I'm a done dinner, darling."

He pulled up a stool at the bar and watched his new girlfriend. She was something else: drop dead gorgeous, outrageously funny, wild, free and wonderful. Sure, it had only been a few weeks, but he already knew there would never be another woman for him. He felt like a bit of a dingbat, and certainly hadn't admitted his feelings to anyone, but it was as though he'd finally met his other half.

She ran her eyes over him and forced herself to look beyond the physical. It was hard. It was all so new and she couldn't get enough of his body. Their passion for each other was all-consuming and it was difficult to even get out of bed. When they did, they were constantly searching for places to hide, where no one would see the hurried undoing of buttons and zippers, the tearing of lace knickers, and the frantic, breathless sex.

Calypso emptied her mind of that now and concentrated on reading him. The ethers around him shifted slightly and she waited for them to open, so she could move through. She blinked a few times to get a new perspective ... and tried again.

Everyone waited.

Nothing happened.

She turned away, had a sip of water, and then tried again. Nothing. Nothing. Nothing.

Calypso's gut twisted into a thousand knots. She shook her head, as though trying to free her gift. Nothing worked. Her eyes darted around the room, looking, looking for the other realms that had always been so clear up until that moment. It was a total first. She'd spent her whole life accessing other realms, easily entering the paranormal doors, but suddenly she'd lost the key.

Franz sensed her panic. "Callie, are you okay?"

Scott stood, as though readying himself to catch her. "What's going on?"

She drew her focus back into the present, and into Scott's curious stare. Their eyes locked and held, and everything was fine. Calypso nodded and her eyes filled with light as she beamed at him.

"I'm sorry, everyone, but I've lost my powers."

There was a rush of comforting suggestions.

"No, you're just tired."

"Or drunk?"

"PMS?"

"Have a big glass of water."

"It must be God's will."

That brought Calypso back to reality. She'd thought the nuns had left.

Calypso held up a hand, asking for silence.

"It's okay, and it's temporary," she assured everyone. "I'm not concerned. In fact ... I'm thrilled. It's a hereditary thing.

It happens to us Shakespeare women when we meet our one true love." She moved around to the front of the bar and into Scott's arms. "That's you," she whispered in his ear. "We're meant to be together."

"Thank Christ for that." Scott chuckled. "I thought I was going bloody crazy."

*

Back in Birdland, Calypso stared at her friends. How could it happen twice? Shakespeare women only ever loved once. Didn't they? Two true loves? It was unheard of. Calypso had been raised on the romantic mythology of her clan. Every single generation spawned another great romance. But only one. One witch, one true love.

Yet she couldn't deny what was happening to her any longer – and she'd obviously spent weeks trying. She'd fallen in love and lost her powers. And every inch of her being knew those two facts were totally interconnected. Was she destined to love twice? And if so, what the hell was she going to do about it?

Gisella and Franz sat quietly and watched her for a while, and then Franz couldn't help himself.

"So, Callie, liebling, how is Taran?"

Chapter 35

Prevent shaving rash by wiping the skin with
vodka first

Taran was as happy as a wasp in a glass jar. His day had been
a write-off. He'd been unable to paint so he drank instead.
He'd paced Simon's apartment, emptied his liquor cabinet,
and tried unsuccessfully to call Finn three times.

Taran knew he was there – he just wasn't picking up.

Eventually he threw on some jeans, grabbed his wallet, and
headed out. He needed to clear his head, so headed toward
Primrose Hill. He was restless; wound up, despite the copious
amounts of booze he'd consumed. He was anxious about the
opening, but not overly so. He had enough confidence in his
work. It was his personal life that he had no control over.

Taran kicked an empty Coke can off the pavement. He was
angry with Calypso. Why did she have to be so difficult? She
was like tax forms ... a pain in the ass to work out but unfortunately essential. And without her, how would he ever solve
things with Finn? His ultimatum was clear.

Taran missed his brother. He knew Finn missed him. He
could feel him. They were twins with *that* type of bond. It
was the most important relationship in his life, yet he'd been

careless with it. What on earth had possessed him to sleep with Finn's girlfriends? Some of them weren't even that attractive. It was a question he'd been asking himself a lot these past few weeks.

Taran paused and looked into the window of Baker's Second-Hand Books, as if the answer would be there.

And it was.

Perched up on display was *Speak of the Devil*, his mother's autobiography. There she was, dressed in her High Priestess robes, sprawled across a sacrificial altar: *The True Story of Brigid Dee, Straight from the Devil's Mouth*.

Taran rolled his eyes and kept walking. His mother was the type of woman who ate her young. She made Joan Crawford look like mother of the year. He shoved his fists deep into his jeans. That was unfair. She was perfectly nice to two of her three children.

Taran had always prided himself on reaching adulthood relatively unscathed by her, but that wasn't really the case. He thought about all the times she'd call to him and Finn when they were young, "Oh, you're so alike ... which one will I choose?" And then she'd reach out her arms to Finn. Taran's mother seemed to enjoy rejecting him. She often said the only thing that needed to come in pairs were shoes.

Taran understood it now. Finn was more likable. He always had been. And kind. He would always give his mother a quick hug and then return to Taran's side, to show where his true loyalty lie. The twins were inseparable, and Taran adored his brother, but that didn't stop Taran from nursing a deep-seated desire to beat Finn. And in the affections of women he'd won, time and again. Not just one girlfriend, but a string of them. He was never again the rejected one.

Until Finn himself rejected him. Taran got it. He should've stayed away from Tye. But he'd been punished enough. At first Taran thought Finn just needed some space; that he'd come round, like he always did. But Finn wouldn't budge and had refused to see his brother for six months.

It was long enough. Taran wasn't able to give Finn what he'd asked for. He'd tried, but it wasn't going to happen. Instead, Taran would face his twin and ask for forgiveness. For now he knew what it felt like to be heartbroken, and was ashamed that he'd ever hurt Finn. Taran would work at earning Finn's trust back – however long it took.

Taran finally made it to the top of the hill and stopped to take in the view. Two London skylines stretched out before him. He swayed a bit and realized that he was still quite drunk, so picked a spot under a tree and sat.

The sun was setting. He watched the usual cast of joggers, walkers, dog owners, Frisbee throwers and families. It was like something from a film. He almost expected Keira Knightly to totter past in a bustled gown, or Mary Poppins to swoop by on her umbrella ... or one of the zombies from *28 Days Later* to hobble up the hill.

If his life was a movie it would go straight to DVD. He needed to liven things up. No more moping. Enough of the hermit act. Forget about Calypso. He'd emailed, he'd called, she'd ignored. It was time to move on. And the minute he was sober he would.

But while he was still drunk, he might as well have some fun. He grabbed his phone and brought up Laura's number. Then, through his beer goggles, texted: *Fished work. Would love to ketchup. Meat Ewan there.*

*

Calypso woke with a start. Another dream of Bangkok. It took her a moment to realize how far from that city, and that time, she actually was. She knew she wouldn't sleep again, so threw on some clothes and headed outside. It was cool, so she zipped up her jacket and began to walk. She knew where she was going. Her mind was like a dog, chasing its tail round in circles. She needed to go to the one place in Vienna that might calm it.

She turned up Kärntner Strasse and headed toward the opera house. It was a beautiful evening, and although late, the concourse was still busy. There were families on their way home from dinner, couples strolling hand in hand, pausing to look in the windows of jewelry stores and boutiques. She passed a string quartet. Further along was a woman playing a piano. She had no idea how she'd managed to get her instrument into the pedestrian thoroughfare.

She turned left into Weihburggasse, and left the hustle and bustle behind. The Franziskanerplatz was quiet. She passed the fountain in front of the Franziskanerkirche and she stood for a moment. She loved the smaller baroque church, and the adjoining monastery, with its renaissance façade. Being a witch, she didn't have to like *the Church*, but she certainly appreciated its art and history, both beautiful and bloodied.

Calypso noticed some free tables at the Kleines café and took a deep breath. Their table was empty. She walked over and claimed it.

Kleines was her favorite Viennese cafe. She'd been there with Scott a number of times. The last time had been just after they flew back from Thailand, after *that trip*, or the Second Chance Saloon as Scott often called it. She could almost feel Scott take his place at the table with her, and smiled, ever so slightly. Should she order two coffees?

She caught the waiter's attention. "Ich hätte gern eine Tasse mélange."

The waiter nodded. "Noch etwas?"

"Das war alles, danke."

Calypso relaxed back and watched the occasional passerby. The waiter returned with her coffee and she sipped the frothy drink. Mostly, she just thought about her dream. She thought about Thailand.

*

"Me no speak Engrish."

Calypso waved her hands around in front of the hotel receptionist's face, as if that would help. "My boyfriend went to get dinner. *Dinner*. But he's not back."

The young guy behind the desk shrugged. "No Engrish."

"Does anyone here speak English?" Calypso was frantic now.

"No Engrish okay!"

That's what you get for three hundred baht a night, thought Calypso. She wanted to go looking for Scott, but didn't know where to start and felt it was best to stay close to the room. She turned and climbed the stairs, making sure she locked the door behind her. Inside, she pulled a chair up to the window, and searched the street below. Where was he?

The city that had been so much fun earlier in the day suddenly seemed menacing. They'd taken a boat up the Chao Phraya River and spent the afternoon at the Grand Palace. Scott had been in a great mood, but Calypso was feeling jetlagged, so they returned to their hotel and he'd told her to have a nap while he went and found something to eat for them. Seven hours ago.

She curled up on the bed. If only she could tune into him, but that was impossible with Scott. Even though her powers had eventually returned, she was never able to use them on him. She yanked the sheet up over her head to block out the noise: music from bars, people yelling on the street, a woman calling to someone in a nearby room. The constant hum of an unfamiliar city ...

The door flew open and Calypso leapt up, confused. It was nearly light outside. The streets were quiet now. She must've fallen asleep. It took her a moment to realize that Scott was only just entering the room.

She launched herself at him. "Where the fuck have you been?"

"Sorry, baby, sorry." Scott was clearly drunk.

"I've been frantic with worry!"

Scott stumbled a bit and flopped down on the side of the bed. That was the moment Calypso realized his face was swollen and bruised and his shirt was covered in blood.

"Jesus, you're hurt." She clawed at his buttons and pulled off his shirt.

"I'm okay, Callie ... I'm okay."

Scott's eye was black and swollen, his chin was grazed and his lip had split. He had a series of deep purple bruises down his stomach, a gash across his chest and some cuts on his arm. One of them was deeper than the rest but had been tightly wrapped with a tourniquet made from his boxer shorts.

"Fortunately they were clean today." Scott chuckled.

Calypso burst into tears. She ran her fingers over him. Apart from the one on his bicep, the other cuts were superficial and the blood had dried.

"You should see the other guy," Scott weakly joked.

"Who did this?"

"There were three of them. They just wanted my wallet."

"They could've killed you."

Scott agreed. "There was this American guy who saw them drag me into an alley. He just barreled toward them like a goddamn beast ... I guess he freaked them out enough for the two of us to fight them off."

"Was he hurt?"

"Lost a tooth. Perhaps some broken ribs. He was a mess ... but a bloody hero. Without him ..."

Calypso was reeling. "When did this happen?"

"I dunno, babe ... hours ago. I'm so sorry, I know I should've come back earlier, but we were in shock, and went for a drink. One drink turned into six. Or sixteen. Fuck, I don't know. I'm just happy to be alive." Scott held her tight.

Calypso ran her fingers across his chest. He needed a salve for his wounds. And then she noticed something else about his chest: the amulet he always wore, the one she'd had especially made for him, was missing.

"Did they steal the amulet?"

"No ... I gave it to my buddy ... ah ..." Scott's face fell, and he looked concerned for a moment. "Fuck ... what was his name ...?"

Calypso waited. Scott had a memory for names. He remembered the names of every waiter in every restaurant they ever went to. In his opinion, it was only polite.

"I was calling him Chuck ... He reminded me of Chuck Norris the way he went at those guys." He shook his head.

Calypso was furious that he'd given his talisman away. She'd spent so much time designing it and having it made. She went to her bag and removed a small jar of salve made from various oils, goldenseal and coptis root. "This will stop the bleeding and make sure there's no infection," she said as she rubbed it onto his injuries.

Scott grabbed her face, and lifted it toward him. He was staring at her with such intensity that she suddenly felt frightened again.

"Wild abandon, Callie."

"I don't understand, Scott."

"I got a second chance. It's the only way I can live now. There's no other choice."

And that was the way they both lived, together – until he died, two years later.

*

Calyspo wiped a stray tear from her cheek. She glanced around, but she was the only customer left at the Kleines Café. The franziskanerplatz was empty, Vienna silent around her.

The waiter approached, and cleared her table. "Ist alle ok bei Ihnen?"

"Yes, I'm fine. Danke." She was now. She paid for her coffee and made her way back toward her apartment.

"Wild abandon," whispered Callie to herself. "There's no other choice."

*

The next morning, Calypso bounded down the stairs and joined Gisella and Franz for a large breakfast of pastries, bread and cheeses. She was relieved to see Gisella had finally decided to eat for two.

"You had a good sleep?" Gisella asked through a mouthful of Nutella.

"Nope, but it was an enlightening one." Calypso poured herself a juice and gathered together a plate of black bread and cheese.

"What do you plan to do today?" asked Gisella.

She smiled at her friends. "I'm going back to London to win Taran back. And nothing is going to stand in our way."

Chapter 36

Drink damiana tea to increase sexual energy

Calypso called Megan the minute her plane landed in London. "Any idea where Taran is at the moment?"

Megan almost cheered. "I knew you'd come round. Going to grovel are you?"

"Don't be ridiculous ... I don't grovel. Beg, perhaps, but never grovel."

Megan grabbed a cloth and wiped down the bar. "His door was still shut when I left Simon's a short while ago. I think he went out last night so he's probably sleeping off his hangover."

"Still in bed?" Calypso sighed. "How convenient."

"Hey Callie, I have an appointment at one today. It's a bit embarrassing, but I was wondering if you'd come with me."

"Not the gynecologist again."

"No! Gawd, that was a one off. This is for a wedding dress."

Calypso burst out laughing. "Oh Megan, I'd love to come with you." She paused. "I've never seen you in a dress before."

"Funny ha ha."

"I'll meet you at the pub at twelve. Now where does Simon live?"

Megan gave her the address and less than an hour later, Calypso was standing on Taran's doorstep, waiting for him to answer the bell.

She rang the bell again. A few seconds later ... footsteps. The door opened, and there was Taran, his hair mussed, his eyes sleepy, all glorious muscles and golden skin, nothing but a towel around his waist.

"Surprise!"

It certainly seemed to be a surprise, judging by the look on his face. "What are you doing here?"

"I came to apologize. I should never have thrown you out."

Taran looked strangely upset – almost unwell. He didn't speak, so Calypso continued. "I'm asking for another chance. Asking nicely. Groveling really." She smiled, sheepishly. "And normally I'm not big on groveling."

Still nothing.

Calypso stuck her hands on her hips, annoyed now. "Well aren't you going to bloody say something? Or are you just going to stand there looking like an idiot?"

Taran glanced over his shoulder and then back at Calypso. "Callie, I didn't expect you."

Calypso shrugged. "So you're not dressed. That's fine by me. Invite me and we'll put that fact to good use."

"Christ, Callie ... I'd like nothing better, you've got to believe me ... it's just—"

And then a voice – a female voice, with rounded vowels and a syrupy edge – called down the hall. "Everything okay, Taran?"

Horror flooded Calypso's body from the feet up. By the time it hit her face, she was backing down the stairs.

Taran held his towel tight and followed her, stumbling slightly on the bottom step. "Please, Callie, she doesn't mean anything. I never expected to hear from you again."

Calypso nodded, polite, detached. "Of course. No need to explain ... Sorry for interrupting."

And with that she turned and ran.

Taran bolted after her. "Callie, be reasonable ..." He made it to the end of the street before the wolf whistles and honking horns reminded him that he was wearing nothing but a towel.

Chapter 37

Whiskey stimulates the heart and arteries

Calypso was furious! She was upset that she'd put herself in such a vulnerable position. And she was absolutely ropable at the hot tears that were burning her cheeks over Taran. She'd promised herself three years ago that she'd never shed tears over another man, yet here she was blubbering away in the back of a cab.

Of course he's moved on, she thought. *I made it clear it was over. But he's won the Speedy Gonzales award for how quickly he's done so.*

Calypso wasn't one of those women who were hung up on their man's past. She was fully aware of Taran's past. She'd read the piece in *Art Monthly* that briefly mentioned his appreciation of art, but mainly his appreciation for women and lots of them. She'd flicked through an article about his parents in *Hello!* magazine where his mother actually said he had the morals of an alley cat. And there had been a piece in *The Guardian* that concentrated on his romantic conquests more than his artistic achievements. But she'd never witnessed any of this behavior when they were together so it didn't worry her. She didn't think about it. In many ways, she appreciated his history. He certainly knew what he was doing in bed, which was a huge bonus. And it was always better to have a man who was bored of playing the field than one who dreams of doing so. Calypso just *knew* she could trust him. More proof that she had the psychic powers of a baked bean now.

She blew her nose. So much for being ready to love him and start living again. Instead she was faced with a reminder that life didn't always pan out as planned.

It was a bitter and extremely embarrassing pill to swallow, especially after everything she'd realized while she was in Vienna. She'd been given a second chance at true love, but she'd rejected it and that true love had quickly moved on to some silly cow with a very plummy voice.

Her mood lifted slightly when she arrived home and found her father sitting at the bar. He was thinner and paler, but he looked as pleased as punch to be up and about.

Calypso gave him a hug. "Should you be down here?"

"Don't you start," he said. "I'm well enough to manage the bar for a couple of hours while you girls go shopping."

Of course, Megan's wedding dress.

Alf noticed how red her eyes were. "What's up, my girl?"

Calypso's eyes welled up again. "I went to Taran's on the way home from the airport. Poured my heart out. Told him I want another chance – and then realized he was there with another woman."

Alf nodded, as he always did when he was processing information. Nod, nod, nod, at nothing in particular. "Still, you'd ended it. You didn't expect him to sit around waiting or moping, did you?"

"Ah yeah, for a while."

"Callie, love, he's a good lad, but he's only human."

What? Was her father defending him? Calypso's eyes narrowed. "You barely know him."

"I know him well enough. You need to call him and sort things out."

"I'd rather swallow spiders than call him."

"Then you're a weirdo. He had no idea you'd want him back, so sleeping with someone else isn't a crime."

It was all too much for Calypso. She knew her father was right. "Can we talk about something else?"

"How was Vienna?"

"Good." Calypso took a handful of peanuts and began munching. "Gisella is fine now."

"Pregnancy hormones are mysterious things. Your mother was like a rabid dog for the first trimester with you. She bit, she barked, she howled … even foamed at the mouth a few times, but chocolate usually helped that." Alf gave his daughter a wink. "I knew whatever she was carrying was going to be quite a handful." He ruffled her hair. "With Nell, she spent most of the pregnancy cleaning cupboards."

"You called?" Nell appeared behind them both. She was wearing a blue and white polka dot dress with pumps and a cardigan. She gave her sister a hug. "I'm coming shopping with you and Megan."

"Great. We'll have fun." Calypso smiled, but it didn't quite reach her bloodshot eyes.

"Who died?" Nell joked.

Alf said, "She's upset because she's been poking around in the Cauldron, unable to mix magic drinks lately."

Calypso stared at her father in shock. "How the hell—?"

Alf looked almost defensive. "While there's life in this ol' guy, I'll always know what's going on with my girls."

Calypso chewed on her lip to stop herself from crying … again. She was nearly thirty, but sometimes he still made her feel like a child – a safe, well-loved child. He never babied her, and he was never uncomfortable with her adult needs, but she was his daughter and his role as father continued to be important to him.

"So I'm guessing you've worked out the connection to Taran," Nell added.

Calypso put her hands on her hips. "You saw it too?"

Nell pushed a short lock of her hair over her ear. "Helen Keller would've seen it, Callie."

"I thought we Shakespeare women were only meant to have *one* true love."

"What a crock of horse manure," a voice called from the door.

Batty sauntered in wearing a camel-colored trench coat over a red slacks. She had topped her outfit with a red hat. It was a brighter entrance than Harrods.

"There are numerous examples of Shakespeare women loving more than one man. Julanne Shakespeare had her one true love and when he was beheaded in the Battle of Flodden Field she was pleasantly surprised to find love again with the Earl of Bridgewater. Her powers disappeared both times."

Calypso was astounded. "But you've always said that we—"

Batty cut her off. "It's a rich tapestry of tales we Shakespeare women weave about ourselves, but it's not always steeped in fact."

"So it's lies," Nell said, equally mortified.

"All family histories are built on ... exaggerations." Batty turned on her daughters. "What would you rather? The truth? Let's try Ruby Shakespeare, who *died* at the hands of her one true love. 'She didn't see that one coming,' everyone said. Well of course, she bloody didn't. Her powers didn't work around him. Or how about Patricia Shakespeare, who met her one true love and thought '... not this time around'. And instead married a blacksmith and was by all accounts extremely happy."

"I think those stories are wonderful," Nell said.

"At least they're honest," added Calypso.

"I apologize if you feel I've mislead you, girls. Especially you, Callie. I didn't realize you took it so literally."

"How else were we meant to take it, Mum?"

Batty reached out and took Alf's hand. "I was just telling my tale. Yours will be different. But mine … just one. One true love."

Alf locked eyes with his wife. "Me too, Red."

"Like my outfit, Alf?" Batty twirled for him.

"You look like the cat's meow," Alf chuckled. "Obviously not my cat though … the one you gave away."

Batty stopped mid-twirl.

He gave the girls a wink. "Like I said, I don't miss a trick."

Megan sauntered in and looked at all three women. "What's going on?"

"You're shopping for the most important dress of your life. I need to be there," Batty said.

Nell nodded. "Ditto what Mum said."

Megan looked at Calypso. "Did you tell them?"

Calypso shook her head. "I thought you did."

Batty gave a huff. "Haven't any of you learnt yet that nothing is a secret around here?" She glanced at Nell. "Apart from yours." She kissed Alf and headed toward the door. "Let's go."

"That's right, Bettina," he called after her. "And I knew about my cat long before you blurted it out at the hospital."

Chapter 38

Chartreuse is a digestif, often believed to be secret to a long life

Something Etc was a delightful bridal showroom in a converted mews house in Notting Hill, owned by Patty Pfeiffer, part rock chick, part fairy princess, and bride lover extraordinaire. She'd been married six times, so knew a thing or two about wedding dresses.

"So I saw Megan doing stand-up and she was talking about her upcoming wedding." Patty poured the women each a glass of champagne as she regaled them with how she'd met Megan. "The audience was in stitches." She looked at Megan. "What was that one that had everyone howling?"

Meg was already regretting coming. "A seal walked into a club?"

"No ... the one about the dress. 'Why are wedding dresses traditionally white?' "

"Because all household appliances are white," Megan finished.

Patty hollered with laughter. "I loved that! And I thought, this woman has to wear one of my dresses. She's just awesome."

Megan blushed and took a huge swig of courage. She felt like an idiot dragging everyone along to watch her try on a dress.

"Megan's not a huge fan of dresses." Batty stated the obvious.

"I thought I might get married in jeans," Megan added.

"My dresses are different. There's not a meringue in sight." Patty refilled her own glass. "And while that whole boho thing can be lovely … it's not for Megan." She cast her eyes over the Shakespeare women. "I know who you are. And while I'm not actually *psychic*, I am gifted. I *sense* wedding dresses." She stood and handed the bottle to Calypso.

Both Nell and Batty held out their glasses for a refill. They *sensed* they needed it.

Patty stared at Megan.

Megan squirmed in her chair and pretended to look at her nails.

Patty turned on her heel and marched out of the room.

"She's bloody weird," Calypso whispered.

Batty gave her daughter a light slap. "That's not nice. People say the same about me all the time."

"But you *are* weird." Calypso smirked.

Batty ignored her daughter and seized the moment she'd been waiting for. "Megan, Alf and I want to do something special for your wedding."

"Batty you don't have to—"

"Hush!" Batty snapped. "You're like another daughter to us. This is what we want. We need to do … something … To mark the occasion."

Megan stared at her sneakers for a moment. "Well, I was thinking … I'd love to have the reception at the pub."

There was an audible gasp from Batty.

Megan felt like she'd overstepped the mark. "If it's too much, I can have it somewhere else."

Batty waved a hand in front of her face. It took a moment for her to find the words. And then she started to cry. "Megan, it means so much to me that you'd choose the pub for such an important day."

"I love the pub, Batty."

Batty wrapped her arms around the woman she'd helped raise since childhood. "We'll throw you the best damn party the pub has ever seen."

"Just some snacks and beer really."

"There'll be more beer than the London Beer Flood," Batty announced melodramatically.

"And that's saying something," Nell said.

"Megan," Patty's voice cut through their laughter, "I got it. Come and try it on."

"Let's get this over with then." Megan slunk off.

"She looks like a dead man walking," Nell said.

"That's marriage for ya." Calypso sniffed. "Anything left in that bottle?"

Nell poured another round and the women sipped in silence.

"I feel like we're at the undertakers." Calypso giggled.

"Actually, a black dress would suit Megan," Batty pointed out.

"Promise not to laugh." Megan's voice sounded shaky from behind the curtains.

"Promise." They all glanced at each other.

"Shut your eyes."

They all did as they were told.

A few seconds passed and then. "Okay, open."

Calypso, Batty and Nell opened their eyes and looked straight at Megan, dressed in what could only be described as the wedding dress she was born to wear.

Batty burst into tears again.

Megan looked horrified. "It's not that bad is it?"

Calypso walked over to her best friend and took her hands. "It's perfect, Megan. You're perfect."

"It is, isn't it?"

The women all stood back and soaked it in. It was a simple ivory shift dress made from wool crepe. It had long lace sleeves and an embroidered hem at the knee. It was feminine, classy but very different. Just like Megan.

Nell circled her, staring at the detail on the dress. "It's the loveliest dress I've ever seen."

Patty was beaming. "I think she should dye her hair pink," said Patty, and everyone agreed. "And if she's not comfortable wearing heels—"

Megan looked like she was about to protest, but Patty stopped her and finished.

"—you can wear boots with that dress."

Megan broke into the broadest grin of her life. "This is it. This is the one. I love it."

Calypso and Nell both hugged her.

Batty threw her arms up in the air. "Simon will love it."

Megan jumped up and down. "I know, I know ... but more importantly ... I do too."

*

Thirty minutes later, all three Shakespeare women and a very happy Megan exited Something Etc. Batty led the way, talking excitedly about the wedding she'd throw. Nell was texting Percy, letting him know she was dropping by. Calypso was suggesting they should shop for wedding boots while they were on a roll. And Megan was not looking where she was going – and ran smack bang into Simon's mother.

Penelope Apsley reeled back in horror once she recognized Megan. Megan's face drained of joy and was replaced by complete hurt. Penelope went to say something but stopped when she saw the bag Megan was carrying: *Something Etc ... For every bride.*

"You and Simon are getting married?"

Megan just nodded, mute.

Penelope's shoulders sagged. She looked at the other wo-men for the first time, first Nell, then Calypso, and then Batty. Embarrassment flooded her face, and she squared her shoulders back again.

She turned back to Megan. "Make him happy. Please."

"I will. I do."

Penelope gave a nod of her head and then disappeared around the corner.

The women all looked at each other, taking it in.

"That was awkward," Nell said.

"She makes my monster-in-law look positively angelic," Batty admitted.

Calypso slung her arm around Megan's shoulders, and they all headed off. "I know you've got the dress, Meg ... but have you actually considered what that means?"

"What's that?" Megan asked.

"That you'll have to adopt, 'cause, honey, that gene pool just needs chlorination not procreation."

The women all howled with laughter as they made their way up Portobello Road.

Chapter 39

A hot toddy at bedtime clears congestion

Nell made her way through the main foyer of the British Museum of Romance toward Percy's office. She waved at Rachael and Natalie, two of the museum's loyal volunteers.

"Hello, stranger," Natalie called. "What brings you here?"

"I just wanted to see how Percy was doing."

Rachael lowered her voice. "Not great. I mean, he's well, and manages to get most things done, but I think he misses you."

Nell felt a stab of guilt. "Did the Byron letters eventually arrive?"

"They did, but Percy hasn't decided how to display them yet."

Nell rolled her eyes. She'd spent three hours going through ideas with him and then another two hours writing a report for Percy that explained exactly what to do once the letters arrived.

"How's life at the Nat?" Nat had been wildly excited that Nell was going to work at an institution that bore her name.

"Really busy," said Nell as she made her escape. She couldn't bear to answer more questions about work. She just wanted to have a quick look around the museum and then go and see Percy.

She wandered through the stars of the silver screen room, and into the royal room. Victoria and Albert, Bertie and Elizabeth, Edward and Wallis, Elizabeth and Philip: all had displays there. She cut through the Charles and Diana room, where a new Camilla exhibit stood to one side, much to Percy's disgust. It had taken years before he's finally agreed to install the cabinet.

"Percy, we don't judge history, we simply display it," Nell had reminded him.

A few more pieces had been added to the William and Kate showcase. Nell noticed a layer of dust over everything. Some displays needed rearranging. Oh good god, the Harry and Chelsy display had reappeared. Percy felt Chelsy was a lovely girl and an obvious match for the younger prince. He'd never wanted to remove the display. Nell made for the door. She'd been gone six weeks, but already the place was coming undone.

She trotted up the stairs and knocked on the door of Percy's office.

"Yes ... ah ... come in then."

She entered and found Percy teetering on the top rung of a ladder as he reached toward the top shelf of his bookcase.

"What on earth are you doing, Percy? Be careful!"

Percy glanced down at Nell and grinned. "Dear child, how wonderful. I didn't know you were dropping by."

"I just sent you a text to tell you I was on the way."

"I've lost my phone, Nell."

"We also discussed it last week."

"Did we? Oh ... yes, I can recall now."

"Didn't you write it down?"

"I think I did ... but I seem to have misplaced that diary you got me."

Nell held her breath as she watched him grab a folder. "What are you looking for?"

"My accountant wants all the records for the … ah … tax thing."

"You mean the ones I filed here in the drawer." Nell marched over to his desk and pulled out a neat, well-marked folder. "Percy, get down."

He did as he was told and finally stood before her, beaming. "Good to see you, Nell. We miss you around here."

"So I can see. The whole place is falling apart."

Percy looked offended. "I wouldn't say it's falling apart, but yes, there are a few adjustments to make. I'll get there though."

"Oh Percy, I feel dreadful. I wish I could help."

"Don't be silly. You've been given the opportunity of a lifetime at the National Museum. You're a lucky girl."

"I don't feel so lucky. Especially when I come back here to the place I truly love and find it in such disarray!"

"What do you mean, the place you truly love?"

"The BMR, obviously." Nell stared at her old boss. "You do realize how much I love this museum, don't you, Perc?"

The look on his face was proof that he didn't have a clue. "I thought you were fond of it, of course. And loyal, because that's your way, Nell."

"This is the most beautiful museum in London – hell, the whole of England."

Percy flushed, and had to remove his glasses before they fogged up. "I … I'm flattered … and … well, Nell … if I'd realized you liked my museum so much, I would have offered you a proper job. In fact, you should have asked for one."

The two stood there for some time, staring at each other in disbelief. Finally, Nell spoke.

"I didn't ask, because I didn't want to pressure you. I know things are tough financially."

"They're not that tough. And I always harbored a little dream that with you here full time, we'd turn this place into a real tourist destination. You've got the business sense that I seem to lack, Nell."

Nell was livid. "Oh, Percy. I want to work here, but now I'm committed to the National. Damn it! I could just throttle you for being so polite."

"I could say the same for you, so don't unleash that redheaded temper at me, dear."

Nell plunked herself into a chair. "What a mess."

"Yes, yes, a dreadful mess." Percy took his glasses off, polished them and slipped them back on, all the while smiling at his young protégé. "But, Nell, in my experience, you're extremely good at cleaning up messes."

Chapter 40

A shot of Ouzo will ease toothaches and insomnia

Calypso and Batty arrived back at the King and Mistress to find Taran and Alf at the bar together. Calypso quickly surveyed the scene. Taran was halfway through a pint while her father leant toward him, hands flailing animatedly around. They both threw their heads back and laughed. They looked like they were having a grand ol' time until they noticed Calypso, and simultaneously froze. Her father looked as guilty as Taran did. If Calypso wasn't so upset about seeing Taran, their behavior would have been comical.

Batty swept into the bar and shooed Alf from behind it. "Time for you to rest. Go on, upstairs."

Alf looked relieved; he'd been given a get out of jail free card. He threw Taran a look of support, as one would if one was holding the only parachute as the plane was going down. "We'll finish our chat some other time." *If you find your own parachute.* "Good to see you, son."

Calypso raised her eyebrows. *Son?*

"And I agree, now's a good time to mention the other thing." He patted Taran on the back – and didn't stick a dagger into it while he was there, which surely most loyal fathers would've done – and then made his way out of the bar.

Calypso was furious. Had they taken her father's brain as well when they removed part of his liver?

"What was my father was talking about?'

Taran shuffled uncomfortably. "There's something I've been keeping from you."

"You mean apart from your penchant for women who speak like they've got a broom up their arse?"

Taran gave an amused snort. "Inserted broom? No ... not something I usually look for in a woman."

Calypso gave him a withering look. He matched it. Batty picked up a cloth and wiped the bar nearby. She didn't want to miss this.

"Cal, I wish I could rewind this morning's events. Both you turning up at my door *and* me waking up with Miss *Broom-up-her-arse* ..."

Calypso almost smiled. "Was that her actual name?"

"Yes, it's from the Old English name for town sweeper."

"More like town slapper."

Taran raised an eyebrow and smiled. "Jealousy suits you. It matches your eyes."

Calypso folded her arms. "Get on with it."

"This morning means nothing. Should mean nothing. But there is something I've been keeping from you that's important."

Calypso wasn't sure she wanted to hear any more so she decided to be facetious instead. "You're married? Gay? A month to live? A Republican?"

"If you shut up for two seconds, I'll tell you."

Batty hid a smile as she rubbed at a non-existent spot on the bar.

Taran ran his fingers through his hair. "I overheard a conversation—"

"Get to the punch line while I'm still young, will you?"

Taran ignored her and continued. "Your father was on the phone …" He paused for a moment, unsure of the best way to broach it.

"Taran knew about your father's melanoma before we did," Batty said. She looked at Taran and shrugged. "You did the right thing, honey."

Calypso felt the floor beneath her shift. "How long before we knew?"

"A couple of days. I came here after you left me in Paris. I overheard Alf on the phone with his doctor."

The floor dropped away. "You knew, but said nothing about it to me in Vienna, or in Cornwall? You knew he had cancer and you still managed to have a party with me!"

"I knew you'd get yourself worked up over this."

Calypso was standing now. "Too bloody right I'm worked up. How could you keep this from me?"

"Alf thought it was best to wait."

"Conveniently for you, who got to continue our shag fest."

Taran tried not to smile … but failed, which just made Calypso even more furious.

"How *dare* you not tell me."

"Weren't you the one who thought it would be best to not tell Eleanor?"

That shut her up.

Batty wiped down the bar beside them. "And he tried to tell you."

Calypso looked at her mother in disbelief. "Did I ask for your input?"

"It's true, I did try." Taran gave Batty a grateful smile.

"Your father wouldn't let him speak. A bit like you really."

"He made it clear he didn't want me to tell you then."

Calypso sighed. "That night upstairs?"

Batty looked at her daughter and Taran. "Isn't it time you just let go?" She placed the cloth under the bar and walked out the back.

"I'm sorry." Taran sounded as tired as she felt. "For not telling you about your dad. For what you saw this morning."

"I should've called," Calypso admitted. "I just turned up there expecting you to … be waiting."

"Until last night, I was." Taran looked ashamed. "Every second I was with her, I knew it was wrong, but not because I felt I owed you. You ended it, remember? It was wrong because I didn't want to be with her. She wasn't you." He leant against the bar, exhausted.

"The minute something happened with us you went straight back to being Taran the shagmaster."

"Flattering name, but a single one-night stand hardly wins me bachelor of the year."

"Your past speaks for itself, Taran."

"So does yours, Callie."

"What's that supposed to mean?"

"How many times have you hurt me? How many times have I rolled over to hold you, only to find the bed empty? You have a history of acting a certain way, just as I have."

Calypso nodded. "True, but I never hurt you with someone else." The minute she said it, she regretted it, because she had, constantly.

"No one living, no. The difference is, I understood. I didn't like it, Callie, but I forgave it." He looked into her eyes, imploring. "Forgive me."

"How can I be sure you won't run off with the next piece of arse you find halfway attractive?"

"How can I be sure you won't simply run off?"

Touché!

"Who is she?"

"An ex. She called, I was drunk, and thought why not? After you dropped by this morning, I told her the truth about you. She left. It's over. Cal, let's forget all this."

"You still reek of Eau de One-Night Stand. How can I forget?"

"Fine, don't forget. Let's just move on."

Calypso looked at him and knew she had no more arguments to offer. He really hadn't done anything wrong. She'd thrown him out. She'd rejected him. Sure, knowing he'd been with someone else hurt, but what did she expect? That he'd take a vow of celibacy? And she couldn't kick him out now when she knew she couldn't bear him to be with someone else. The only reasonable solution was to chain him to her bed so no other woman could ever put her dirty paws on him.

She moved toward him, draped her arms around his neck. "Okay, but if I even catch you looking sideways at anyone for a while, you're history."

"I didn't think you were the jealous type."

"I'm not, normally. And I think the freedom to flirt is essential, but I'm taking that freedom away from you until you prove yourself to me."

"Babe, you can take it away for all eternity. There's only one woman I want to be watching from now on."

He leant down to kiss her, but she pulled back just before their lips touched.

"Let's just hold off on any physical contact until the sting of where you've been this morning wears off." She stepped away from him with a resigned grimace

"I'm not a complete slob. I did shower."

"Perhaps you could have a disinfectant bath. I'm not big on sharing."

"I'm sorry, Cal."

"Shhh." Calypso cut him off. "Look."

Enid was floating above the bar, watching them.

"Oh great, the pervy ghost. Usually she shows up when we're naked," Taran whispered.

"I told you I'm watching you," Enid hissed from the corner.

"Got that loud and clear."

Enid's vaporous form rushed toward him and hovered within an inch of his face, which immediately drained of all color. "One day you'll thank me," she screeched, and disappeared into thin air.

Taran and Calypso looked at each other, eyes wide.

"She's creepy, man."

"Yeah, she always scared me as a kid," Calypso admitted. Something about Edith's appearance had unsettled her.

Taran took Calypso's hand in his. "Why do you think she's keeping an eye on us?"

"No idea ... but I have a feeling we'll soon find out."

Chapter 41

*"I only ever indulge for medicinal purposes.
Fortunately I'm a raging hypochondriac." Lady
Jane Hurley*

Nell watched as Julian inspected a piece she'd never seen before. His expression was serious, his head bent toward it. His hair kept flopping forward and he'd brush it back and continue the assessment. Nell wondered why he didn't get a haircut, but then decided she liked it longer. She liked a lot about Julian.

He suddenly looked up and grinned. "Hello, Nell. Didn't notice you there."

Nell blushed. "I didn't want to interrupt."

"You're not. Come and check this out." He handed her a magnifying glass and made room for her at the table. "I've never seen anything like it."

Nell hovered over the medallion. It was stunning. At first glance, handmade silver, probably, dated between the twelfth and thirteenth centuries. She held the magnifying glass over it and took in the finer details.

"It has a small loop of silver to show that it was once worn around someone's neck. Yet it's heavy, and the inscriptions point to it not being simply ornamental. Perhaps it was a talisman."

"I've considered that but it's unlike anything I've seen from that era."

"Where did you get it?"

"This is from the estate of Lady Jane Hurley."

Nell's eye's widened. "So it's true, she did leave everything to the museum?"

"Not quite everything," Julian said. "She left this to me."

Nell was floored. "Julian, at the risk of sounding rude – why?"

Julian shrugged. "The museum got the rest of the collection. I got this."

"Did you know her well?"

"I'd say we were friends." His eyes misted over and it was obvious that they were.

"Was she really as strange as the press makes out?"

"Most people thought she was barking mad. I found her fascinating. We often met and discussed history. She had an amazing knowledge. The odd thing about this piece, though, is I've never seen it before. She introduced me to every single piece over the years. It was all carefully catalogued and kept. She took great care in making sure I knew the history of everything in her collection. But this ... it was on her bedside cabinet when she died, with a note for me. No one can re-member seeing it, ever. Apart from her lawyer, who'd drafted it into the will. I certainly have no idea where it comes from." Julian motioned to the piece. "Turn it over."

Nell gently turned the medallion and held it closer to the light. There was an inscription on the back.

"What does it say?"

"Your guess is as good as mine. I've had Niamh Wilson from the ancient languages and symbology department at Oxford check it out and even she has no idea what it means."

"What did Lady Hurley's note say?"

Julian motioned to an open letter on the desk. "It's there. Read it."

Nell unfolded the scented sheet of paper and scanned the shaky handwriting, and then read out loud: "'Dearest Julian. I have left you a piece of the puzzle. I have reached the final chapter. Enjoy your own book. Forgive me for being so cryptic. Warmest regards, your friend, Lady Jane Hurley.'" Nell looked at Julian. "I think everyone was right. She was bonkers."

"Perhaps. I never saw it. If she were crazy why does she apologize for being cryptic?" Julian shrugged. "She was always immaculate, perfectly groomed and manners were of the utmost importance to her. Hardly signs of a crazy woman."

Nell stared at the medallion. It tugged at something deep inside her. But then, it's why she loved history: you're bound to remember some of it on some level.

She shook her head, breaking the spell the piece had over her. "It's very strange, Julian. What will you do with it?"

"I'll store it here until I gather more information on it – if I ever do." Julian looked excited for a moment. "We can search for answers to this together, like detectives. Obviously not tough ones. More like Enid Blyton characters. How does that sound?"

Nell moved to the other side of the cubicle and shuffled a couple of books around. "That sounds like fun, Julian." And it did ... but ...

"Anything bothering you, Nell?"

"No ... no, nothing ..."

"You're a dreadful liar."

"I am, yes."

"Want to go for a beer?"

"That would be nice, but ... ah ... I should really discuss something with you first. Here, at work. It's about work you see."

Nell tidied another couple of books. "The thing is – I'm not sure how to say this, Julian."

"As much as I'd appreciate you tidying my whole desk, Nell, it's best just to blurt it out. Just say, 'Julian, I'm not happy here. I want to go back to the BMR.'"

"Julian, I'm not happy – how did you know?"

Julian shrugged. "Like I said, Nell, you're easy to read, although I have no idea why."

"I'm so sorry. I feel dreadful. You were kind enough to give me the job—"

Julian held a hand up. "Enough, Nell. Working in one's dream job is such a rare and wonderful thing. I'm thrilled you have the opportunity. You deserve it."

"I'll stay here until you find a replacement."

"Thank you. I'd appreciate that."

"And ..." Nell twisted her fingers together. "I was thinking ... seeing as we won't be working together any more ... perhaps you'd like to have dinner with me ... sometime."

Julian broke into a large, toothy smile. "Wow, Nell, that would be grand."

*

One hour later, Nell raced back into Percy's office.

"Good lord, Nell, what's happened?"

"Nothing, Percy, everything is fabulous."

"Did you forget something?" Percy asked.

"Yes, I forgot to tell you that I want full pay and benefits."

Percy broke out into a huge grin. "How wonderful. Now that you've sorted that mess out ... what will we do with the Isabella and Richard Burton display?"

Chapter 42

Gargle with vodka and warm water to sooth a
sore throat. Swallowing is optional

Calypso woke and for a moment wondered where she was. That wasn't unusual. She travelled so much that often it took some time to get her bearings. This morning though, she quickly realized it didn't matter where she was (Taran's room), or what country she was in (England, obviously), because Taran was wrapped around her.

It was a lovely way to wake up.

"Whadda you gotta do today?" came a mumble from somewhere around her neck.

"I've got a date with the Spanish Inquisition. I'll experience some flaying, some stoning, a taste of disembowelment … and probably finish with some time on the rack."

"Lunch with your grandmother, eh?"

"I bargained it down to just coffee. Lunch would include a full crucifixion." Calypso rolled over and climbed on top of Taran. "Big day for you, mister."

"Please don't remind me until I've had caffeine."

"All eyes will be on you tonight."

Taran let out a deep breath. "Hopefully all eyes will be on my work."

"Are you excited?"

"I'm more excited about you sitting on top of me at the moment."

Calypso slipped her hand under the covers. "So that's what they mean by *rise and shine*."

Taran let out a deep groan and reached for her. Calypso slapped his hand away.

"You've got a *huge* ... night tonight. You need to conserve your energy." She leant down and whispered into his ear, "So you just shut your eyes, lie there and think about good reviews and accolades and art critics, while I do this ..."

*

At the other end of the apartment, Megan took a moment to reenter her body before she opened her eyes. Simon was staring straight at her, assured and amused. He knew he sent her to places she'd never been before. They were a regular Lewis and Clarke in the bedroom, exploring new areas, new countries, completely new continents.

Simon traced a finger around her navel, which was still covered in a slight film of sweat. "So I was asking you if you wanted to keep the name the C Spot?"

"That was just before you hit my G spot. I missed what you said after that." Megan rolled onto her stomach and stared up at her boyfriend. "I like the C Spot. And we can play on the name. The New C Spot."

"The C Spot, discovered! Finally." Simon laughed at his own joke.

Megan giggled, at his enthusiasm rather than his joke. "Stop by for a C Spot to eat."

"Not bad, Meg, not bad." Simon was on a roll now. "Sit, C Spot, Sit … Good dog."

Megan groaned. "Thankfully you're the business brain, not the main act." She twirled one of the hairs on his chest. "Are you sure this is what you want?"

Simon tilted her chin upwards, so he could look into her eyes. "I've never wanted anything more. This life I'm building with you is so exciting."

"But what if it fails?" Megan said.

"The business might fail, but we won't."

Megan nodded, and rested her head back on his chest. She inhaled his scent. She could hear his heart beating. Nothing else existed.

*

Batty was packing away her tarot cards and purifying the reading room when Alf scarpered in and shut the door.

What are you doing, Alf? Who's looking after the bar?"

He held a finger to his lips. "Don't jinx it. Empty in there, apart from Harry." He marched over to her, and took her in his arms.

Batty's eyes lit up. "Well, look who's feeling better!"

"I saw you sweeping the stockroom earlier and thought, 'I've got to get my hands on that woman by day's end.'"

"It has been way too long, Alf." A look of concern crossed her face. "We should speak to your doctor first."

"Already have, Red. I called and said, 'No time for an appointment. My wife's sweeping the stockroom in slim-fitting slacks, doc. Today's gotta be the day.' Doc said he hopes he is as enthusiastic at my age. He gave us the green light."

Batty beamed at her husband. "Old people sex. The poor thing was probably traumatized."

"Not at all. We gave him something to aim for, love." He ran his fingers through the curls he so adored. "What do you think we should do?"

"I think we should ... do two things." Batty gave her husband a sexy smile. "Firstly, I think we should stay at the Ritz tonight."

Alf looked confused. "I don't follow."

"I've always wanted to stay at the Ritz, but never have. If there's one thing I've realized lately, Alf, it's that our whole lives revolve around the pub and our girls. And that's fine. I love our life, but we need more. Just you and me, darling. So that's the first thing. A suite at the Ritz."

Alf let out a booming laugh. "Fine idea. Count me in. And the second thing?"

Batty winked at her husband as she pulled him toward her. "And here's the second thing ... the only thing, my love."

*

Calypso made her way through the main bar and noticed Harry, propped up in his regular place. "Your glass is empty Harry. Where's Dad?"

"No idea, Calypso. Everyone's disappeared. I think that fox has come back and your dad is dealing with it. There are some strange sounds in the side room."

"Would you like another cold one?"

"I'd be mighty grateful."

Calypso slipped behind the bar and poured Harry a beer.

"Your dad's looking much better now. Was bloody worried for a while." Harry looked like he was about to burst into tears, but then suddenly perked up. "He tells me you've met someone. You might settle down."

Calypso visibly blanched. "Yes, I've met someone, but that doesn't mean I'm going to 'settle' down. I think Dad needs to halve his meds."

"Settling and stagnating are two different things. Clear water will settle, Calypso – muddy water will stagnate ... remember that."

Calypso nodded, but didn't look sold. Harry was hardly Plato. As much as she adored the old guy, and felt for him since his wife passed away, he wasn't exactly a shining example of how to live one's life. Harry had been stagnating up against the bar for years.

Harry watched Calypso carefully over the rim of his glass. "I wasn't so different to you, lass. I wanted freedom when I was young. That's why I went away to sea. But loving, truly loving ... That's the ultimate freedom. Everything else is just fear, and that's what ties you down."

Calypso looked into Harry's creased old face. Poor bugger was obviously pining into his pint. "You must miss Nancy so much."

"That I do." Harry stared at the beer for a moment, but then perked up. "But I've met a lovely lady. Peg's her name. Quite a cracker. Makes me laugh and laugh."

Calypso stared at Harry, totally at a loss for words. Harry's eyes twinkled and he gave her a cheeky smile.

"It was one helluva romance, but Nancy died, darlin', not me." A pause, and then, "At my age, you can't take death too seriously."

Chapter 43

*The juniper berries in gin relieve menstrual
bloating*

Calypso glanced at her phone for the third time in five minutes.

"Are you expecting a call?"

"Just checking the time."

Nell grabbed the phone from her sister. "Turn that thing off. And be nice."

Calypso leant back in her chair and surveyed the room. It was dim, with thick drapes, heavy furniture and a lifeless energy, which meant it was always empty. Calypso wondered how it stayed in business. Her grandmother and her cronies seemed to be the café's sole clientele. "I hope you told Gran to be nice to me too."

Nell reached across the table and took her sister's hand. "It's one coffee, Callie. When did you last spend time with her?"

"I saw her for her birthday," Calypso huffed.

"Over a year ago. You completely forgot her last one."

A wave of shame washed over Calypso. "Okay, I'm a dreadful granddaughter, but it's not like she's that fond of me. You're the favorite."

Nell didn't argue. It was true. "That doesn't mean she doesn't care about you." Then Nell added, with uncharacteristic bitterness, "You're in her will."

Calypso felt heat rise up her cheeks, as it always did on the rare occasion that Nell mentioned, even inadvertently, Granny Emma's will. Calypso would never be comfortable with inheriting everything. Nor would she ever understand why she did. "I've been meaning to tell you, Adelein sent you a message."

"Adelein of St Nectan's?"

"No, Adelein of Clapham."

Nell looked completely baffled. "Why would the Faun send me a message? What did he say?"

"Your inheritance is coming. Something about the missing piece of the puzzle."

"Huh?"

He kept saying Cane Cata Juel."

"Do fauns drink?"

"They eat a lot of mushrooms."

Nell clapped a hand over her mouth. "You don't think it means Gran is about to die, do you?"

Calypso shook her head. "You'll inherit property and money off her. Those things aren't important to wood folk. He would only pass on a message he felt was of great importance *from his perspective*."

"What do you think it means?"

Calypso noticed Eleanor entering the café. "No idea, but let's ask Gran. You know she loves hearing about our Fey friends."

"You're awful, Callie." Nell giggled.

Eleanor made her way through the room with a look on her face more suitable for someone about to have a root canal. She gave both her granddaughters a peck on the cheek. "What are you two giggling about?"

Calypso couldn't help herself. "I was just giving Nell a message from a fairy."

"That's not the appropriate term, Calypso," Eleanor chided. "My friend Dominic at the library prefers the term homosexual."

Nell and Calypso both nodded solemnly while their feet kicked at each other under the table.

"I've already ordered your tea, Gran," Nell said, as the waiter arrived with their drinks.

"Thank you, dear." She poured herself a cup of Earl Grey and then turned to Calypso. "How have you been?"

"Good ... yep," Calypso said. "Happy birthday by the way ... for last month."

Eleanor sighed. "They come around quickly. We might as well make a toast to the next one now."

"Suits me," Calypso said. "Then no one can say I forgot it."

Another swift kick from Nell under the table.

"You look well, Gran," Nell said.

"Thanks to powder and a dash of rouge. I've barely slept at all, with this sciatica." She smiled at Nell. "How's Julian?"

"He's good, Gran. A very nice man."

"He's a handsome boy, isn't he?"

Nell hesitated, then said, "He's charming."

"Does the museum have rules about employees dating?"

Calypso rolled her eyes. Her turn was undoubtedly next.

"Actually, Gran, I was going to talk to you about this." Nell had already worked out how to deliver the next bit of news with minimum fuss. "Percy has offered me a full-time job at the BMR, and I've accepted."

"But you can't work for free," Eleanor barked.

"Full pay and benefits. Plus I'll be doing what I love."

Eleanor looked like she was about to cry, something she hadn't done since Alf first brought Batty home. "But the

National is the best museum in London, Nell. Don't blow this opportunity."

"I've had such a lovely time there, and learnt so much. And now I can return to the BMR and put that experience to good use. And of course, it means Julian and I will no longer be colleagues, so I've asked him out."

Eleanor clapped her hands in front of her. "Call me Cupid, but I knew it. He comes from quite a wealthy family you know."

"Let's not get too excited yet, Gran. It's just a date."

Eleanor refrained from asking any more questions. She knew Nell well enough not to pry at this point. That would come later.

Instead, she turned to Calypso. "And what about you?"

Calypso could tell by the look on her grandmother's face that she was steeling herself for the usual answer: "There are a few guys but no one special." Normally it would take pigs flying for her to share personal information with her grandmother – but she was still feeling guilty about missing her birthday. What harm would it do?

Calypso brushed some invisible lint from her jeans. "Yeah ... I ... er ... met someone ... special."

Calypso waited for the usual lecture about boys not liking easy girls, or choosing a man who could provide, but instead ... complete silence.

Eventually, she raised her head and looked at her grandmother. Eleanor was staring straight at her, eyes glistening. One understanding nod, and then Eleanor reached her hand out and placed it on top of Calypso's. "I'm so very happy for you dear."

It was a moment so unexpected, so filled with emotion, that both Calypso and Nell searched the room for something to say, as though the words would be hanging alongside the dusty drapes. It was Eleanor who came to their rescue.

"I do believe this calls for a celebration. Let's order some cake." She grabbed the menu and buried her head in the dessert section. "And Calypso, you can pay for it, seeing as you missed my birthday."

Chapter 44

Pear wine helps combat cellulite

Calypso and Nell stepped off the street and straight into a gigantic cobweb.

"Holy Spiderman," Nell whispered. "What is this?"

One of the gallery attendants handed them a program. "This explains the inspiration for Mr Dee's exhibition, and contains a summary of each piece."

"Thanks." Calypso took the program and looked inside.

The Web of Life: Taran Dee takes us on a moving visual exploration of the interconnected threads between the events and the people who have shaped and inspired him. Each portrait symbolizes a thread, weaved into the fabric of his destiny.

Calypso and Nell pushed their way through the crowd. The guest list was like a who's who of *Hello!* magazine, with wall-to-wall socialites, minor royalty, and the occasional A-lister – mix together, add Krug, wait for the froth to rise.

"I think I just stepped on Princess Beatrice's foot." Nell giggled. "Are they all here for Taran's work?"

"That or the free champagne."

Calypso took a moment for her eyes to adjust to the dim lighting. The walls were lined with paintings of varying sizes.

There was spot lighting above each piece, which gave the room a nocturnal feel. The pieces were attached to one another by numerous delicate silver wires. The wires shimmered like the fine-spun thread of a spider's web, or the threads of life.

"The goddess weaves Taran's Fate, each person interconnected and destined," Nell said.

"Or maybe he's an arachnologist," Calypso whispered.

They moved from a few smaller pieces to a large one. It seemed to be a self-portrait, with two versions of the artist. At the forefront was Taran, only with blond hair. Behind that image was a smaller, darker version of himself.

"That's Finn," Calypso explained. She opened the program and read, "'Two forces, masculine, feminine, dark and light, the essence of life. One cannot exist without the other.'"

"Brace yourself, Callie ... There's one of you."

Calypso turned and her own image bore down on her. Embarrassed heat rose to her cheeks and then in one tidal rush flooded her whole body. Everyone nearby was watching her. Everyone waited for a reaction. She didn't give them one. How could she? One glance at the canvas and she was completely overwhelmed. He had truly captured her, not only her physicality, but also her spirit.

Nell read from the program. "'Love, the force all threads emerge from. The point all threads return to.'" She looked at her sister and tried not to laugh. "That's a lot to live up to."

Calypso was as red as a beet. "If I wasn't so moved I'd kill him."

"Who's this one?" Nell guided her sister away from the staring onlookers and to the next portrait. "It looks like the spider."

"It's his mother."

Nell burst out laughing. "Okay, that one speaks for itself."

"Yeah, I look forward to meeting her."

*

Calypso noticed Taran on the other side of the room, standing with Simon and Megan. He seemed nervous and his eyes scanned the room. Then he saw her ... and he looked like he'd just seen sunshine after fifty years in a cave.

"There's Spiderman." She took Nell's hand and led her across the room.

"Here they are!" Megan and Simon were even speaking in unison now.

"You look lovely, Nell." He gave Nell a peck and winked at Calypso as he put his arm around her. "You too, my gorgeous firestarter."

"This is amazing, Taran," Nell said. "I'm quite speechless."

"I didn't know you could knit," Calypso teased.

"I didn't know he could build *web*sites." Simon had been waiting to use that one.

Megan gave him a slap. "Oh, Sime, so lame, so lame." She turned to Calypso. "Shall we do the rounds? There's one of Simon apparently."

Calypso pulled an embarrassed face. "Twenty quid says mine's bigger, Simon."

"Unfair bet, Cal, Simon's is a weiner." Taran gave a look of faux comprehension. "Oh, you mean his painting?"

"Where do we start, Taran?"

Taran led his friends toward the back wall. "There's no beginning, no end. Each thread is its own journey, and yet essential to the total. The weaver links the experiences together in surprising ways."

"By weaver you mean the Goddess?" Nell asked.

"Is that what it means to you?"

Nell nodded. "Yes. She weaves together the tapestry of our lives, right?"

"But we have free will, so really we construct our own webs," Calypso said.

"We still can't escape destiny," Nell pointed out.

Taran gave Calypso a quick squeeze. "Try though you might." He paused in front of a large painting in an ornate oval frame. "You could say this is the starting point for the exhibition. It's what led to here."

Taran waited for his friends to say something, but the piece was met by a deadly silence.

"I like it," Simon offered, rather meekly.

Nell reached out to Calypso. Megan stared at the painting, for once, speechless.

"Are you okay, Cal?" Taran asked, alarmed.

Megan regained her voice, but only spoke to Nell and Calypso. "It's a coincidence. It's not exactly like him, right?"

"Who? What's going on?" Taran asked.

Calypso was like a deer caught in headlights. She couldn't move, she couldn't take her eyes off the painting of a man who looked so much like Scott. It wasn't identical, it was just a strong likeness … except that the subject looked like he'd been in a fight, and hanging around his neck was Scott's one-of-a-kind amulet.

"Around his neck. Where did you see that?" Calypso's voice was barely a whisper.

Taran fumbled at his shirt collar and undid a few buttons. "You mean this?" He drew back his shirt and showed her the amulet from the painting, hanging around his neck – a web with a spider made from a flawless black tourmaline in the center.

Calypso reeled back as though he'd hit her. She'd know it anywhere. Hanging around Taran's neck was Scott's talisman. Turn it over and engraved on the back would be *Two threads*.

Calypso felt the blood drain from her legs. She blinked a few times but nothing changed. There was no mistaking it. She'd had it made for Scott. She'd designed it herself. It was a completely original piece of jewelry, which was why she'd been so upset with Scott when he'd given it away.

"Are all your teeth real?" Stupid question when she already knew the answer.

Taran's eyes widened. "I had one knocked out. I was in Bangkok and—"

Calypso had heard enough. She glanced at Megan and Nell, who were as horrified as she. Calypso felt faint. *This can't be happening, not here in public.* She needed to escape, immediately. "Excuse me … I have to …"

Disappear again. And she did, quickly, through the crowd and out the gallery door before anyone could stop her.

*

Taran looked absolutely stricken. "What just happened?"

"Buggered if I know, mate. Some weird dental thing," Simon said.

They both turned to Nell, hoping she could shine some light on Calypso's behavior, but she was already pushing her way through the crowd, after her sister.

Simon turned to his girlfriend, who was in tears. "Meg, what's going on?"

Megan's face crumpled. "The guy in that painting is Scott. It doesn't look exactly – it's an eerie likeness."

Now Taran felt sick. "I painted that guy from memory. I only met him once."

Megan nodded. "In Bangkok. You saved him. And he gave you that amulet."

Taran shook his head. "No, the guy who gave me this was Ando. His name was Ando."

"Scott Anderson – known to his mates as Ando."

Taran grabbed Megan's hand and dragged her out of the gallery. Simon followed hot on their heels. Taran needed air .

He hit the pavement outside and turned to Megan. "Are you telling me the guy I saved in Bangkok was Scott? The man I spent one life-altering night with was *the* Scott?"

Megan was just as confused as Taran. "I was with Callie when she designed that amulet. There's no mistaking it. That's Scott on that wall."

Taran ran his fingers through his hair. How could this be happening? He clearly remembered the night he met Scott. The moment he stumbled across him being beaten. The ensuing violence. The attackers retreating.

"Run, you bastards," Scott had yelled after the men. And then, ignoring his injuries, reached out to Taran. "I'm Ando … and I owe you my life."

Taran shook the outstretched hand. "A drink should suffice."

Taran slammed back to the present when he heard Nell running towards them. "She drove off before I could stop her."

"Should we go back to the pub?" Simon asked.

"She won't be there," Megan said.

Nell agreed. "She never goes home when she runs away."

"Yes, she does," Taran said. "She goes to the cottage."

"You're right. What should we do?"

Taran was shifting quickly between two places, two times.

Nell sensed his distress and reached out to him. "What happened the night you saved Scott?"

Taran pressed his forehead. He felt like he was about to crack. "I didn't save him. He saved me." He felt like crying. It was ridiculous. He'd only met Scott the once, but it had been a turning point in his life. Taran looked at the others, who were waiting for him to speak. "That night … it was important. To us both."

"This is too strange to be a coincidence, don't you think?" Megan asked quietly.

"There's no such thing as coincidence," Nell said.

Taran nodded. "Scott told me that night that he felt his 'number was going to come up' soon, and he was worried about his girlfriend. It was clear how much he adored her." He paused for a moment, emotional. "He said, 'You'd look after her.' I disagreed. I told him I'd fuck her up, like I fucked everything up. But he had this … faith in me. 'You'd be good for her. And mate, she'd be good for you.' Of course, I just thought it was the vodka talking … I never expected …"

"Of course not," Nell finished.

"You don't think Cal will do anything stupid, do you?" Simon said.

Taran knew damn well she could. "She's impulsive. And she drives like a maniac. She'll be halfway to Tintagel by now."

Simon looked at his watch. "I can make a call and get us a plane."

Megan stared at her fiancé. "Who are you? James Bond?"

"It belongs to my family, but they never use it and the pilot is loyal to me." Simon looked at his friends. "We'll fly into Bodmin and rent a car there."

Megan was in. "It would be quicker than driving."

Taran nodded. "Great, let's do it."

"What about your opening?" Nell asked.

Taran gave her a resigned grin. "Some things are more important, right?

Nell reached out and gave him a hug. "Scott was right," she whispered.

Chapter 45

Detox the liver with grapefruit wine

Calypso's heartbeat was as loud as her breath, and just as ragged, as she ran through the forest. The orbs of light were waiting for her, expecting her, but for once, they didn't come down to greet her. There were no whispers or giggles. They silently lit the path all the way to the glen and Adelein, who was waiting.

Calypso was nervous. She knew the Faun would not be pleased with her, but she'd come this far and her mind was made up. But before she could speak, Adelein nodded.

"I know why you're here. Follow me."

"Thank you, Adelein."

The Faun turned and walked deeper into the forest. "I will guide you in but you must find your own way out."

"Of course." Calypso had expected that but hearing it unnerved her. Would she be able to find her way out of Summerland without Sylph dust? She'd been trained beyond the veils, and knew how to pass through different layers of reality, and still return. She was banking on that experience to get her through – and home.

The Faun led her into a circle of Fey folk who had already lifted the first veil. There was no time to waste. If she was going to return, she needed to do so before dawn.

Calypso lie in the centre of the circle and closed her eyes. It was too late to change her mind now, even if she wanted to. She felt the first shift. She could hear the buzz of power as she passed from one tier to another.

The ceremony began.

The Fey folk chanted and sang. The melody started quite low, but rose note by note as the veils lifted. Higher and higher they sang. To anyone walking nearby it would've sounded like thousands of crickets in the thick of summer. But to Calypso, who used each note to move further away from the earthly realm, the sound was like someone rimming a crystal glass, only clearer, brighter, a hundred times magnified. Each note held all the mysteries of the world. It was pure joy and beauty and Calypso basked in it while she could. She drew strength from the sound, because she would need it later. That much she was sure of.

The buzz grew louder and her own energy exploded as the Fey folk hit one completely pure high note, so high even dogs wouldn't hear it. It was the bridge she crossed as she left the dense human realm and began to move through the layers toward Summerland. She drifted, she floated, she soared. She flew faster than light and sound, yet was filled with stillness. She fell into a state of slumber, yet all her senses were alert, a heightened awareness took hold.

Adelein's voice rang out, "Safe journey, friend."

She was alone. She opened her eyes and took a moment to get her bearings. She was surrounded by a dense mist, and could barely see her hands in front of her. The air was still, and while not dark, it felt like twilight. An eternal one.

Calypso knew where she was. She'd been this far in her training before.

"Right … so far, so good …" Calypso took in her surroundings. She was at the edge of a dense forest. Shards of light pierced through sections in the trees, in an otherwise dark and overbearingly quiet place. She noticed a stone staircase leading up and, left with no other options, took it. The woods around her were unlike any she'd seen before, yet not entirely unfamiliar. The area was thick with gnarled trees that seemed ancient in energy. Given the human propensity to destroy the natural surroundings, Calypso realized that these trees were not from another place, but another time. As she grasped the reality she was in, the spirit trees began to disappear, one by one, until she was surrounded by space and nothing. She continued up the stairs, one determined step at a time, wondering how long they would continue.

And then she saw a door. Calypso had been trained well, and knew that doors were never to be taken lightly. She turned, and as she suspected, the stairs she'd just climbed disappeared one by one behind her. With space beside her, and nothing behind her, she had no choice but to take the door in front of her. It was always the best option. So she opened it and – with a touch of apprehension and as much determination as she could muster – she closed her eyes and stepped through.

She fell.

Her petrified scream echoed around the realm. Her body hurtled toward her fate. In that moment, she had the strangest thought. She remembered her grandmother Emma telling her how sometimes souls leave their bodies just prior to their actual death, if it's going to be a particularly traumatic one. Calypso stepped out of her screaming, hurtling, falling body and viewed it from above. From that angle she couldn't understand what all the fuss was about; she felt quite detached from her human fear. She cocked her head and watched herself with what could only be described as amusement, although it wasn't even that, but something we can only feel in pure spirit form.

The physical Calypso plummeted through the air, terror across her face, arms flailing, grasping at nothing in a vain attempt to survive. The spirit Calypso found it all fascinating: her fear of death, her desperate attempt to hold onto a life that she hadn't truly been living for some time. And with that realization, she slammed back into herself, opened her eyes, and realized she wasn't falling at all. She was sitting on a chair.

Calypso quickly got her bearings, as, section by section, the room came into focus. She was seated at a dining room table. The room was nicely furnished, but had a heavy air to it. There were photos of children on a sideboard. She heard the clink of cutlery, and watched as a woman came into view. Calypso realized with horror that she'd come face-to-face with herself, twenty years in the future.

Her first reaction was delight at how well she'd aged. But then she noticed the faint lines around the eyes and mouth that told of sadness rather than laughter. She stood and walked to the sideboard for a closer look at the photographs and realized they weren't her own children, but Nell's. She wasn't a mother. She was the doting aunt.

She felt breathless. This couldn't be her life. This was no life. What had happened to her that she'd ended up here? She realized with horror that she was being watched. She swung around and came face to face with her older self, standing behind her. She could see her and was staring at her with such contempt.

"You blew it!"

Calypso stared into her own aging face, into eyes that were filled untold regret. Those eyes drew her in and in … falling and tumbling through the lost chances, missed opportunities. As she fell a hand reached out for her again, and again, and again … She screamed as she reached for it.

"Taran!"

Everything went black. She sensed him first: she could smell him, the heady scent that drove her wild. She reached out her arms in front of her and touched him. Taran didn't say a word as he laid her back and slipped off her clothes. She couldn't see a thing, but she could feel him, and hear his breathing as it became more and more heated. He slid into her and they both cried out. There was the sound of drums in the distance. Or perhaps it was their heartbeat, together, as one. Calypso disappeared inside her head, and then merged into his. She lost awareness of where she ended and he began. All she felt was pure pleasure and a ferocious need for him. More and more and more, their lips and breath and hands and whispered words devouring each other, until they both exploded, their whispered promises carving their way across the universe.

Then he was gone.

And Calypso opened her eyes and realized she was lying in a freshly dug grave. She heard voices above. Crying.

"Hello?"

But no one answered.

And then the first shovel load of dirt hit her in the face. And then another.

"Stop! I'm not dead!" Calypso screamed. "I'm not dead."

The dirt kept coming, she grabbed at the side of the grave, trying to claw her way out, but the grave got deeper, and deeper, and the damp, foul soil kept filling up. And all the grief and anger and sorrow she'd felt for three years came barreling out of her body in one heartbreaking howl. She was at Scott's side as he died. She was at the viewing of his body. She was at the funeral, the wake and Ash Cottage, where she broke apart. She hurtled back further. She was in Bangkok, pacing the room. She was in the bar, with Scott and Taran. She saw their bond, that one brief but profound moment they shared. She saw Taran look at her. She saw Taran smile at her. And Calypso realized she'd made a terrible mistake. She wasn't at all prepared for this journey. She should've spoken to some of the wood folk, or her mother, or at the very least googled "How to return from Summerland." Google probably would've also shown results for *not possible* and *death* ... It dawned on Calypso that she had just signed her own early warrant.

"I'M NOT FUCKING DEAD!"

And just like that the grave fell away and she was surrounded by mist. She ran her hands across her body. She grabbed at her chest. Her heart was racing. But she couldn't let her fear win. Three deep breaths – she could do this.

She cocked her head and heard it ... the sound of oars on water. She walked toward the sound, setting one foot carefully in front of the other. She needed to reach the side of the lake, but couldn't risk stepping into it. No one had ever returned from under that lake.

One step ... and another ... to the edge.

The surface of the lake was like cobalt-blue glass. Calypso could see her reflection in it. She stared at her own features for a moment, feeling herself drawn in by a powerful force toward the lake. She blinked and broke the spell, berating herself for being so naïve. It was a one-way ticket into that lake. She glanced back at her reflection, which had now morphed into the face of a stranger with hideous features and a silent scream so morbid, Calypso almost caught it and started screaming herself. But she didn't. And as soon as the creature realized it had no power over her it darted away, to the depths of the lake that entrapped it.

"The lake of lost souls."

She could see them all clearly now. Below the surface of the lake were countless souls, swimming by in an endless dance of sorrow. Some moved slowly, weighed down by the lake and the events that led to them being trapped there. Others darted to the surface, and for a moment it looked like they'd break through … but they'd stop, horrified, as they realized they were stuck under what appeared to be an indestructible mirror, in which they'd see their own reflection and start to scream.

Calypso turned away. She'd seen enough. She'd heard about these souls, but nothing had prepared her for the misery in their faces.

"As in life, so in death," she said to herself. Freedom from misery didn't come simply through death. It came through love, of oneself and others. That much she knew.

She stepped back from the water's edge and listened for the sounds around her. She couldn't hear the oars any more, but there were gentle slaps, water on wood. The mist was now lucent enough to see the boat waiting for her. The mists parted ever so slightly and Calypso noticed the oarsman standing at the rear of the ornate boat. He was wearing a long dark cloak and hood, although the hood was positioned back far enough to see his craggy face.

He watched her for a moment. Waiting for a reaction, Calypso thought. Or just waiting. He was in no hurry. He had all the time in the world … and beyond.

She looked at the boat. She had no idea how long this part of the journey would take. She'd heard from her grandmother once that it depended on the person making the journey. Some people crossed the river quite quickly. Others took years.

She stared across the lake and the mists evaporated and there, on the other side, standing at the water's edge, was Scott.

Calypso's heart leapt. She could see him clearly … his smile, the lift of his hand as he waved to her. And the shake of his head as he told her not to cross.

Calypso took a moment to study him. There were subtle changes. Not in him, but how she felt about him. Scott was still perfect in every way to her, but suspended in time. He seemed so young, while she'd been forced to grow up through losing him. She was three years older and wiser and more damaged. Three years of growing and sinking, of grief and joy and new love. Three years she hadn't shared with him. Changes, events, time he hadn't witnessed, at least not in human form. Three long years etched on her soul. She was a different person now. And yet Scott stood before her, exactly the same as the day he died – and suddenly she realized she'd outgrown him. She still loved him, she always would, but she'd moved on. Despite the pain and the struggle and her apparent inability to do so, she had in fact moved on.

Calypso realized how foolish she'd been to visit the Summerland. There were no answers for her here. Answers weren't as important as the questions. There was no unfinished business. Death finishes it for you, whether you like that or not. It was over with Scott. It had been for both of then, the moment he died in her arms. And as heartbreaking and awful as it was at the time, she accepted it now. Her greatest betrayal to Scott was not surviving, or even falling in love again, but not embracing that.

Calypso realized she didn't want to get into that boat. It was not a journey she needed to take right now. She had to get home.

She gazed across the water at Scott. He grinned, and held his hand to his chest. She was there, in his heart, as he was in hers. And in that instant the mists closed and he disappeared from view. She couldn't see him any more, but she felt him. She smiled. She'd felt him fly free from her once before, but this time was different. This time was okay. It still hurt that he didn't get to live a full life, but it hurt her, not him. He existed in a space where he knew he'd lived exactly as he'd meant to, for the time he'd predetermined. He had lessons to learn and had done so.

He had lessons to teach others and had achieved that. He'd done exactly what he was meant to do.

"Christ, you're a pain in the ass."

Calypso staggered backward as Taran stepped out of the mist behind her.

"How did you get here?"

Taran drew a packet from his pocket. "Sylph dust. I thought Madam Linzbichler was freaking nuts when she gave it to me, but apparently she's not. You are."

Calypso was horrified. Putting herself at risk was one thing, but what if Taran couldn't get home? Sylph dust was no guarantee. "You should never have followed me here."

"I'd follow you anywhere, Cal."

"I don't need you to ride in here on a white horse and save me."

Taran did a mock search around him. "I could've ridden a horse here?" He grabbed her with more force than he normally would. "You crazy idiot. You should never have done this, and definitely not without Sylph dust." And with that he kissed her, it was deep and long, and as close to home as she'd ever get, despite where they were.

"Don't get into that boat, Cal," Taran pleaded.

"I'm not going to. I made a mistake. Whatever happened between you and Scott is in the past, and that's the one thing I need to let go of."

Taran lifted her chin and looked deep into her eyes. "Hey, you and I will talk about it. And I'll tell you all about what a great guy he was, and what an amazing night we had, and how this stranger believed in me when I needed it most ... and some of his passion for life rubbed off on me and motivated me to paint. Cal, we can revisit it all ... but we'll do it at home, with a wine ..." He gave her a grin. "It's more normal that way, babe."

Calypso had tears streaming down her face, but almost laughed anyway.

"Now, Nell told me how your magic has disappeared around me, which under normal circumstances bodes well for me. But it ain't great here, because we need it."

Calypso nodded. "Give me the Sylph dust. We're going home."

"You can do this, Cal."

"I know I bloody can."

Taran handed her a small packet of white powder. "I wasn't the only person at my opening with a bag like that in my pocket," He laughed.

Calypso glanced around the lake. She didn't want to show how frightened she was, but she'd also heard so many tales about this place. Getting out of here wouldn't be easy.

The mists shifted and Calypso realized that the darker energies were now aware of their presence. Summerland and the realms around it were as dangerous as they were safe. As with all light, there was a flipside of dark, and those energies would feed on them and off them if they caught them. It was time to leave. Returning from Summerland was always hazardous; especially once these energies took hold.

"You want to hurry up, Cal? This place is creeping me out."

"I just need to think this through."

"Think fast."

"I'm trying."

Taran shut his mouth. But it was too late. Everything around them began to vanish. The vibrations shifted and swallowed them and Calypso knew they were in danger. There were eternal mazes of energies and layers. Once lost in them it would be impossible to find a way out. Spirit drifted through the realms quite easily, but being in human form, they were unable to sense the very subtle shifts that were necessary to get them through.

Taran held her close. "It's okay. Don't panic." It was obvious from his voice that he was.

There was a sense of motionless. Nothing. Endless nothing. It began to engulf them.

"Oh Taran, I'm so sorry ..."

Taran held her, kissed her. "It's okay. I'm with you. That's all that matters." He tried to cheer her up. "And it could be worse ... we could be in Hackney. I went there once and that was hell."

Calypso giggled. But they both knew they were in deep trouble. Calypso tried to shift the veils, but she hadn't used magic in a while, so couldn't raise the energy they needed. They sank deeper away from any reality, and into nothing, a despondent eternity ... There were creatures around them. Shadows of tortured souls. Circling, circling, bearing down on them, pressing the breath from them ... when suddenly a woman appeared before them.

"YOU SHOULD NOT BE HERE!"

Calypso and Taran screamed as this creature rushed toward them. Taran grabbed Calypso and held her tight, turning to face the creature himself. And then ...

"Enid!"

"I told you I was keeping an eye on you," Enid snapped. The ghost stared at Calypso and Taran, whose eyes were wide in disbelief. "Honestly ... I don't know what you'd do without me. Come on then."

"I didn't think you'd recognize us with our clothes on, Enid."

Enid snapped her head back and glared at him. "I don't have to save you. Just her."

"Point taken," Taran mumbled.

Enid moved between them and guided them away from the abyss. They flew through dark tunnels and alleyways. The smell of sewage filled the air. It was dark and cold and there were screams that chilled Calypso to the bone.

"This is a great place," Taran said. "We should bring the kids here for holidays."

"This is no place for children. Or anyone. Come this way."

Calypso had the overwhelming sense that Enid had existed within the abyss before, which is why she knew it so well. The pace quickened, the energy jolted, as they moved into a more familiar space. The vibrations became familiar. Calypso had worked with these energies before, although not with Taran around.

There was light up ahead, but Enid stopped. "I don't go any further." She looked at Calypso. "You will find the way."

Calypso gestured toward Taran "My powers don't work around him."

"You also thought you only had one," Enid snapped, as if Calypso were quite stupid.

Calypso breathed deeply. Enid was right. She had allowed family myths and legends to control her for too long. She knew these vibrations. She glanced at Taran. He'd come in to save her, but really he had no idea how to do that. She owed him, and would get him home safely.

Calypso turned to Enid, searching for the right words, so the ghost truly understood what she meant to her. But Enid shook her head.

"I've watched you grow up. It's my duty to make sure you're safe." And with that, she disappeared, back to the pub where she herself felt secure.

Taran looked nervous. "Any more creepy realms to traverse?"

Calypso giggled, as she dipped her finger into the bag of Sylph dust. "Hold onto me, Taran. And don't let go."

"That's exactly what I intend to do, Cal."

Calypso closed her eyes. She refused to allow negative thoughts to govern her. She knew how to do this. The veils shifted. Further ... and again. She was there, she could feel it, she blew them wide open and the remnants of the dark energies evaporated behind them. She was back in that space she'd missed so much. Back and then some. She felt more powerful than ever before. The cobwebs that had collected in the corners of her mind were swept away. And she knew exactly what to do now. She pulled Taran toward her. It needed to be exactly right or they'd never get out. There was one force more powerful than them all. She held him, pressed her lips against him and he responded ... and she moved onto him. He was so deep inside her that they became one. Together they got lost, this time in each other, because nothing else existed. It felt like they were traveling that way for hours ... perhaps they'd been missing for years.

Then the energy exploded and familiar smells surrounded them, familiar sounds, orbs of light rushing toward her ... the rustle of leaves, and a burst of light ... and they were back in the forest.

Calypso lay on the ground that was so achingly familiar to her and tried to catch her breath. She reached out for Taran and lay a hand on him. He moved ... and moaned a bit. It was not a soft landing, but it was one helluva ride.

Taran opened his eyes and smiled at her. "That was great, but I was thinking perhaps Greece on our next trip."

He drew her onto his chest. She could hear his heart pumping, the adrenaline still high. They looked at each other, aware of what they'd just experienced.

Taran broke the silence. "That was a close call." He began to laugh. "Hard to top that for an interesting night out."

"We can certainly try." Calypso laughed too, as absolute relief flooded her.

"Dinner and a movie won't cut it after that. Not very exciting."

"Sounds just perfect to me."

"Cal, baby, next time you need to release the past, how about you just do what other chicks do ... you know, talk about it over coffee with friends, or take a workshop, or something."

Calypso began to laugh. "I will, Taran. I promise I will."

Their clothes were scattered around the glen floor. Taran scrambled for his and tossed hers at her. "C'mon, the others are back at the cottage."

Calypso looked confused. "What others?"

"Nell, Simon, Megan." He buttoned up his jeans and pulled Calypso to standing. "Simon flew us down here. Cool little plane."

"Oh Taran, I ruined your opening night."

"You have the rest of your life to make up for it." Taran smiled at her. "So let's get on with it."

Calypso hesitated for a moment, but Taran gave her hand a yank and they moved forward, one step at a time, the forest orbs lighting their way.

Acknowledgments

This book has been a long time coming, and there are a lot of people to thank. Unfortunately the ones below are the only ones I have remembered.

To Chicky Linzbichler: This book started with you. I appreciate your years of unwavering support. I am lucky to have you in my life.

I thank Joel Naoum and the crew at Momentum for helping me dust this one off. It means a lot to me.

Thanks to Rosemary Serluca, Ken Atchity, and Chi-Li Wong. Also to Mike Kuciak, not only for the years of support, but the recipe for the Mike Tai.

A heartfelt hug to Samantha Beeston, who came up with the name, *Trouble Brewing*, and Tony Beeston, who was plying us with wine when it happened.

Thanks to Warren Gibson who must surely be over the mileage. To Ulrike Sturm and Markham Lane. Also to Alison

Nancye, who shares International Release of Fabulous Books Day with me.

Many thanks to my gorgeous stepsons, Oscar and Tadhg for putting up with a stepmum who would rather write than cook, and for both embracing dunno pasta, dunno pizza and dunno pie. You rock!

And to my darling boys, my world, Indy and Raffy: I regularly drift off mid-sentence (because I've just thought of a new storyline) and I often forget to feed you (because I'm writing), but somehow you've turned out to be wonderful young men anyway. I love you both.

Finally, my guy, Dominique Sweeney. Thank you for the love and support, the way you threw yourself into critiquing this book, and the enthusiasm you had for the characters. Now that's romance.